THE LORD'S SCANDALOUS MISTRESS

An Oxford Set Novel, Book Two

AVA BOND

First edition published 2022.

Cover Art by: Forever After Romance Designs.
Edited by: Tracy Liebchen

ISBN: 9798426633674

This novel is entirely a work of fiction and all characters and events are fictional. Any resemblance to actual persons, living or dead, events or localities is entirely coincidental.

This novel contains scenes of a sexual nature, as well as allusions to sexual assault and violence.

CHAPTER 1

E*astbourne, Sussex, December 1814*

As a young matron of good birth, pleasing looks, and in a respectable marriage, Mrs. Isabel Hall was an important member of Sussex society. She expected to lead out the matrons at various public balls, attend the theatre in her family box, and contribute to the local charity collectives. But what she had never expected was for her husband to stumble through the doorway of their home, covered in blood, in the middle of the night.

Pierre Hall staggered into their house at ten-thirty, just as Isabel was locking up for the night. The front of his shirt was soaked crimson. He collapsed onto the hallway floor as soon as the door was closed behind him.

"Mrs. Gilbert," Isabel screamed, the shock hitting her hard. She ran forward and was joined by her housekeeper.

"Let's get him on the sofa, ma'am." Isabel and the housekeeper dragged him into the front room, a stain of red coating the carpet.

Whilst Mrs. Gilbert went for hot water and sent the butler for the doctor, Isabel held Pierre's hand. It was an odd scene to play out in one's drawing room, a space where she would have entertained her mother-in-law or other matrons of the town, where gossip and the latest fashions were discussed. Never had their drawing room housed so much drama.

"I'm done for, wife," her husband said. His colour was very weak, it was true, but Isabel, who was always praised for her practicality, ignored his terror. With tentative movements, he jerked himself forward, and more out of instinct than true matrimonial duty, much less love, Isabel kissed his clammy hand.

"Tell me what happened to you." She had no idea what might have caused such an injury to her husband. Perhaps he'd been set upon by bandits. Pierre was a businessman, and the impression she had always received was that he was rather stuffy and strait-laced ever since their first meeting at her father's office. He liked to maintain that everything was orderly and correct, from how he never paid the servants a shilling more than they were owed to how he refused to dance on any occasion. It was not good practise, he said. Eighteen months of marriage to Pierre had not changed her initial view of him, nor deepened their connection, sadly. She was fond of him; she forced herself to be. Isabel was sure that Pierre felt something towards her.

"I'm going to die." His breath was laboured as he pawed at his front.

"Stop that," Isabel begged him. She was scared he would make things worse.

He raised his puppy-fat face to hers. His grey eyes were bloodshot. "You need to do something for me. Promise me that you will. Promise."

"If it's within my power," Isabel said. The desperation on Pierre's face was scaring her. As yet, there was no sign of the doctor. How long would it take the butler to cross the streets of Eastbourne? It wasn't the largest of places...

"Jamie... He's a good boy, really," Pierre said, referring to his wastrel younger brother.

Isabel kept her face emotionless. Her views on Pierre's younger brother were not polite. To her mind, James Hall was the worst sort of man.

"He got mixed up with the wrong sort, with the Wareton Gang." His voice dropped lower, and Isabel crouched closer, down on the floor beside the settee, nearer to Pierre.

"What did he do now?" They were so close they were almost sharing the same breath. Isabel could smell blood and what she suspected was vomit.

"You need to help him."

"Please stay calm," she begged. She doubted his fear would help.

"It'll damage all of us," Pierre said. This time his voice was reed-thin as if his breathing had been affected. Isabel could not claim much knowledge of medicine, but she knew that if the injury to his chest had affected his lungs, Pierre wouldn't be able to breathe. And then he was right; he would die. Her eyes went to his face, and her panic started to mount.

She leaned closer. "What has your brother done? You have to tell me."

"There's money involved. He took some... bonds and the like. They're..." Pierre's voice was wobbly, jumping from word to word.

The front door of the Halls' townhouse was thrown open, and in marched Mr. James Hall. Pierre's dratted younger brother. He fancied himself a rake-in-training. At least that was the impression Isabel had always gotten of him. Getting to her feet, Isabel crossed to her brother-in-law.

"Tell me what happened to him." She tried to keep the

desperation out of her voice; she did not like being vulnerable in front of James.

"They're going to hang me." James's normally arrogant expression was gone, and he looked as white as a sheet. For the first time, James appeared older than his big brother. Isabel could feel herself growing angrier with the pair of them.

"I burnt the paperwork," Pierre said.

"One of the men made away with the rest." James collapsed into the nearest armchair. "I can't go after him. They'd know it was me." He rubbed his eyes, then lowered his hand as he surveyed the drawing room. "She could go."

Heaving himself up as much as possible, Pierre looked at his wife. "Do you know the Hurstbourne estate?"

"Yes, of course." Isabel was familiar with the grand home, a good ten or so miles away from where they were in Eastbourne. It belonged to the great family of the district, the Earl of Hurstbourne, and his famously glamorous and beautiful children, Lord Lynde and Lady Viola. The estate was also close to her own maiden family home in Alfriston, so she had grown up in its shadow, hearing all about the stunning Lyndes.

James scrambled up and grabbed Isabel's hands in his own. "You have to intercept the man. Cut the blackguard off as he's making his way to the magistrate."

"What? I cannot. He will be miles ahead of me." If the man had set off straight away, he had a definite advantage. If the man rode as fast as he could, he'd be at the estate in two hours, less perhaps.

"He's injured," wheezed Pierre. "He doesn't know that you'll be lying in wait for him. He'll take the main road. He'll think—" He paused to cough, and Isabel noticed more blood ooze through his fingers. "You can catch him if you leave straight away. Go the back route."

"Don't be a coward." James's fingers dug into Isabel's small wrists as he pulled her close, away from Pierre. "You don't have much choice; he's got something on all of us. Including your father. Yes, that's right, your precious Mr. Blackman's involved too."

Isabel had turned and looked back at Pierre, but her husband seemed past caring. He turned his face away from the pair of them, and his skin was sweaty and pale in the firelight.

"The incriminating documents will be in his travel bags," James said. "You'll need to steal the papers back from him before he can get to the earl. He's the local magistrate." He made the last point as if Isabel was an idiot when she knew all too well the power the Lyndes wielded in the area.

"I can't," Isabel whispered. If it involved shooting someone... She shuddered at the idea of it. "But won't he have such a head start? Besides, I should stay with Pierre." She crossed over to crouch down beside her injured husband. After his outburst a moment ago, Pierre had fallen back amongst the cushions, all his colour gone. Tentatively, Isabel dabbed at his mouth with her handkerchief.

"Nonsense," James said, drawing closer and dropping to his knees to intimidate her by his presence. "If we are to survive tonight, it's down to getting those papers back. Now, my girl, you'll take the quicker route to the estate. You've got some time. The earl is elderly; there's a chance he won't be woken until morning. The problem is if his son is back for Christmas. Never mind that." He fixed her with a brutal stare. "You need to lie in wait and shoot the officer. It's better you go, far less suspicious than me going. We can lie and say you're abed if they come to check on us."

From the pocket of his velveteen jacket, James pulled out a heavy pistol, which he pressed into Isabel's hands. It was cold to the touch, and the feel of it chilled Isabel down to her toes. She knew, then and there, that she could never fire it at another human. Unable to bear it, she scrambled away, across the salon and towards the door, but James was quicker, cutting her off.

"But I—I've never fired a pistol," she said to James in desperation.

Pierre swore.

"We're counting on you," James said. "It's a new design. Just point and aim. Then shoot."

Isabel shook her head. She couldn't do it. James pressed himself closer, leaning forward and whispering in her ear, his breath heavy. "Your father could lose everything for this. Your whole family will be damaged, and then what will happen to you... as a widow?"

Isabel looked into James's face. He wasn't lying. He seemed to know that Pierre was done for. His eyes narrowed on her as he saw that he had hit upon a nerve—her desire to protect her family.

"Very well," Isabel said, feeling as if she was entering a battle without knowing what the war was for.

TWENTY MINUTES LATER, ISABEL WAS RIDING THROUGH THE countryside late at night, dressed as a man, with a pistol in her hand. She did not much fancy her chances of success. She wasn't familiar with smuggling. She wasn't familiar with business in any of its forms; it wasn't considered ladylike. She had been kept ignorant. Nor was she familiar with what her husband had been up to on this fateful night.

The irony might have made her laugh if she wasn't so scared.

"Dear God, keep me safe," she muttered under her breath.

It was madness, she kept telling herself. Utter and complete madness. Perhaps, it might have been more worthwhile if it had been done for love. But she wasn't in love with either of the Hall brothers. No more than Pierre was in love with her. She knew he wasn't, or he wouldn't have sent her out here on her own. It was being done for the love of her family. Then again, she thought ruefully, her father had married her off to a man she didn't know, so what good had familial love done her?

Isabel straightened in her seat. Her bottom was sore. She had never ridden like a man before. Her nervous stomach had settled, so she was at least wide awake. The cold of the night and the dread of James's threats kept her so. Great wintry gusts of wind were driving across the flat marshes, digging into her back. She would have liked to have stayed in the house to wait for the doctor, but there wasn't time. Both Pierre and James had insisted on that. They'd insisted that she be out of the house and on Pierre's horse as soon as she was dressed in his clothes. She wore his oldest suit, strapped to her with a belt. If anyone in polite society saw her now...

With a strangled laugh at the idea, Isabel slowed her horse down. Up ahead, the road widened and split. One route led towards Alfriston and all the sights of her maiden family home. It would be familiar. Comforting. Knowable. Secure. It was so tempting to run back there and hide, but she knew the truth would come out, and then what would the rest of them face?

Never in her life could she have imagined that she would end up in this position. And the lulling promise of an Alfriston welcome called out to her. But she had her duty first, which was to save her family.

Would the paperwork in that officer's bag expose her family and have them out on the street? How far would it stretch? Just to the Hall or wider still? Would it stop at her sister Agnes's marriage to Mr. Miles? Ruin Thomas's budding legal career? Humiliate her father and mother to all of society? Would she dare fire the pistol? She had her doubts, but perhaps she could hold him at gunpoint and get him to hand over the papers. As if she were a highwayman. *Stand and deliver.* Yes, that might work.

Isabel nudged her horse onwards, taking the pair of them farther away from the temptation of her family home and towards Hurstbourne Manor.

The great house was much talked about in Sussex society. It was agreed upon that Hurstbourne Manor was one of the most picturesque buildings in the county, if not the whole of England. Since the Blackmans were in trade, they had only been invited to the public Yuletide ball that the Lyndes had held when the countess was present. But that was many years ago before the great scandal that had engulfed the Lyndes, and never in all her six years of being 'out' had Isabel been invited to the great manor. Agnes, Isabel's sister, had always hoped that they might see the Hurstbourne heir, Lord Nicholas Lynde, during one of their trips to the local assembly rooms. Something about that name conjured up flights of fancy in Isabel's mind. Even on this December night, during the fear and terror of the last few hours, Nicholas's name seemed to stir something in Isabel's mind and awareness in her body. Back at the house, James had mentioned him in passing, and Isabel had struggled to control herself.

It was a girlish infatuation. You must focus.

In their youth, Agnes and Isabel had imagined that when Lord Lynde was down in Sussex, he might dance with one of them. Sometimes locals claimed that he visited the estate for hunting. Once, Lady Viola Lynde had been at the Brighton Assembly Ball, but her older brother had not been in attendance. Viola had been the belle of the ball, glistening in the centre of the room in a shimmering ivory dress, but nevertheless, Isabel had left the evening disappointed. The gossip sheets wrote about Lord Lynde and his daring friends, nicknamed the Oxford Set, and their exciting exploits. But Isabel liked to go further and focus just on Lynde. Imagining everything about him. About his strong jawline, his slim but handsome physique, how he boxed at Kingston's, how he was thought of as the quintessential Corinthian gentleman, the most gallant of the Oxford Set. It was written about in coded language, but Isabel had summarised as much. In her most girlish and silliest of moments, Lynde had been a true Adonis to her.

One of the sketches of Nicholas had even been part of a ritual that Isabel conducted whilst at school. But that had been over twelve years ago when Isabel had only been sixteen. Her girlish fascination would not help her now. She needed to make sure that Lord Lynde's father, the Earl of Hurstbourne, did not receive the officer because that would mean...

It was dark. She blinked. Only the moon and stars guided her, and whilst her knowledge of Sussex was extensive, she did not know the grounds of the Hurstbourne estate. She slowed her horse to a brisk trot, sitting up in her seat to gaze this way and that.

She had to decide whether to enter the grounds and wait for the officer's arrival or linger outside the property. Slowly she edged the horse onwards, past the entranceway to the estate. The gates had been left a little ajar, but there were no lights on in the gatehouse. An oversight, she told herself. But one that might work to her advantage. All she needed was his bag. She didn't want to kill him. If she could startle the officer's horse, the soldier would be thrown off, then she could get to the bag without anyone being hurt. Provided the fall didn't do any serious damage to him.

Isabel climbed down and secured her horse to a nearby

secluded tree with this idea in her mind. They would not be visible from the road. Hurrying forward, Isabel located a large branch and then crouched down amongst the trees and bushes near the gatehouse, waiting for the officer.

The woods were dark and dense, letting very little light in from above. The gatehouse was likewise gloomy, although presumably, this was just because it was so late at night. Occasionally the moon swung out from behind the clouds and gave Isabel some idea of her surroundings. But at least it wasn't raining.

Crouching down on the woodland floor, Isabel rested her back against a tree and let out an unsteady breath, her emotions threatening to overwhelm her. As a distraction, she rubbed her arms against her sides, bustling from one foot to another to keep warm. She wished James had given her his greatcoat because the slim jacket that belonged to the stable boy was not very covering or as thick as her husband's. She would freeze, she thought, as she huddled amongst the bushes of the estate.

Isabel was close to giving up hope and had lost track of time when she heard the unmistakable sound of an approaching horse. This had to be the officer, and she readied the branch she would use to trip the horse and rider. For a second, she thought she could hear multiple men talking, but she ignored the idea. Perhaps he was drunk and speaking to himself. Thankfully, the moon came into view, and Isabel could make out the solo rider approaching through the soupy darkness. Something about the set of his jaw and body, visible even in the dim light, spoke of authority. He rode through the gate.

She sank low to the ground and jabbed the stick out, catching his horse between its legs. The horse lurched to one side, and the rider was thrown off. This was better than using a pistol.

Isabel hurried forward and grabbed the horse's reins, forcing herself to ignore the yelling of the fallen man. If he could cry out like that, he must be fine. Her hands moved over the large horse until they alighted on the saddle bag, and she started rummaging through it. But the moonlight was not *that* good. She would have to settle for removing the bag from the horse altogether. Her hands shook as she struggled to loosen the straps.

Click.

A strange noise came from behind her, and Isabel spun round.

"What the blazes?" Five feet away from her was a tall man. He had his pistol raised, moving with a pace that shocked her. She caught sight of his glowering gaze and little else. His intense eyes were striking, deep and shockingly blue, visible even in the moonlight. He had the sort of immediately pleasing face that sucked the breath out of her lungs; she felt dizzy with it.

Maybe that's the fear. Glancing around, Isabel knew there wasn't time to get back to her own horse. She would need to make a break for it, regardless of how much of a criminal it made her. Out through the park, jump the low edges at the end of the estate, and then make her way back to Alfriston. That was her only choice.

Isabel took off running, the saddle bag flung onto her back. She'd always been fast as a child, but now that she was wearing trousers, it made her footfalls quicker. She darted into the safety of the dense woods, the man following in hot pursuit.

CHAPTER 2

Lord Nicholas Lynde was having one hell of a week. First, the outrageous choice Viola had made at her almost-wedding and their father's reaction to it, and now, today's turn of events. He heartily wished the entire last twenty-four hours to go to the devil. It seemed that scandal was doomed to dog the footsteps of his family. Nothing ever went to plan. Still, it was his duty, as his father delighted in reminding him, to be at home and to ensure that he was never the one to bring anything shocking down upon them. Being here, in Sussex, ready and able to support the community, that was his role. Tonight, that meant stopping a smuggling ring.

That was why Viscount Gregory Silverton was here too. Silverton seemed to know a great deal about the ins and outs of this local Sussex smuggling ring. Rumours had persisted through the Oxford Set that Silverton was a spy, that Baronet Verne, another member of the Set, was too. The two of them had supposedly played an elaborate part in the capture of three of Napoleon's best ships, which had led to roles in the Home Office... Nick had laughed it all off. Previously. It seemed to have a lot more weight when Silverton suddenly said he needed Nick's help. Still, it was meant to have been a lark and nothing more.

Now, his friend was groaning on the ground where he lay. More importantly, the man who'd rendered him so was rifling through Silverton's belongings.

Nicholas swore and jumped off his own bay, drawing and cocking his pistol. Someone was loose on his land. Near his family home. A criminal. It wasn't to be borne. He made a beeline towards the man. Sharp grey eyes flicked up and saw him, and before Nicholas could even level his pistol, the chap was off, cutting into the forest that clumped around the edges of the estate. If the young man knew the area, he'd be able to hide in the dense woodland for hours, and the evidence in Silverton's bags would be gone.

"Get back here," Nicholas shouted as he charged after the young man. But the criminal was quick, damn him, with the sort of pace that was possible when one was lithe and not burdened with the four whiskies that Nicholas had consumed earlier in the day.

The forest was thickly planted, with brambles that reached up and grabbed at Nick as he ran through the trees. The figure in front of him seemed to almost dance with a grace that surprised Nicholas, the man's agile movements cutting through the thicket. The criminal must be very young, Nicholas reasoned as he thundered on. Any delicacy in his movements was gone, leaving a cold fury in its place.

The moon, his only source of light, plunged suddenly behind a cloud, and the woods went dark. But Nicholas trusted his gut; he'd seen the boy and kept moving towards the point where the fellow had been. Quietly. Silently, in fact. When the clouds parted, pouring bright moonlight down through the leaves, he saw a flash of the intruder's face, eyes raised to the dark heavens. The two of them were far, far closer than before. Nicholas had the thief in his arms in three quick steps, holding him tight. His hand covered the boy's mouth as the other went to clamp around the man's arms, securely fastening the criminal in his grip. But he met a strange resistance when he brought the chap's body flush against his. This man seemed to have breasts.

"What the devil?" Nick said. There was no way in hell he could have been outpaced by a woman, and what was she doing being a criminal?

Nicholas lifted his hand up to yank the hat from the culprit's head in one quick movement. Immediately a cascade of fairy light, blond hair tumbled out from the loosened cap. It seemed to glow in the moonlight as if it had been spun by silver magic. For one brief, fleeting moment, he looked into a face that the moonlight seemed designed to illuminate as if nothing could have rendered her more lovely. It framed each of her features with a particular joy. She had a soft little chin, quizzical eyebrows, large wide eyes, and high cheekbones. She also had a handsome set of curved lips that made Nicholas wish never to see this woman dressed in boy's clothes again.

He had been about to acknowledge her feminine state when the young woman drew her leg up in a quick, decided manner, powerfully driving her knee into Nicholas's balls and knocking him down sideways. It hurt like the very blazes. It hadn't happened to Nicholas since he was at school, and the sensation removed his ability to speak for many seconds. Finally, he dropped to the ground, his hands leaving her and going to his groin protectively. She darted off into the woods, along with the stolen saddlebag. Nicholas lay where she'd left him, sprawled on the woodland floor, the ache in his balls acute.

"Frig," he said as he got to his feet once the pain had subsided. He started to make his way back towards Silverton and the gatehouse at a slow, careful pace.

He found his friend on his feet, although in a worse state than him. Silverton's cries had woken the gatehouse and its owners. Coming to Silverton's side, Nicholas pulled his friend's arm over his shoulder, to help Silverton towards the gatehouse.

"Who was it? Did you catch him?" Silverton's face was little more than a grimace.

"No. He got away." Nicholas wasn't quite comfortable revealing that a woman had manhandled him or showing his error in front of someone of Silverton's reputation.

"Blast it. I can't walk on my leg," Silverton swore.

"Really?" Nicholas tried to keep his tone neutral, but it surprised him to see Silverton so vulnerable. Wasn't this something his friend was used to?

"Yes." Silverton strained down to feel his left leg. "I think it's fractured, but it might be broken. Can you send for a doctor? I can't be sure."

"I didn't need your diagnosis. Let's go to the experts." Nicholas took more of his friend's weight and hurried them towards the cottage. They made their way through the door of the gatehouse. Old Mrs. Peters, in a large blue nightdress with her hair tied up, was stood in her kitchen looking worried, her soft cheeks and weak chin wobbling.

"No need to fret, missus. We need to use your settee," Nicholas told her. "Mrs. Peters, this is my dear friend, Silverton. He has been attacked by a thief who is still on the ground. Send your husband up to the manor to raise the alarm. Do you have any brandy for Silverton?"

The woman rushed off to search for some alcohol.

"You're in good hands." Nicholas stared down at his friend. "I've known the Peters for years. I'll go for the doctor myself."

Silverton's countenance was pale beneath his tan. His debonair face was tense; he looked for all the world as if he might faint. His dark eyes crinkled at the edges as he tried to shift on the settee. He dragged his fingers through his brown hair and winced at the movement. "I don't think I'm going to be of much use to you in this smuggling enterprise."

"Or with anything else," Nicholas said.

Silverton had alerted him to the Wareton Gang in the first place. They had bumped into each other by chance in Eastbourne. Nick had prided himself on staying away from the more dangerous side of things, whether that be *ton's* man-hungry debutantes or matters more scandalous. Still, when Silverton had asked that Nick come along tonight to help, he hadn't felt he could say no. That was only this afternoon, and now this.

Silverton had left out how serious this all was. He had promised it was just some drunken locals, but it seemed far more organised than that.

Mr. Peters had set off to the Manor for the manservants to search the estate for the thief, Mrs. Peters told them. Nicholas had planned on continuing the search for that slim, womanly intruder himself, but she would have to wait. Someone that striking couldn't hide forever. It would be faster if Nicholas went for the doctor himself, as he had already suggested.

Striding to the door, Nicholas yanked it open. "Stay put," he called back to Silverton.

"Wasn't planning on anything else. Just as well we looked through the contents of my bag before we left, isn't it?" Silverton said as Mrs. Peters bent over him, lifting a spoonful of brandy to his mouth.

Grimly laughing, Nicholas left the cottage. He made his way to their horses before his eyes were caught by something moving in the trees. Drawing his pistol, Nicholas edged forward until he realised what he was looking at. A large, black horse tied to one of the trees close to the gatehouse. It must belong to the young woman he'd seen in the woods, although for the life of him, he couldn't understand how that delicate being could have ridden such an intimidating-looking animal. Her possession of such a striking creature told him something, although his sluggish and weary mind could not quite piece it together.

Untying the horse, Nicholas led it back to the other animals and secured it to the same post before swinging himself up into the saddle of his own mount. He rode the bay back towards the open road and out of the gates.

The nearest doctor would be in Alfriston; Doctor Forde had been his family's physician when Nicholas was growing up. He steered his horse to the left at a brisk canter. If he could have the doctor roused and back here within the hour, then his old university friend would not suffer too much. A mission such as this one would distract him from thinking about the feminine intruder who was stirring the most erotic thoughts in his mind, centred on that mane of her hair. Instead, the journey to Alfriston would let him go back through the events of the last twenty-four hours and piece together what it could all mean.

He had travelled down to Sussex yesterday with his irate father and baby sister. They were leaving London in disgrace. Lady Viola Lynde had been engaged to the eligible, if juvenile, Duke of Mortimer since the end of the Season. The duke was a good four years younger than Nicholas's own thirty, so a trifle young to be wed, but Mortimer was smitten. He was also heir to a great estate and name. Viola was vivacious, blonde, and the daughter of an earl. So, a good match, society had concluded, even though Viola was lucky to have landed it at twenty-four. At least, that was what the *ton* mammas would say. But Nicholas had seen Viola's face after the engagement had been announced and known that it was a mistake. His sister had accepted Mortimer's proposal for all the wrong reasons. Nicholas had tried to convince his father of this, but Hurstbourne wouldn't listen. His tired, worn face had looked his son up and down with distasteful fury.

"Viola knows what is due to her position and name. It is time you learnt the same lesson."

Hurstbourne might have had a point, having married late himself. Since he'd only provided the family with the one male heir, the pressure was mounting on Nicholas to find a bride. No one knew better than Nicholas to never mention his father's own disastrous marriage. Nicholas had decided that next year, the summer of 1815, he would wed, which meant he would need to start taking the game seriously and look for a suitable bride. The problem was, the hunt for a girl was far more fun in theory than the reality of trailing through ballroom after ballroom. Unfortunately, it seemed that Viola had come to agree with her brother's views on matrimony. On the day of her wedding, at the actual altar itself, as many society matrons as could be called back from their estates over the festive season had watched in fascinated horror as Viola refused her intended.

It had been tempting to remind the Earl of Hurstbourne of their earlier conversation about duty. Lynde had stared at his fairylike sister from the front pew of the Mayfair church.

"You can't make me do it. Not with all of the pressures of death on my head," Viola declared to the assembled throng before she threw Mortimer's hand from her arm and ran down the aisle, dropping her bouquet of imported lilies as she bolted from the church.

"Bravo," whispered Jasper Mavor, the Duke of Woolwich, one of Lynde's friends from the Oxford Set. Lynde glanced back at the duke. Jasper looked more broken and twisted than ever, his wife's recent death affecting him. He seemed embittered; his cruelly sensual lips twitched into a grin at Viola's performance, and his old charm peeked out at her show of defiance. "She's a scandalous Lynde, through and through. Should stop anyone else commenting on my wife's death for at least a week."

Turning, Nicholas had looked away from Jasper. He was still fond of Woolwich, as he was of all the members of the Oxford Set. Thankfully, though, only Woolwich and Trawler had been in attendance to watch Viola wed. Not everyone was based in London, nor were they tempted to make the journey down, which had made it a lot easier and had the added benefit of meaning there were fewer eyes to witness his sister's dramatics.

Woolwich's caustic comment at least had the power to lighten the mood. But Nicholas had had to wipe the smirk off his face when his father glanced in his direction. Hurstbourne staggered after Viola. Likewise, the rest of the *ton*, all abuzz, left the beautifully done up church and headed home, tongues wagging. The Lyndes had left London the very next day, with every single gossip sheet bearing their disgraced name. There had always been rumours about them, what a daring, shocking family they were, and now Viola had added weight and force to the idea that the Lyndes were infamous.

"You'll not be able to come back for next year's Season," Hurstbourne had said as their carriage cut through the edges of London.

Viola was sat stoically enough and did not respond to her father's comments. She had pulled a great bundle of blankets down and wrapped them around her legs.

"I will need Viola's help, Father," Nicholas interjected, trying his best to keep the peace, even at the cost of a compromise on his part. "If I am to manage society and find myself a bride."

There was a pause after Nicholas's comment. Viola glanced up at him, her little cherubic face alight, but it was snuffed out when their father replied.

"You can't marry before your sister. My god," Hurstbourne muttered. "She's already on the shelf. No one will take her now... Disgraced." His father had placed his hand on his own chest, his expression pained. "Can't you get one of your blasted Set to wed her? They're nearly all single."

"No," Viola said.

Hurstbourne took no notice of her and continued speaking, warming to the idea. It had once been floated when Viola was a debutante, but Lynde had never embraced it. The Set consisted of spies and libertines, one married man and a widower. They were not for the likes of his virginal little sister. She deserved better than them. He glanced at her. Then again, maybe none of them could quite match up to his sister, the firecracker.

Again, Viola said, "No, Father. I don't wish to marry anyone."

"If you're not careful, you're going to end up as an orphan," Hurstbourne bit back at his youngest child. "You'll drive me to it. My doctors don't give me much time, and if you carry on like this..." His tone carried the full weight of his statement and silenced both of his children. No one said another word until they reached the Sussex estate for Christmas.

"Do you think he's lying?" Viola asked as soon as Hurstbourne had gone upstairs to rest.

"No," Nicholas told her. He had known his father to twist things to his advantage, to try and force his children to bend to the wills of the *ton*, but to lie? It was not in the Earl of Hurstbourne's nature. "Viola." Nicholas caught her arm and gave her a quick brotherly hug. "You know I will support you with whatever you choose."

"Thank you." She had returned his hug before stepping back. "I wonder if you'll always feel that way."

She slipped from the room, leaving Nicholas to ponder

what she meant. His sister had always been a little wilder than most debutantes, but surely, she must want what every woman desired? A comfortable and secure home to call her own?

The following day, Nicholas had gone to the nearest large town, eager to get away from the gloom of his familiar residence and to try and brighten their festive season with some pretty Christmas trinkets. It was here, in the shrill, bright, December day on the Eastbourne promenade, that he'd seen Silverton. Two hours later, after a hearty meal and a long chat, Lynde was vaguely aware of the small danger of a couple of 'smugglers.'

"The truth is..." Silverton had paused here; he had laid out the barest facts, trying not to give too much away. "We're really trying to find out who's supporting the Wareton Gang."

"It's always about the money, you mean?" Lynde asked.

Silverton nodded. "It's just a tip-off, but it could be something."

"What do you need from me?"

"Your father is the magistrate of these parts," Silverton stated. "It would be useful to have you there as a witness."

"Is it serious then?" Lynde pressed. Silverton had made it sound as if it were just a couple of men sharing an illicit bottle of French brandy, nothing more.

"I doubt you'll even need a pistol," Silverton replied.

Lynde remembered laughing at this. He wondered where the rest of the Set, who Silverton would normally have roped into helping with this sort of thing, were. Trawler was dealing with something in town, and Verne... No one seemed aware of where Verne had gotten to, Silverton said.

"I'd be glad to help out. Time to play my part in the defence of the country. Besides," Nicholas added, his father's remark at play in his mind, "in return, you can come home with me for the festive season. We need some company about the place to brighten things up a bit."

Silverton had looked rather dubious at the idea of this, but he'd agreed. They'd clinked glasses, and Nicholas wondered if he couldn't play at being a matchmaker. His father's idea lingered in his mind. Killing two birds with one stone. After all, he wouldn't say he was a good judge on what attracted women to men, but Silverton was older than him, perhaps around thirty-one or two, mysterious, with dark hair rather than Mortimer's fey blond curls, and a touch more exciting to someone of Viola's sensibilities.

It had seemed such an easy plan in the tavern at midday. But after the flying bullets, screaming attacks, and a couple of men determined to fight to the death, matchmaking seemed like a distant memory. The smuggling party had shot at least three of Silverton's men, one of whom had died in Nicholas's arms. Nicholas had been grazed by a bullet and wondered if they would make it out of there alive. He had glanced at Silverton in anger; here he was, risking his life for something he didn't even fully understand.

Silverton had been lying next to another of the injured men, pressing his handkerchief against the man's wounds. It had happened ever so fast. In a blur. There was a flash of a figure trying to make a break for it, which was all that Lynde had needed to roll forward, lift his pistol, and fire. He'd caught the man somewhere in the chest, the adrenaline pumping through his body. He had watched as the man staggered and dropped his satchel. Another had appeared, taller than the injured man, and Nicholas had overheard a tiny part of their conversation.

"I'm shot." The injured man's tone was etched with fear.

"Where's the bag? We need it."

"Too late. Take me back to Isabel." His speech was slurred at this point, and Nicholas jumped back up, knowing the bag was what Silverton needed. He fired again as he got to his feet, hitting the injured man again. Killing him, presumably. The pair of them had collapsed out of sight, and Nicholas had grabbed the satchel.

He crawled back to Silverton, and they made their way outside with Silverton's surviving colleague, a balding Irishman named Walsh. Once at the nearest tavern, they pored through the bag, looking at the names in the lamp light. All the while, Nicholas kept asking Silverton and Walsh to tell him more.

"Do you know these names?" Silverton asked, holding up a sheet of paper.

"Some of them," Nicholas replied, glancing through them. They were the names of respectable family men throughout the county: lawyers, bankers, tradesmen, and landowners, some of whom Nicholas had known all his life. If Viola's disgrace didn't tip his father over the edge, then the news that half the county was in on the cut just might.

"We don't need to punish all of them. Some might just be taking some French wine. Not ideal, but hardly worth executing them over," Silverton said, more to Walsh than Nicholas. "It's about finding the men who have funded this."

Walsh, a rotund but practical-looking man, nodded. "Money's always the key."

"I've got it," Silverton said after several long moments. "Does the name Hall mean anything to you?"

Nicholas had shaken his head, and they had agreed that Nick and Silverton would go to Hurstbourne while Walsh went to collect the bodies of the dead men.

God, if Hall had done worse than injuring his friend, Nicholas thought, as he rode along the road towards Alfriston, he would kill the man with his bare hands. He wanted answers. Not just from Hall but from Silverton too. The night had been clear, which meant it was easier to ride but chilly. The cold night air bit at Nicholas's limbs as he made his way into the village and up the narrow, Tudor-built streets. He had grown up around here, when his father had let him off the estate, and he had a peculiar fondness for the place, although he could not often enjoy it since he was swamped by desperate young women keen to marry. At two o'clock in the morning, however, Nicholas thought himself safe.

He slowed the horse outside Doctor Forde's home, hopping down and then rapping on the door and waiting for the servants to emerge. He hoped that Forde was not out on another emergency. The door opened, he told the young boy what had happened, and the child dashed up the stairs. The household stirred and awoke at the news that Lord Lynde's dear friend was injured. Nicholas was grateful for Doctor Forde's speedy greeting and the servants who readied the doctor's horse.

As he stood to the side of the street, unseen from the main walkway, a lithe figure dashed past, moving with a pace that Nicholas thought he recognised. Silently, he edged forwards, his eyes following the shape of that person. It was the woman from earlier. He was not close enough to make out the size of her as he would have wished, but the silvery, shimmering hair loose around her shoulders gave her away. Nicholas felt certain he would have recognised those strands of hair anywhere.

She darted from building to building, keeping to the enclaves and doorways as much as she could. Nicholas watched her as she hurried along the silent and empty street. She was a local. It was impressive that she still moved at such a pace even though she must have walked or run miles from the edge of his estate all the way to Alfriston. She continued along the street, and Nicholas followed, edging his way after her, seeing where she went. Then he turned back to the doctor's home when he realised her destination.

Doctor Forde joined Nicholas in the street. "All ready?"

"Which family lives up on that road?" Nicholas asked once they were both on their horses and riding through the town.

The doctor glanced up, his watery eyes blinking as he viewed the road that the woman had taken just moments ago. "That leads to the Blackman home."

Nicholas nodded in thanks, then spurred his bay on. Doctor Forde followed suit, and they cantered back towards Hurstbourne Manor. Nicholas wondered how he would link the name of Hall, and that mysterious young woman, to the Blackman family, but most of all, how they were all connected to the dangerous Wareton Gang.

CHAPTER 3

Lottie, a sharp-eyed maidservant, let Isabel into the Blackman kitchen when she knocked at the door. The servant girl recognised Isabel right away and thankfully asked no questions, despite the late hour. Her pleasant round face nodded without judgement, and she started up the fire and fetched Isabel first a glass of whiskey and then some hot tea. Then, bless the girl, she wrapped several blankets around Isabel, who by this point was drooping in the armchair. The entire time though, the saddlebag was still held tightly in Isabel's arms.

Only when Lottie listened to reason and went off to her own bed did Isabel get up. Her clothes were dusty and stained, and she was grateful the noise hadn't woken her parents. Mrs. Blackman was likely to scream half the village down at the sight of her eldest daughter dressed as a man and having run from the law.

Despite the late hour and the risk, Isabel waited for the house to fall silent, waited until the only noise was the fire in front of her. Then she eased the bag open. She had no idea what she was looking for. But anything that linked her father or her family to the smugglers would need to go into the fire. Sheet after sheet of paper was eased out and looked through. They hadn't used any sort of code, the fools, so she made quick work of it. It seemed obvious from these pages that the Halls had been profiteering from what seemed like a collection of local businessmen, presumably including her own father, roping them into schemes that only paid back a fraction of the profit the gang pocketed.

Beyond tired, Isabel got to her feet. She tipped most of the pages into the fire, keeping only one page back. The page that listed James Hall as the key leader of the Wareton Gang. It would be her leverage and her revenge. It was a means of preparing for a battle. There was a repeated reference to someone named 'CH' on the page, but she had no idea what that could be. She imagined she could use this proof to chase James out of her marital home. Folding it up tightly and hiding it down the front of her stays, Isabel settled back amongst the blankets to wait for the arrival of dawn.

She loved her family home, a pleasant-looking townhouse constructed in the last fifty years; it contained every modern luxury. Mrs. Blackman had decorated the place to the height of sophistication but elevated comfort over style. It meant that the Blackman girls had been raised in relative sumptuousness; at least Isabel had always thought so. They had nice books, fashionable clothes, bonnets, ribbons, and scarves from either Brighton or London. The girls had received lessons with a piano and painting master. Unfortunately, neither skill had grabbed or held Isabel. She thought of the sheet of paper wedged in her strays. She would have been better at business than her father, but that was not an option for someone like her.

Stretching out her small fingers, Isabel contemplated her wedding ring, a simple thin gold band. After tonight's events, she would like nothing better than to cast it off.

When dawn came, she snuck out of the kitchen and up the servants' route to her sister's bedroom. Clara was a good three inches shorter and much plumper than Isabel, but even so, it would be far better to return to Eastbourne dressed in her sister's clothes. Besides, Clara would need to be her alibi should the need arise.

Isabel slipped into Clara's bedroom. It was a mess; a spiral of clothes, books, and shoes on the floor. Lying still, asleep amongst the scattered items, was Clara. She was a small, well-rounded, red-haired girl with a vast array of freckles, vivid blue eyes, and a generous personality. Isabel wondered where Clara had come from; she was so different from her older, more sombre siblings. But despite their differences, Isabel adored her youngest sister.

"Wake up," she said, edging forward into the bedroom.

"Uhuh," came the undignified response from the centre of the bed. Despite years of reading romantic gothic novels as soon as they were published, there was something delightfully unromantic about how awful Clara looked when she had just woken up. Isabel neatened her own clothes in response.

"Gah," Clara said when she opened her eyes and saw Isabel. "I almost didn't recognise you."

"Hush," Isabel said, "I can't explain it. But I need your help."

"Is it romantic?" Clara asked, sitting up in her bed.

"I'm married." Isabel realised how simultaneously revealing and tragic her reply was, yet she had no desire to correct herself.

Clara was soon out of her bed and listening to Isabel's requests. First, find her sister a dress. Next, Clara was to be Isabel's alibi. Third, they needed a carriage to take them to Eastbourne and Milbourn Street, where Isabel lived.

"I will smuggle myself into the carriage," Isabel said. "And if anyone should ask, I spent the night here with you because you took ill on our trip out yesterday."

"I spent the day reading, with no one near me," Clara replied as she dressed, scrambling into her clothes, her red curls bouncing around as she moved through the bedroom. Ribbons flew up in her wake, followed by slippers and stockings. Clara gathered her longest dress, a bright green one with little yellow birds decorating it. "You can keep it," she said as she held it under Isabel's chin. "It will suit you more than me. And I haven't had the time to get it shortened." She sighed. Her lack of height was one of the many things that Clara disliked about herself.

Thanking her sister, Isabel started to dress. It was nice to get out of Pierre's suit of clothes. She wondered what she would tell Pierre and James about the satchel as she did so. She supposed they would be grateful to her; no, she would insist on their praise. It was thanks to her that they were saved. She deserved some credit, and she had managed it without anyone being killed.

Within the hour, Isabel and Clara were on their way to Eastbourne. On reaching Milbourn Street, the place she was supposed to view as her home, although it had never really felt as such, Isabel was dismayed to discover her mistake. The two Halls did not feel relief or anything approaching that emotion. No, when the door swung open, Isabel was greeted first by the weeping Mrs. Gilbert, and behind her, a group of servants, all dressed in black. It was then Isabel realised that she was a widow.

Pierre was dead. It hit her like a stone, but Isabel felt no stirrings of grief, only shock.

The news was confirmed by her mother-in-law, who was sat in the drawing room. The cold, haughty eyes of Mrs. Emma Hall took in the sight of first Isabel and then Clara. "Where have you been? God, go and change into something more appropriate. And you," she advanced on Clara, "Go home, child, and tell your family that your sister is a widow. My son..." Her breath hitched in her chest, and she turned away.

Clara looked around at Isabel. Leaning down, Isabel kissed her little sister's cheek. "Send Mama when you can," she whispered. "I will go and change at once."

She made her way, footfall after shaky footfall, her hands holding onto the banister, up to the first floor. At the end of the corridor was James Hall. He was positioned in front of her bedroom.

"I said you were at your parents."

"That is where I stayed," Isabel said. "Excuse me, I need to..."

James's hand stopped her in her step. He was not even touching her, but Isabel did not want to get any closer to him. He wasn't as tall as he'd like to be, so the two of them were almost the same height. He was famed for his handsomeness, but she thought he looked more like a rodent up close.

"I was worried about you," James said.

"I don't believe you," Isabel snapped back. She could feel her heart beating faster than was normal, but she didn't care. On account of this arrogant fool of a man, she was a widow. A brief, terrifying thought occurred to her: As a widow, Pierre's control of her was gone, and she was far more vulnerable to James. The man didn't even have the decency to look sad about his brother's death. "Now move," she told him, trying to banish her fear. "I need to dress for the vicar."

"Mother will take care of all that." James blocked her entry again, pressing himself closer to her. The scent of him, a mingling of alcohol and sweat, made Isabel feel as if she might throw up. "I've no objection to you changing in front of me."

"Have you no shame? Pierre has just died." She stared at

his face, trying to detect some sign of grief in the man's features. But James looked bored and annoyed, little more.

"There's some emotion. I thought it was locked in you." James reached out and jerked Isabel's chin up to meet his gaze. "Pierre was never much of a lover of women, so I doubt he aroused...."

Isabel raised her hand again. From his stance, from the way his eyes caressed her body, it was clear that James thought Isabel would be easy pickings now. "No, no, pretty one, not again." He grabbed and held her hand, bending it back and to the side of her body until she smarted at the pain of the movement. Whilst he did that, his thin lips grazed the skin at the side of her jawline. "My brother was an idiot in a lot of ways. But he's gone now. Wouldn't it be better to do as I say rather than risk being sent off to Hodgkin's?"

The name of Doctor Hodgkin lingered between them and chilled Isabel to the bone. The infamous doctor ran an asylum located in Hastings, some fifteen miles along the coast. That cursed place was intended to control women, to scare them. It worked. Most people in the area never spoke of it, other than whispers that the cries of the women could be heard at night along the shoreline.

A memory returned to her; James had sent a girl there before. He had made a nuisance of himself with the maids in her household. One poor girl especially. It had occurred four months ago when the poor girl had started to show. But subsequently, when she'd asked what had happened to Jessica in the hospital, Pierre had told Isabel to mind her own business. The guilt twisted through Isabel. This was how James operated, moving through women before discarding them. But Pierre hadn't liked to hear criticism of his darling younger brother. And it seemed that James had no reservations about packing Isabel off to the terrifying asylum as well. The threat was clear; do as James said, or she'd end up there too.

"Get off me." Isabel stomped her heel down hard on James's left foot, and he released her. She staggered backwards away from him, her arm still sore from his grip.

Noises were coming from downstairs, the sure sound of his mother, her heavy steps nearing the staircase.

"Tell me," James snarled. "Did you get the papers?"

From below, there was the sound of Mrs. Hall on the steps. "Hurry up, gel, will you?"

"I got them. I burnt all of the papers; they're gone." Isabel was so relieved she had kept that piece of paper proving his guilt. That would keep her safe from the asylum.

James let out a sigh and stepped aside, giving Isabel space to get to her bedroom. As she pushed open the door, he called after her. "Did you shoot him?"

As Isabel closed the door on her brother-in-law, she replied with grim satisfaction. "No, the man lived."

She slammed the door shut and leant back against the wood, sucking in a breath. She could hear the Halls talking as James made his way down the stairs to join his mother. But that brief snatched moment of quiet was a godsend. Shuddering, Isabel felt tears form in her eyes. Poor, pitiful Jessica. She felt more for her than she did her own husband.

Letting out her held breath, Isabel moved unsteadily forward.

Her bedroom was at the rear of the townhouse, and she had tried to make it as much her own room as she could. It was hers. Pierre rarely came in here. Their monthly visitations took place like clockwork, straight after her period had finished and only for one night a month. Any more wouldn't have been godly, Pierre had always assured Isabel. This was a practice he had read about, and he believed it the surest way for her to fall pregnant. It had never worked. Isabel assumed that either she was barren, or his theory was mistaken.

When she had queried this assumption, Pierre had said

it wasn't her place to know more. The outcome was that the bedroom remained hers. Decorated in the palest of blue, with appropriately chosen, well-made wooden furniture, it was her sanctuary from the Halls. It was where her favourite books of poetry lived, where the miniatures of the Blackmans were, and where all her sewing and jewellery was kept. She had always had an unbroken agreement with Pierre that this room was to be kept private and for her.

Stripping out of the happy green day dress, Isabel pulled out her only acceptable mourning gown. It wasn't crepe, and the skirt was more grey than black, but there was a handsome black velvet ribbon at the waist. With little to no warning, it would have to suffice. She wondered when she would feel some sadness at Pierre's death, but she couldn't make herself feel grief for him.

There came a knock, and Isabel assumed it was a maid to help her lace up the dress. She unlocked the door and was amazed to see Mrs. Hall, who pushed her way into Isabel's bedroom.

"What are you doing in here?" Isabel asked.

"James is talking to the undertakers." Mrs. Hall glanced over Isabel's gown. "No. That dress won't do at all."

"I don't have another."

Her mother-in-law let out an annoyed little huff. "Turn around then, and I'll do you up. You had better send for your father."

"Clara will let them know what has happened."

"I meant for your allowance. You will need him to cover your costs."

"Won't—" There was an uneasy pause in which Isabel stepped back and looked at her mother-in-law. The woman seemed cold as if it had not hit her that her oldest son was dead.

"No, my son won't have to pay for you. Not without a child."

"Child?" Isabel's question tumbled out of her mouth without thinking about it.

"Are you increasing? Because we would need that to be verified. I am surprised that Pierre wouldn't have told me immediately were that the case."

"I am not," Isabel said. "Increasing, I mean." She wasn't. She couldn't be. She had just finished bleeding, and there hadn't been a chance for Pierre to visit her yet. A weight shifted in her mind; that meant only one thing. She wasn't ever going to be. Ever. She would never be a mother. She couldn't remarry. The idea turned her stomach, the idea of letting another man do to her what Pierre had done. No. God, no. Never. But the consequence of it—she would never have a child move within her, nurse at her breast, or call out for her in the night. Never have those sparkling summer picnics on the beach she'd dreamt about, or just the simple everyday task of teaching her child to play the piano. Or read. Any number of little things that Isabel had envisioned vanished in an instant.

"Now you start to cry," Mrs. Hall snapped, her doughy face creasing. "I suppose that tells us what you really cared about. It was just about the money."

"I don't understand."

"The only way you would receive your widow's portion is if you had at least one living issue. My son was generous enough not to specify what sex it had to be. But you have even failed in that."

"My father would never have agreed to that."

"It was a cut deal because you were so long on the shelf," Mrs. Hall added. "I suppose we now know why. No dowry. No children. Little to no beauty. What good are you?"

"Get out," Isabel snapped. She had always tried her best

with her mother-in-law, no matter how dislikeable Mrs. Hall had always been. But now she realised she didn't have to deal with her anymore. Even if it meant crawling back to her father. Even if it meant moving in with her younger sister and becoming a maiden aunt. At least she would never have to deal with Mrs. Hall or her evil son again. Straightening to her full height and drawing in her chin, Isabel spat the words out. "Get out of my house. And take your vile son with you. Don't either of you darken my door again."

Mrs. Hall's whole face dropped, her jawline sagging and her eyes bugging at being spoken to in such a manner by her once meek daughter-in-law. Isabel crossed to the doorway and yanked it open. "The lease is paid here until September. That's a good nine months. I will find a solution for myself by that point, I am sure."

"If you drag my dead son's name through the muck by whoring your way through society—"

Isabel thought of the small piece of paper she had folded close to her breast. That could be used against the living Halls. The thought made her smile, which of course, Mrs. Hall took the wrong way.

"If you were to try something of that ilk, I would have no hesitation calling in my dear friend, Doctor Hodgkin, who is so adept at dealing with unruly women." Having delivered the same threat as her son, Mrs. Hall stormed from the bedroom, down the stairs, and, Isabel hoped, out of her house.

Upon reaching the downstairs hallway, Isabel looked around the sitting room to the welcome and familiar faces of her butler and Mrs. Gilbert. The one she didn't know was the undertaker, who bowed low to her.

"I am sorry for your recent loss; I understand that poor Mr. Hall was set upon by thieves. It must have been very shocking for you."

Isabel stayed quiet. If that was the story that the Halls

wanted to use, she would abide in silence until there was a good reason to contradict it.

The undertaker stepped closer and handed her his card. "Mr. Chism, at your service, ma'am. I will arrange for the funeral to take place tomorrow. I understand from your family that only Mr. Hall's brother will be attending."

"I will be there too." Isabel saw no reason why she should miss it. She wanted to say goodbye to her husband, convention be damned. "And any of the servants who wish to attend will be given the day off, should they want to say their goodbyes."

Mr. Chism nodded, his pale, pointed face a little sweaty at the edges at her flouting of society's rules. "Then 11 a.m., at St. Mary the Virgin Church."

Isabel watched Mr. Chism leave her house. Tomorrow would not just be a chance to say goodbye to Pierre but to confront James over the money she was owed as a widow. It was she who'd risked life and limb the previous night. She was owed at least something. It was she who had been tackled and pulled up against that solid brick of a chest and live body.

That man from last night. He had known she was a woman. She didn't know who he was, but ever since she'd left his presence, he had stayed in her mind. Their interaction had been for less than a minute, but the feel of his hands on her body, holding her, touching her, his palms encircling her waist.... Isabel felt sure she would remember the feel of him for longer and with more excitement than she would ever recall Pierre. What a shocking way that man had behaved. How frightened she should have been. But Isabel could admit to herself that the rush of giddiness in her belly, the feel of his fingertips on her skin, had been exhilarating. Especially in contrast to the eighteen months of marriage to Pierre.

There was a cough, and Isabel glanced up to look at the

butler and Mrs. Gilbert, the two of them watching her with equal amounts of sympathy and concern.

"Could you fetch me the accounts of the household?" Isabel asked. If nothing else would set her straight and remove the fluttering in her belly, surely a good, hard look at the extent of the Hall corruption would help.

❦

THE DAY OF THE FUNERAL DAWNED WITH HEAVY SLEET, AND in part, Isabel was grateful; it would mean a smaller number of people in attendance. She was also relieved to put down the account books because they revealed how much the Halls had woven her father into their web of deceit. If Isabel's calculations were correct, poor Mr. Blackman had been funding much of the smuggling.

Her father stood next to Isabel in the church, and it was all she could do not to yell at him in frustration. But he was here to be supportive, and few others were prepared to risk the sudden downturn in the weather. Mr. Hall was in the opposite pew. As the vicar read, Isabel glanced back to give a nod of thanks to the handful of servants who had attended. But on the first of these glances, she was surprised to see a man she didn't recognise at the back of the church.

As she looked over her shoulder, the man's eyes lifted and met hers. Isabel felt a frisson of excitement and fear bubble up within her and journey from her chest to her stomach in a fizz of energy. She was certain he was the man from the forest. How had he found her? He was tall, dressed all in black as was proper, the severity of the garments emphasising his chiselled, handsome features, with a strong jawline and sensual lips, along with a light sprinkling of freckles that added a roguish air. Those blue eyes looked about the church with unquestioned authority.

God, she scolded herself, she was gawking at an officer of the Crown. One who could recognise her. Or must at least have suspicions over Mr. Hall's sudden death.

Isabel looked away as the vicar finished his speech. The servants filed out. Mr. Blackman took her arm and led her out of the pew before Isabel could think of a reason not to follow him. How could she explain it to her father? *Don't introduce us, please?* She doubted it could be explained without...

But her father marched on, dragging the reluctant Isabel in his wake, before pausing next to the man. "Good of you to attend my son-in-law's funeral." Mr. Blackman's voice was low and cautious, and Isabel glanced up at her father. What did he make of it all?

The officer was positioned close to the door. He nodded to each of them in turn.

"I understood someone might attend because of the manner of his death," Mr. Blackman started to say before there was a small outbreak of an argument at the lectern between the vicar and Mr. Hall. "Excuse me," Mr. Blackman muttered, "I will return in a moment." And off he bustled hurriedly, leaving Isabel hoping against hope that the floor might open and swallow her whole.

"Thank you, sir, for attending my husband's funeral," Isabel finally settled on.

The handsome man removed his hat and dipped his head in the manner of aping respectful courtesy before taking Isabel's hand in his. He was even better looking up-close, Isabel realised, much to her own annoyance. Horribly, unfairly so. Those eyes were a soft alluring blue and seemed to have the power to draw her into their silken depths. It made for such a contrast to his build, which, given his muscular shape, could have overpowered her in seconds. It was strange to think that she was rather thrilled by the idea of this. When their eyes met, she hoped he was aware of the challenge she was issuing to him.

The man dimpled in answer to her question before resuming a more serious expression. The smile brightened his face; it suited him. "I'm afraid I never had the pleasure of formally meeting your husband." There was an odd sort of emphasis on the word 'formally,' and Isabel wondered if this man might have fought Pierre. "But I find myself as a stand-in magistrate, and given my father's position in the county, I had to attend Mr. Hall's funeral to best offer my sincere regret over his passing. And, of course, to find the men who committed such base crimes. Allow me to introduce myself, Mrs. Hall. I am Lord Lynde."

CHAPTER 4

Nicholas watched her expression change with utter enthralment and delight. The young Mrs. Hall knew he was the man she had fought; she wasn't a good enough actress to mask that. But she hadn't known who he was in terms of his position in society. That had at least surprised her. Shocked her. There was a strange amusement in watching her expressive face move with this new information. Adapt to this shock and then steady itself to resume the fight. Her flushed features calmed themselves into a more sombre look.

Mrs. Hall wasn't his normal type, Nicholas mused. He preferred curvaceous brunettes with wide laughing mouths and flashing eyes, neither of which Mrs. Hall possessed. But her strait-laced manner appealed to him. She was handsome, he allowed. He suspected some of the Oxford Set would call her more than that, but Nicholas was not at present willing to give out too many compliments, given that she was dangerous, scandalous, and a criminal to boot.

In the dim light of the church, her face was still recognisable as the dashing girl he'd grabbed in the woods. The question was, how much did Mrs. Hall know, and how involved was she in the smuggling ring? Given her willingness to throw his friend to the ground, Nicholas told himself trusting her would be a mistake.

"It is good of you to come, my lord." She bobbed a curtsey.

"Even in these unfortunate circumstances, it is a pleasure to make your acquaintance."

Mrs. Hall made to step back and retreat, but Nicholas followed her, still holding her hand in his. Nick's heart lightened as she slid her hand along his arm to walk with him. He led them both forward out to hover under the out-jutting roof of the church, away from the protective eyes of her father and brother-in-law. Above them, the rain beat down; the noise would blot out any questions he chose to put to her. That was if he trusted her enough to answer them.

"I must extend my family's deepest apologies for your unfortunate loss." He wondered if it was his bullet that had mortally wounded her husband or if it had been fired by Silverton or Walsh. It didn't much matter; his actions against the gang had rendered her a widow.

He seemed to remember some medieval myth in which killing a man meant one had to provide for his family. Nicholas cast a glance over her. He might not provide for much, but he'd be willing to fulfil some of the husbandly duties she might be missing. Nicholas swallowed; that was an unpleasant thought of his. She deserved better, even if she was a criminal.

Mrs. Hall released his arm and stepped back to gaze out over the graveyard. She looked too young to be embarking on widowhood. Her slim figure, dressed in heavy black, contrasted against the paleness of her creamy peach complexion, and her brilliant hair was pinned back under a black lace-trimmed bonnet. She turned around to look at him, her expression neutral and contained, as if the feelings he assumed she would be experiencing were nothing of the sort. She appeared to be in utter control. A few drops of the rain had landed on her cheeks, but she was not at all upset.

"Lord Lynde, I had no idea you would be in the neighbourhood. I am sure many other duties might occupy your time more valuably."

Nicholas realised the cheeky madam was trying her best to dismiss him. His hackles raised, he grinned at her. The respect he'd initially felt had morphed into something else. He resolved to treat her like a criminal.

"No, indeed," he answered, stepping closer to her. She came up to his chin; the very top of her head would brush against the underside of his jawline if he were to pull her close. It was odd to realise that that was the pose they had been in previously. Her earlier victory would not reoccur. Nicholas drew out a snowy white handkerchief and raised it up to dab at Mrs. Hall's face, removing the raindrops that decorated her cheeks. "I consider it my duty to care for the unfortunate peoples of my county. Especially in the face of crime."

He paused and watched her expression contract with awareness. Stepping closer still, he realised he could smell her perfume. It was jasmine, exotic and alluring. The expensive kind that women wore in clubs or gaming halls. It did not seem a good fit for a young society matron.

He pocketed the handkerchief square. "Where were you when your husband was attacked?"

"At my father's. Looking after my sister."

"Your sister is lucky to have someone so devoted to her care," Nicholas said, whilst wondering how many members of her family were caught up in the smuggling scheme and how young they started them off.

The youthful widow, so close to him now, looked no more

than twenty-five or so. If she had been corrupted, she must have been no more than an adolescent when it began. Again, a medieval idea occurred to Nicholas, but this time it was of him rescuing her. Would she not be looking for protection? He looked over her features again, cursing her for that direct gaze that so threw him off his guard. *No, do not be charmed by a pretty face. That way lies ruin.*

"Of course," she said, looking up at him, "I will forever feel guilty that I was not at home to say goodbye and ease my husband's parting from this world."

"One can tell how much it has affected you," Nicholas said. Judging by her stony expression and unruffled exterior, Nicholas had his doubts over the Halls sharing a loving marriage. Maybe it was a marriage of convenience, one built on extorting money and spreading disaster in its wake.

"I appreciate your concern, your lordship. It is not often we see the Lyndes about with the common folk."

"My father is kept busy at Parliament."

"And you?" Her tone was sharper, and she coloured.

Nicholas raised an eyebrow at her. She was trying to imply he was lazy or too... too much of a snob to mix in her society. Which was true, he realised, at least from her perspective. He did love coming back to Sussex when he could, but there was not enough time to attend the functions she would have frequented.

There was a sharp cough from behind them, and Nicholas turned and looked at the two men who had been arguing in the church.

"Lord Lynde." The older of the two, a grey-haired man of around fifty-five, spoke first. "I am reliably informed of your title by our vicar. All is resolved now. Please accept my humble apologies for earlier. I am Mr. Harold Blackman. I am honoured to have your father's acquaintance, and I should have recognised you. You are the image of him." Mr.

Blackman had a wide open face, with deep lines that furrowed around his grey-blue eyes.

Nicholas shook the proffered hand of the older man before glancing at the younger. "And you must be Mr. Hall. I convey my sympathies for your brother's passing."

They continued to linger in the entranceway to the church, the grave-lined cemetery spread out before them.

"His murder. Set upon like that. I wish I had been there," the younger Mr. Hall said. From the paperwork Silverton and he had found and briefly flicked through, Nicholas remembered that this one was James, and the dead one had been Pierre.

James turned his gaze from Nicholas to Mrs. Hall, his expression transforming into one of hunger. Nicholas hoped Mrs. Hall knew what she was doing. For a moment, he noticed her delicate neck contract as if she were swallowing, and he had the brief impression she was ill at ease with James. The idea of leaving an innocent young woman alone with someone involved in the smuggling gang—Nicholas stopped himself. He knew she wasn't innocent. He had a dear friend at home unable to walk; that proved she was as guilty as her in-laws.

"Yes. If only the law had been there to stop it," he said, aware of the double meaning of his words. Nicholas would have bet money that James had been there that night. "Excuse me now. I should be heading home."

"Do come and take tea with us in Alfriston whenever you can," Mr. Blackman said into the strained silence. "I am sure my wife and daughter would be thrilled to make your acquaintance. My youngest child is a great friend of Prudence Pendleton, the Marchioness of Heatherbroke. Her husband is an acquaintance of yours, I believe?"

This was why he'd avoided local society. Avoided it like the plague. In London, matrimonially minded mamas were the norm; it became the game for all, and Nicholas was too good-natured to want to hurt anyone's feelings. Be it the fathers, the brothers, hell, Mrs. Hall might try and force her younger sister on him to get him off the scent. Her delicious jasmine scent.

There she stood, watching him, as cool as anything, and Nicholas assumed he must have misread her earlier fear. In her striking black get-up, that frigid beauty wasn't scared of anything. For all he knew, she was the ringleader of the entire Wareton Gang, manipulating both the Halls and her father to her whims.

As his carriage drew up, Nicholas replied, "I would be pleased to attend tea. Thank you for the invitation."

He watched all of them out of the window as his carriage drove him back towards Hurstbourne. He was going to go to that blasted tea. But first, he'd call on the guilty Mrs. Hall, he decided. After all, he had her horse to return, and he was curious to see how she'd explain that one.

HURSTBOURNE MANOR WAS NOT AS CALM AS NICHOLAS would have liked. In fact, he hardly recognised the place. He'd left Silverton lying stretched out on a settee in one of the downstairs rooms, close to his father's study; that at least was still the same. But now, all the papers were strewn here and there, and a maid was crying in the corner of the room. On top of all of that, one of their finer tea sets was lying broken on the floor. The ordered drawing room with striped, yellow wallpaper and elegantly picked pieces did not seem big enough to house either Silverton or Nicholas's angry younger sister, Viola. She was red-faced and as furious as Nicholas had ever seen her, close to stamping her foot, her flushed face as pink as her cerise gown.

"Get up. I insist you stand," she was yelling when Nicholas pushed open the door.

"I'm afraid I can't." Silverton watched her with the sort of patient weariness that always wound Viola up. Nicholas knew that his sister did not respond well to being told what to do; she had a fierce temper and was familiar with using it. That, however, was not Silverton's way.

Viola wasn't listening; she flew over and grabbed Silverton's legs, trying to get him on his feet. "I won't be forced to wed one of your friends," she said over her shoulder.

Nicholas had gone to check on the maidservant, who ceased her crying when he approached. "What's wrong, Bessie?" he asked her, with as much kindness as he could.

"Oh, sir, Her Ladyship said I'm to move the gentleman... but you said, and then..." Bessie's words trailed off as Viola started to speak again.

"What's the meaning of this?" Viola shouted. "You took Father up on his suggestion that I should wed one of your Set. Then you decided you'd force me to do it?"

"Lord, girl, I haven't even asked you," Silverton said.

Nicholas forced himself not to laugh. It seemed like his idea of matchmaking was not going to work out. It had only been a mild notion, but Viola was too much of her own woman to be led around. And Silverton... Well, he looked ready to murder Viola and far more inclined to wed Bessie of anyone in the room.

"He really has fractured his leg," Nicholas said.

There was a pause in which Bessie slipped out of the chamber with the broken shards of the tea set. Viola looked between her brother and the injured man on the settee. The fury seemed to go out of her, but nevertheless, she folded her arms, her pretty face frowning at the pair of them. "You promise?"

Sitting down in a nearby chair, Nicholas nodded. "Utter and complete fluke, the injury."

"Can I know what the hell is going on?" Silverton asked. "I assume madness must run in your family. I hadn't even proposed."

Viola laughed at this. "I'm afraid I see matchmakers everywhere."

Nicholas wasn't quite as thrilled at the Viscount's joke or really any dig at his family's past. Everyone in the Set knew not to mention, or even allude to, Nicholas's mother. The countess was out of bounds to everyone.

"Apologies for any offence given," Silverton added when he saw Nicholas's expression.

"None taken," Viola answered for him. She had moved to sit on the arm of Nicholas's chair. "I think you'd better tell me what's going on."

"Probably not for the best."

Viola gave her brother a furious look. "If you don't tell me, I will just have to continue listening to the servant's gossip who let me know a great deal about the smuggling ring in these parts." Both men shifted in their seats, and Viola grinned with a look that said, 'I've trapped you, haven't I?'

"I will inform you of one or two things, but no telling Father. It'll just...." Nicholas trailed off. Hurstbourne had been looking worse for wear ever since that wedding debacle, and Nicholas had no desire to stir up any issues for his father.

"Of course, I will keep as quiet as the grave. And I'll be a help if I can. But oh, Nicholas, how exciting. And romantic," Viola said.

If anything could have doomed a potential romance between Silverton and his little sister faster, it was this statement. The look that Silverton bestowed on her was one of patent dislike. His handsome face drew in, and his lip curled.

"Madam," he drawled in a cold tone. "There is nothing dashing about the crimes that these men commit."

"Stuff and nonsense," Viola declared. She was far too used to the high-handed manner that most of the Set adopted to be overruled by one viscount. She looked away from Silverton and back to Nicholas. "You had better tell me everything. I know Sussex, and everyone here, better than the pair of you do."

The wisdom of using Viola's knowledge of the area without arising suspicion hadn't occurred to Nicholas before, but now he could see the sense of it. He offered her his hand. "But no getting into trouble or trying to turn criminal yourself."

"Oh, of course," Viola agreed. "Unless you frog march me up the aisle to that one." Silverton gave her another cold look, and Viola laughed. "So, what do you want to know?"

"As much as you know about the Halls." Nicholas wanted to press his sister for details of the widow Mrs. Hall specifically, but this warred with his desire to keep her presence in the woods from both parties. Lord knows why, but part of him wanted to protect Mrs. Hall's name.

"There's the old boot and the older brother, Peter, no, Pierre Hall. He runs a trade, shipping, I think." Viola started to walk around the room, clearly enjoying the drama. "There's a younger brother too, but he's more of your type, the young man about town look. I don't know what he does. Although Eliza Stoppard told me he might have gotten a maid with child. Now, as for his mother, she is—"

"What about Pierre's wife?" Nicholas couldn't help but ask.

There was a pause, and both Silverton and Viola looked at him. He had just cut his sister off halfway through her sentence in order to know more about a young, attractive matron. No, she was a widow now.

Viola's cheek dimpled in a way that he had adopted when he sensed there was someone to tease. "How do you know the younger Mrs. Hall?" she asked innocently.

"I attended her husband's funeral this morning. Pierre Hall is dead."

There was a break in Viola's smile, and her expression dropped, ever sympathetic to the plight of others. "Oh, gosh. Poor Isabel."

I have her name. Isabel. He played with the name on his tongue before deciding that it suited her. There was something about it. Isabel. It felt held in, secure, almost withdrawn. Wouldn't it be nice to see the cracks break in that maintained façade and watch her passion issue forth?

"Ahem." Silverton pulled Nicholas back to the real world and out of his imaginings, where he was busy spreading Isabel's golden, gossamer hair on his pillow.

"Eh?" Nicholas asked.

"You think that the Halls are involved in the smuggling ring?" Viola asked.

"Well," Silverton said. It was clear by the dubious look on his face that he didn't want to risk telling either of them too much. But Silverton had little choice but to trust them both, given his injury. "What we need to work out is who else is involved."

"I doubt it's either of the Blackman girls. I only know them slightly. Agnes, that's the middle girl; she was close to the Stoppard sisters. But they aren't the type. What's the word?" She looked around the room, her gaze alighting on Silverton before she rolled her eyes at him and looked back at Nicholas. "They are very wholesome."

Silverton let out a sigh. "The Waretons have been selling illegal goods for years; any family profiting from that is about as far from wholesome as—"

"I was giving you my insight," Viola said. "Who are the Waretons?"

"Their ringleader, James Hall, is our key suspect. But I believe that he is being funded by someone named Harlington. He is ruthless and responsible for some terrible crimes." There was a pause, and Silverton looked pained. "He has killed several men in his schemes." Silverton moved, the gesture causing his face to contract from the discomfort as he did so. "Bugger it," he swore. His hazel eyes looked between the two of them before fixing on Viola. "He also likes very young girls." Viola was not the sort of person to back away from anyone, but even she took a step back at this remark, her vivacious face paling. "He has a distinctive mark near his mouth." Silverton gestured to his own lips. "I managed to scar him, but the long and the short of it is, he got away to the Continent."

"If you see someone like that—" Nicholas began.

"You don't need to tell me." Viola made her way over to stand next to Nicholas, who squeezed her hand. "I won't go near someone like that."

"What is the best course of action?" Nicholas had his own plan to investigate the Blackmans, particularly Isabel Hall. But now he knew about Harlington and that this went beyond brandy and up to something worse; he would immediately secure more men.

"I won't be much use to you, I'm afraid," Silverton muttered. "I'm going to be laid up for the next eight weeks or so, according to your doctor."

"Is that all you want to tell us?" Nicholas asked.

Silverton looked away from him, not answering, and Nicholas had the distinct impression that he only had half the story yet again. His friend was hiding something.

"We will take care of you," Nicholas said into the silence.

"Thank you."

"Do you think he might be more comfortable down in Winston Cottage?" Viola asked. "It would give you more peace and might provide a better cover for the viscount?"

"Not a bad idea," Nicholas replied. His sister was right. Winston Cottage was at the edge of the estate, with access to the Cuckmere River, which could be rowed down. It was also easy for outsiders to visit without being seen by all the servants. Walsh could be slipped in and kept there, given the size of the estate. "It might be safer. We could consider it our base of operations."

"I appreciate your effort. If I could... if it could just be Walsh and myself. I would not want Lady Lynde to be tied into this. It is my fault other women died and that this gang continues to exist. If I had managed to take care of Harlington, earlier..." His voice trailed off.

"That's decided then," Nicholas said. "We'll get you moved today."

Viola and Nicholas slipped out of the room with promises to fix things at the cottage to Silverton's liking. Nicholas took Viola's arm, and they meandered down the portrait-laden corridor in silence until they were out of earshot of the drawing room.

"Do you trust him?" Viola asked.

"With my life," Nicholas replied. It was the truth. He would have said the same of anyone in the Set. He didn't add that Silverton was hiding something from him. "But he's a spy, and he's good at keeping secrets, so you need to be careful."

Viola nodded. "What did you not want him to know?" Her cherubic face was watching her brother carefully.

"I didn't want him to jump to conclusions."

She laughed. "Heaven forbid that would happen. About whom?"

"I don't want you to, either."

"Mrs. Hall?" she guessed. "The younger? I assume."

"Of course," Nicholas said with some bite.

Drawing to a pause at the entranceway to the servants' quarters, Viola studied her older brother's face. Her expression was quizzical. "I never witnessed you chase a woman."

"No. I never chased one of your friends."

"Are they all too ladylike?"

"I wouldn't want to be forced into the parson's mousetrap."

Viola grinned at the terminology. "I wouldn't call Isabel Hall a friend per se. Although I've nothing against her. She's very sensible. And that would suit you."

"What do you know about my type?"

"As much as I can," Viola said. "Why else would I decide against ever marrying one of your friends? I've read up on all of them. Each is worse than the last."

"Mrs. Hall doesn't have any inside knowledge of me."

"By the look on your face, she soon might. Lud, do you mean to battle it out of her? Or just plain seduce her?"

"Never you mind." Nicholas wasn't sure what he felt. The more he considered the enigma of Mrs. Isabel Hall, the less he understood her. Her refined, cool, handsome exterior contrasted her actions: her riding to Hurstbourne, hiding on his estate, the felling of Silverton. But he was going to find out, and if it happened to involve a tumble in her bed on the way to the answer, then so much the better.

CHAPTER 5

It had been a whole ten days of liberty, or widowhood, as she should be calling it, Isabel realised, as she sat in the drawing room to the rear of the house. Weak sunlight was spilling through the lace curtains and warming her face. Isabel never again wanted to sit in the front room where Pierre had died. The whole of the townhouse was decorated in all the necessary black. She had donned enough black crepe to make her feel fifty, so she at least looked the part of the grieving widow.

Her family had visited in groups. First, her mother, who had been the most comforting. Then her sister, Agnes, who had been the least, followed by Clara, which had been helpful, as between the two of them they set in stone their story for the night of Pierre's death. The one remaining fear she had was what had happened to her husband's valuable horse, which she had had to abandon.

She might have embraced the look of widowhood, but the truth was different. Isabel had noticed how much lighter she felt as she walked around the townhouse, as if a burden had been lifted from her shoulders. First, how she no longer had to endure the monthly visits from Pierre, always over within five minutes, but she doubted she would ever forget the sheer uncomfortable embarrassment of him moving around on top of her. He had insisted from their very first time together that Isabel wear a thick brown nightdress; anything else would be distracting for him, he told her. No matter the fact that the gown itched, Isabel had always kept it on throughout their brief exchanges. He, too, had always worn his long nightshirt. She was grateful that he ensured the lights were out.

Over the last few days, Isabel had gone around gathering up the items that had been Pierre's. His clothes, first and foremost, were sent to his mother. Then she had stripped out his artwork. She planned to sell the pieces. Finally, she had turned her attention to his ponderous books of law, each heavy tome symbolising yet another thing they did not have in common. In the end, Isabel had sent them to her brother, Thomas, who was training to be a lawyer. She also insisted the cook start preparing food that was enjoyable to eat. She had never liked Pierre's fish-centric diet. That could go to the devil. It felt exhilarating to make these small choices for herself at last.

There were other, more important worries, though. Pierre had kept his wife out of his finances, as was common for gentlemen in society. What wasn't standard was the gaps in his ledger or the vast amount he had spent on keeping his mother housed separately. It would have been more logical to have the elder Mrs. Hall live with them, but Isabel would have rather walked over hot coals than admit that to anyone.

Glancing back at the ledger, she resolved to ask her mother-in-law to reduce her sizeable household of fifteen to a more manageable ten. Given that Isabel would manage with just four servants, this seemed a fair enough exchange. If she was going to oversee her husband's estate, and given that

James was such a liability, it seemed sensible. She also felt certain she could ensure that Jessie and the baby were returned to her household. There was enough money for that. That would be a silver lining of the situation.

There was a ring at the door. Isabel got to her feet, thinking the elder Mrs. Hall had come to discuss arrangements, but it was Lord Lynde who entered the sitting room, ushered in by her maid, Lucy. He bowed low to her and then straightened up.

In haste, Isabel dropped into a curtsey. What was he doing here? Had her imaginings called him here? Had her replaying their little scene at the church caused him to manifest before her? On occasion, his image had occurred to her at night in her bedroom, as she lay spread out in the darkness. In the safety of her chamber, his face and form made a far preferable thought than Pierre's. She had called him her dream lover, just to herself, much in the way he had been in her youth. Although now she could claim to know a little more about men. Where all the implications and suggestions led to.

No, but in these dreams, he could be hers' alone. He would come in through the windows of her bedroom. It was to the rear of the house, and there was no balcony nor any hanging vines for him to climb up to her, but it didn't matter. In these little fantasies, she could banish the brutish realities of lovemaking and have him be her Romeo. The candles would be lit around her room so she could watch him as he climbed in through the window. He would be wearing a white shirt, a waistcoat, hand-stitched clothes... all of which he would start to discard. He would remove more than Pierre ever had, leaving him naked. Her mind created a sort of sketch, but she had no idea if it did him justice or not. Then he would walk closer to her, reaching out towards her.

It was here that Isabel's mind stopped. She would have

liked to have continued, but she could not make herself. Isabel realised with sadness that she lacked the imagination to picture what happened next. She did not want to spoil the fantasy by casting him into the same mould as Pierre.

But of course, he knew none of this, and the idea that he ever could have an inkling made Isabel want to climb into a nearby cabinet and never emerge.

Lord Lynde was watching her closely. Isabel pointed at a nearby seat at the table with a jerk of her hand. "Do sit, my lord. Lucy, would you fetch us some tea?"

His Lordship took the offered seat, his bright eyes travelling over her notes and calculations from the accounts. In haste, Isabel shut the book. How rude to try and read what was hers. Why did his eyes make her think that they were indeed back where she'd last conjured him up, in her bedroom? As if, perhaps, he was able to read her mind and wanted things to progress further, past what she'd imagined.

"How pleasant to see you again, Your Lordship," she said, adopting the role of the proper young widow, as if societal rules and practices were an armour.

"Why, thank you." His tone was light. A little frivolous, she decided. "I thought I would take you up on your advice to visit more of the neighbourhood than I had previously experienced."

"So many young ladies will be delighted to hear that," Isabel said, then slammed her hand to her mouth, embarrassed by her curt tongue. "I'm sorry, my lord, I should not have said that. It was not appropriate."

"I'm certain it was innocently meant. Of course, you will have to tell me if any particular females did desire me to call." He was looking at Isabel with a smirk on his lips. She was sure he meant the comment flirtatiously. Searching for an appropriate reply, Isabel drew a blank.

Lucy returned with the tea moments later and set it out

before them. A little part of Isabel pondered the wisdom of her taking tea with a man of Lynde's standing. The Hurstbourne name was rifle was scandal, wasn't that what everyone always said? Something about Lynde's mother, but it was before her time. She poured out the brew, as Lucy slipped from the room. Given what might come out after Lynde's investigation into Isabel's family, both married and maiden, perhaps it wasn't worth worrying too much about his family's exploits.

She offered him a cup, he took it, and their fingers brushed against each other. That was the third time he'd touched her. *Why, oh, why, am I counting?*

Isabel got up from the table in one quick move, putting some much-needed space between them. She could still feel the brush of his fingers just above her wedding ring, the strength and heat of his hand far more stirring than the gold band had ever been.

"How—"

"I've come about a rather awkward business," he cut her off. "You see, the night your husband died, it seems there was a theft."

In her head, Isabel started to pray. She made up her mind, as she watched the handsome lord drink his tea. She decided that he could have the Halls; she'd give them up. He could have whatever money her husband had stolen. He could have her—the idea made her flush, both in confusion and annoyance. That was what she'd promised during the ritual she had done at school. She'd promised herself to a copied sketch of Lord Lynde. Nicholas Lynde. A boy she'd never met, but always wanted to. He could have her. That was what she had whispered to herself again and again. But the bloody man had never materialised until now. Until she was trapped.

Now he was sat in her pretty little drawing room, his handsome frame out of place next to the delicate pastel-coloured wallpaper. He was too late. There was one thing he couldn't have, and that was her family; she would die to protect her father, mother, and siblings.

"Out with it," she snapped, her fear manifesting as rudeness, but Lord Lynde seemed to find it amusing.

"You're not shy about getting straight to the point, are you, Mrs. Hall?"

"Would you prefer it if I was?"

"It is a little odd," he said, getting to his feet and moving towards her. The air in the room seemed to come alive as he stepped within a foot of her. "Because your reputation is of someone who never lets her emotions get the best of her. Perhaps it is delayed grief over your husband's death?"

"Perhaps," she muttered, forcing herself to calm down and nod at him in the most stilted of manners. She was dying to know who he had questioned about her reputation, but she buttoned her mouth upon the subject. "You mentioned some awkward business?"

"Ah, yes. Yes indeed. You see, your husband's horse seems to have been found on the Hurstbourne estate. I asked around, and the beast belongs to Mr. Hall."

Isabel had been awaiting news of the horse, hopeful that the dear creature would be found. She schooled her features into surprise. "It must have been stolen by the thieves who set upon my husband. And have you been kind enough to return the animal? I had lodged the horse's disappearance with the authorities."

"Quite, Mrs. Hall. But that is not the odd thing I meant. The nature of the events that occurred on Hurstbourne estate were unusual. You see, the bandit who stole your horse also attacked a man on my estate before fleeing into the woods with some valuable paperwork."

"Oh, my," Isabel made herself sound as shocked and

appalled as she could, with the added gesture of lifting her hand to her heart as if moved by horror. "How shocking."

"Indeed, although that's not the worst of it."

"No?"

"No. The man whom the bandit attacked subsequently died from his injuries."

"No." Isabel's response was more heartfelt this time, and she immediately felt guilt-ridden and sick. Her hands reached out to steady herself, going towards the nearest chair. The idea of being responsible for a man's death—dear God, no—tears filled her eyes. That was what she had tried desperately to avoid. It didn't make sense. She'd heard the man crying out on the ground. She had glanced the man's way, seen him moving his head. Surely, surely...

Lynde moved nearer, crouching closer and staring up into her face.

"Come now, my dear, dear Isabel, surely, there's no need for the show of tears." His voice was low, creating a strange warmth that infused her body.

With his un-gloved fingertips, Lynde reached up and traced the trail of her teardrop down her cheek. The tear had run into the indent at the side of her mouth, so that is where Lynde's finger came to rest. The gesture was more moving and thrilling than anything Isabel could remember happening to her in years. Lynde seemed to be ready and willing to take his time, each one of his movements well-considered to fit with her quickening breath. Without realising it, Isabel let her eyes drop to Lynde's mouth. His lips were firm and wide, with markers either side that indicated that he liked to laugh. She wondered what it would be like to be kissed by someone like him. Not the fantasy man she'd imagined.

"I..." Her reaction to the news of the death, her response to him, her own tears now... She blinked. She needed time to regroup, to re-strategize. She was just ill-prepared for the realities of facing someone as devastating as Lord Lynde. He had an advantage of her because of her childish infatuation. It was nothing more than that. Isabel moved forward in her seat. She needed to tell him not to touch her. She needed to tell him that he had no right to use her Christian name. She needed to thank him for returning the horse but insist that visits like this were not to continue. She had her reputation to consider.

He didn't move, so when she shifted closer to him, he was still crouched in front of her. Inches away. Breath hitched in Isabel's throat, and then he smiled and bent forward, his lips brushing against her parted mouth, before pressing onwards. He was kissing her. It started slowly, delicately at first. As if it were the most natural and easy thing in the world, as if they were doing something utterly acceptable. His hands rose and came up to hold her face, his fingers touching her hair. His head angled to the right.

His lips were as tender and pressing as she'd always thought they would be. It was sweeter than she'd imagined. Better than cocoa, or ices... because of the way it made her heart pound within her chest. His tongue edged along the seam of her lips, nudging them wider, and Isabel sighed into a deeper kiss. Lynde dropped his hand from her hair, moving it down to her waist. He scooped Isabel out of the chair, lowering her down to kneel on the floor with him. Her knees banged against the carpet, making Isabel start. Waking up her to reality.

She raised her hand, ready to slap him. She didn't know if she was angrier at the kiss ending or his impertinence at such a move. "How—how dare you?"

"Here, let me help you." He offered his hand to help her to stand. She scrambled away from him so that she could feel in control. Her eyes blazed into his as she stared at him, waiting for Lynde to be embarrassed.

But he just grinned. "I knew it would look better loose."

"What?"

He gestured to her hair, and Isabel's hands flew up to her bun. He'd pulled and tugged pieces of it free, his hands ravaging her chignon. If she were a lady, Isabel would have hurried out of the room and made her butler throw him out. But she couldn't leave him alone with the household accounts.

"I think you've insulted me enough for one day, Your Lordship."

"Hadn't you better call me Nicholas?"

"No," she replied.

"I can help you."

"What?"

"With the hair." For the briefest of moments, Isabel wondered if he'd been about to say something else, but his casual nature seemed to take over. His easy grin was back in place. "Pin it up for you. Can't say I'm a natural at it, but I've helped others—"

"Stop it. I will not be insulted so."

"Indeed," Nicholas's smile dropped and was replaced with a coldness that rather disappointed Isabel. "We will return to the issue of the man on my estate."

"It is very tragic."

"Yes, I can see you mean that, given your tears."

"Any death would render me so; it is a difficult time."

"It is odd, even bizarre, you did not feel the same sadness at your own husband's funeral."

Isabel fidgeted where she stood, conscious of his presence in such a small space. If she had thought that one kiss would dispel the heightened tense air between them, she was wrong; it seemed instead to have tightened like a coiled spring.

"You have no right," she repeated.

"You already said that. It might have been a worthwhile point had you not kissed me back."

"Do not be ridiculous." She tried to pull her hair back into place.

"Don't hurt yourself," he soothed.

Isabel dropped her eyes, and he stepped closer. Even his breathing stirred her, she realised. It had to be a magic spell, that silly ritual at school, that explained this desire she had for resuming their kissing. He had initiated it, so one could assume that he wanted her. The fluttering this created in Isabel's stomach was more enthralling than she cared to admit.

"Come." His voice was harder than before, firmer, the charming man replaced with someone who meant business. "You can tell me what really happened."

Forcing herself to look up, Isabel met his eyes. She felt he had known that it was her in the woods that night. But that would mean he thought her guilty of murder. Isabel was about to throw herself on his mercy because perhaps there might be a chance of salvation if she did when the door of the sitting room opened, and in walked her mother-in-law, thirty minutes late for their arranged teatime discussion of Pierre's belongings. She wore a massive bonnet, as if the size of it would imply all the grief she needed to demonstrate.

"Now really, Izzy," Mrs. Hall said. "Do you often greet guests in such a manner? You look a fright. Go and straighten yourself up at once." The woman looked at Lord Lynde. "And who are you, sir?"

"This is Lord Lynde," Isabel said. Her voice had returned to its normal, neutral tones. She walked to the tea bell and rang for Lucy once again. "Allow me to introduce my mother-in-law, Mrs. Hall."

"How do you do, ma'am?" Lord Lynde was all politeness.

Mrs. Hall sank into Isabel's seat, nodding at His Lordship.

Her angry eyes pivoted to Isabel, instructing her to leave the room. Instead, Isabel reached out her hand to Lord Lynde.

"It was pleasant to renew our acquaintance. Thank you for returning my husband's horse to me."

Taking her hand, Lord Lynde bowed over it. "I hope to have the pleasure again soon. Good day to you, madam." And he was gone. The room seemed calmed, and Isabel felt she could breathe, and yet there was a lingering sense of sadness that he had left. Despite the anxiety, or rather despite her awareness of him, she had rather enjoyed their battle of wits. It was better not to dwell on whether she had enjoyed the kiss.

Halfway through her lecture, Mrs. Hall was shaking her head as Isabel lowered herself back into a nearby seat. "And you look as if you were trying to seduce him. Poor man."

"Ma'am," Isabel said. "I called you here today to give you Pierre's remaining personal items. But also, to discuss his finances."

"James has already been to see me about that," Mrs. Hall said as Lucy entered and collected the service. "We discussed it all, and you're to move in with me."

"No, ma'am." Isabel waited until Lucy had left the room before she spoke. "I have looked through the finances, and for the time being, the lease here is paid; we would not get the money returned to us. It is more logical to cut costs elsewhere."

"I'm not losing anything from my household. Between James and you, there will need to be some penny-pinching. Or, as I said before, you can return whenever you like to your father's."

"I looked over what was set aside by Pierre for me," Isabel said. "And from his paperwork, and what my father signed, there should be an annual allowance from his estate, regardless of children, of sixty pounds a year for the remainder of my lifetime. Which is owed to me." Isabel had double and triple checked this. Whilst it was not a vast sum of money, it was enough to retain her independence.

"You may, I suppose, live with me, and let James deal with all this," Mrs. Hall fussed.

"I don't think we would deal well together. Nor do I trust James to manage my affairs."

"You little—"

Lucy's nicely timed return with the tea-service cut off whatever Mrs. Hall had been about to say. Isabel indicated to the girl that she should remain, and Lucy bobbed her head and stayed watching the older Mrs. Hall from the corner of the room.

Sucking in a breath, Isabel continued, "If it turns out that my legacy has been lost or gambled away, I will, of course, be seeking legal recompense from Pierre's business. It would be a shame if any note of scandal," on that word, Isabel placed particular emphasis, "were to be attached to the Hall name. I hope you take my meaning."

The silence stretched until Mrs. Hall got to her feet, nodded her head at Isabel, and walked to the door. She glanced at Lucy and then shot Isabel a nasty smile. "We know what to do with scandals in our family. I hope you do, too." When Isabel made no answer, the older woman said, "It is best that James looks through this all. We will need to rely on him."

With no more threats to issue, Mrs. Hall turned and exited the sitting room, leaving a drained Isabel to look in confusion at Lucy.

"What was that about?"

The maid blushed and studied the carpet. "I wouldn't like to say, ma'am."

A distant nagging thought occurred to Isabel. She was certain that Jessica had been Lucy's cousin and perhaps the maid feared a similar fate. "Jessica's actions have no reflection on you." Lucy glanced up, a mixture of emotions passing over her face, but she didn't reply, so Isabel pressed on. "If any information on her occurs to you, please let me know."

Isabel could tell the maid knew something, but instead of pressing the matter, she let the girl go. However, before she located Jessica, either in the hospital or if she had been moved on, Isabel needed to have her own money in order.

Isabel crossed to the mirror with a sigh and gazed at her reflection. She had flushed cheeks, and her hair was a mess. Her lips, a small line of pink, were fuller than normal, having been thoroughly kissed. When she looked herself in the eye, she did look different. She looked excited, as if someone had lit a spark beneath her and was encouraging her to feel alive for the first time in years. Even her skin seemed brighter; the dullness that had descended on her ever since she wed was slipping away, and the passion she so admired in her littlest sister was creeping into her bones.

It would be daunting to confront James again, a man who should have been her ally, but it would be thrilling to do battle once more with Lynde. And the thought of that made Isabel's mouth curve into a grin, one that would not drop, even though she knew it was wrong to be this happy.

CHAPTER 6

Nicholas had decided that two days before Christmas wasn't an odd time for a social call. After all, he was involved in an investigation where no one would tell him anything, from his chief suspect, Mrs. Isabel Hall, to his own friend, Silverton. The reality was, of course, that he had spent the entire time away thinking about the former anyway. Mooning around Hurstbourne Manor, as if he were a lovesick boy. It was only one kiss. What had come over him? Nicholas excused himself with the justification that he had not had the time for female companionship, what with his sister's wedding and then this trip home. Not to mention a smuggling ring to locate and destroy.

But to do that, he needed more details.

He had gone to Winston Cottage, but neither Walsh nor Silverton were informative enough. They had clammed up when he had arrived and restricted their remarks to the food parcels they were receiving from the manor. No matter what approach he tried, Silverton would not tell him any more information. In disgruntlement, Nicholas had quizzed his sister, but Viola only had a nodding acquaintance with the

Blackman family, and it was limited entirely to the daughters, not the father of the household.

This was why he had settled on the social call and why, on the 23rd of December, Nicholas stood in front of the Blackman house on the outskirts of Alfriston and knocked at the door. He was ushered in by a rather awed-looking maid, who seemed close to fainting on hearing his name. She vanished, and then the drawing room door was pulled open to reveal Mr. Blackman and an assortment of other staring faces, bright, smiling, and hopeful amongst the cheerful fire and colourful wallpaper. In amongst them, he saw Isabel. She glared back at him, whilst the rest of the Blackmans grinned and welcomed him into their family home.

"I hope you don't mind me taking you up on your generous offer of a social call," Nicholas said to Mr. Blackman. "Your husband was generous to invite me over last time we met." He felt as if he were passing through a bower to another kingdom, as if the warmth and affection were not just from the fireplace. An older woman, Mrs. Blackman, had a handsome cloud of greyish-blonde curls surrounding her head, whilst her arched eyebrows watched him with interest. Next, a rather gawky young man with knock knees and badly cut hair, presumably the younger Mr. Thomas Blackman. Nicholas was then introduced to a blonde, matronly woman who held a baby to her chest and was told that this was Mrs. Agnes Miles.

"And of course, you know my older daughter, Mrs. Hall. And—" With a flourish, Mr. Blackman turned and pointed to a plump, red-haired girl by the fire. "This is my youngest, Miss Clara Hall."

"It is good to meet you, my lord." The youngest girl bobbed a curtsey.

So, it began. Nicholas could tell an element of expectation passed around the family between the beaming smiles and looks. Clara was their precious baby, clearly. The family's favoured child. Based on her stance and jewellery, she was also a little spoilt, although this wasn't why she held no interest to him. It was down to the blatant similarity between Clara and Viola, a sort of undimmed youthfulness. They had a similar set to their chins and ferociousness in their expressions. Immediately, he knew he would only ever see Clara Blackman as a sister. She and Viola were just too similar. Nevertheless, he bowed politely to her.

"Very nice to meet you too," Nicholas said. He made no move to advance towards her but glanced around the free seats. "I'm sorry for interrupting your family gathering."

"Not at all," Mrs. Blackman said as she moved over to the bell to order more tea. She had a similar grace to her eldest daughter. "We are delighted to have you in our home. You will have to excuse the informality; we are all very much at our ease. You see, we are celebrating my daughter's birthday."

Nicholas looked to Isabel. That would explain why she was here, away from the security of her townhouse, staring at him with the sort of murderous contempt he was coming to associate with her.

"No, it's Aggie's twenty-sixth," piped up the younger Mr. Blackman.

Everyone turned annoyed looks at Thomas, who was flopped down on the floor, and muttered, "Sorry."

Nicholas resisted the temptation to smile; he knew he teased his own sister as much as this boy clearly enjoyed winding up his.

"Happy Birthday, Mrs. Miles. I was taking the advice of your eldest daughter," Nicholas said, his head indicating Isabel. "Her wise suggestion of making myself known to the best families of the neighbourhood. You must tell me everything you can about the scene; I throw myself on your mercy." His eyes moved around the room, not lingering for too long on any of the women but including each of them in his appraisal of the drawing room.

"It would be a pleasure," Mrs. Miles said. Nicholas thought how plain she was in comparison to her sisters. Her hair was the mousiest, her eyebrows fey and pale, and whilst she had fine blue eyes, they had none of the limpet curiosity of Clara's nor the sensual grey pull of Isabel's.

Everyone had stood when he'd entered except Mrs. Hall, who had remained seated with what appeared to be a six-year-old on her lap. Nicholas moved over to the settee and sat down next to her.

"Hello," he said, turning a bright smile on the young boy. "What's your name?"

"Billy," the child replied. He was tugging at the edge of Isabel's sleeve and avoiding Nicholas's gaze. Nicholas wondered if Isabel had warned him against being at all friendly or if the child was simply shy.

"Is this your son?" He looked up into Isabel's eyes, wondering why he hadn't imagined her as a mother before. It wasn't that she didn't seem the type. His mind conjured up the image of her rounded with his own child in her belly, the swell lifting and softening her contours. Shocked, he blinked away the rather compelling, if overwhelming, idea. Why had that occurred to him? It annoyed him that she might have been in this state previously; it was not an emotion he wanted to explore in any detail.

"No," she replied, moving the boy off to the side, putting Billy between them. "I have no children. He is Mr. Miles's son and my sister's stepchild."

"Here you go," Nicholas said. He passed the boy a tin of mints he kept in his pocket. "Why not offer one to your aunt?" he said without thinking and indicating Clara in the corner. Billy scrambled off with the tin in his hand.

"What are you doing here?" Isabel asked him in an undertone as the maid returned with tea and the bustle of it being served took over.

The family was talking in bright tones. Their excitement for the upcoming festive period was obvious. They were taking turns to speculate on what their presents might be. He glanced at Isabel in her natural habitat. It suited her better than the townhouse; there was a glimmer to her eyes, and her posture was more relaxed. It struck him that something made her uneasy in her townhouse. Despite her recent widowhood, Isabel had not dressed the part today. Whilst she wasn't clothed in the colourful tones of her family, her dove-grey dress seemed to be moulded to her body. Nicholas forced himself to focus on her question, on why he'd come here today. He needed to investigate Mr. Blackman, whose cheerful face and squishy countenance laughed at something his son had said. Never had a man seemed more unlikely to be involved in a dark and elaborate smuggling scheme.

"Just taking your advice. As I told your mother," he replied.

"Nonsense."

"Perhaps I find myself overly curious." He accepted a biscuit from the proffered tray.

"What about?"

For a second, Nicholas wondered if he should be honest with her, mention the links that he knew existed between her father, her husband, and herself. But he still wasn't sure that he trusted her. He went for a white lie. "You did suggest I would be surrounded by eager young misses."

"As soon as they get to know your personality, they'll change their minds," she bit back at him.

Nicholas laughed at this; he rather liked the amount of spirit and grit that Isabel possessed. The room quieted, and all looked over at the pair of them.

"I didn't realise you were such good friends." Mrs. Miles

had sat closer to the pair, her eyes moving between Isabel and himself with a knowing glance.

Nicholas stood; he didn't want to blacken Mrs. Hall's name, at least not amidst her family. "I met Mrs. Hall at her husband's funeral."

"He also found poor Pierre's stolen horse and returned the animal to me," Isabel added.

"Of course, it was the neighbourly thing to do."

"I am sure Lord Lynde would agree with me, sister," Mrs. Miles continued. "It was shocking that Pierre was so set upon, but with such ruffians about, neither Mr. Miles nor I feel safe with you living alone."

"It would be acceptable, dear, if you wanted to move back here," Mrs. Blackman said as she passed, filling up Nicholas's cup.

Nicholas had paused, looking down at the gathered sight of Miss Blackman, the younger Mr. Blackman, and Billy. There were no mints left in his tin now.

"Wouldn't you agree with me?" Mrs. Miles called after Nicholas, forcing him to turn his gaze back to her.

"Lord Lynde doesn't—" Isabel started to say.

"I regret any violence committed in these parts. But I will do my utmost to see those responsible brought to justice."

"My sister's standing within the parish does require her to be housed somewhere safe." From the vehemence with which Mrs. Miles spoke, Nicholas got the distinct impression all was not cordial between the two sisters.

"All Agnes means," Mrs. Blackman cut in, "is that it would be a dear sight, having you closer."

"Indeed," Nicholas added. Although this too seemed regrettable, as if he were commenting on how dear a sight Isabel was. Which was true; she was. But he didn't want her to know that. "What I should have said is, until the neighbourhood is secure, any extra precautions one can take would be wise."

"I can take care of myself, thank you," Isabel said. She, too, had gotten to her feet. "I find I have a slight headache," she added, although Nicholas was certain she was lying. She looked perfectly fine to him. "I beg you to excuse me."

"Please allow me to escort you. That way, if you were to worsen, I would be able to secure a doctor," Nicholas said, with as much courtesy as he could. His plan on quizzing Mr. Blackman was forgotten now with the return of Isabel to his sight. He knew it went against what he had told Silverton, but for the life of him, Nicholas didn't care. He offered his arm to Mrs. Hall, who swallowed before taking it.

Grinning, Nicholas smiled around the room at the assorted family members. It was pleasant to see them all together, but getting away from any matchmaking that paired Miss Blackman and himself was a relief. Whilst it would have been useful to get more information on Blackman, Nicholas couldn't help trusting his instincts that the senior Mr. Blackman didn't seem the type. Exiting the neat, handsome drawing room, the pair of them waited in silence for the maid to return with his coat and hat.

"Such a shame you were taken ill," he said to Isabel. Her hand still rested on his arm, and his eyes kept returning to the delicate pale skin of her fingers, her knuckles, a tiny freckle at the joint of her wrist.

"Here you go, my lord. Madam." The maid bobbed and swung the door open. They walked outside and up into the waiting carriage.

"To Milbourn Street," Nicholas called to his coachman, sitting opposite Isabel. The carriage rumbled away, and Isabel averted her eyes to gaze out of the window.

"Why did you come to my father's house today?" she asked as they left Alfriston. "The real reason, please."

"To see what he knew about the crimes committed in the area."

"He knows nothing. I can promise you that." She spoke in such a rush that it sounded suspect.

Nicholas smiled, his grin dimpling his left cheek in a way that most women of his acquaintance found endearing. Isabel looked away from him. "If I said I believed you..." Nicholas began. She looked back, a flash of eagerness brightening her features. "What would you do for me?"

"You believe me to be a... ummm..." She paused. "Willing to have an affair?"

The idea of trading her sexual favours for protection turned Nicholas's stomach. His idea had been that in return for her knowledge of the gang, of what she'd seen the night her husband had been killed, he would protect the Blackmans and her too. But since she posed the question, he couldn't resist asking, "Why? Is an affair something you wished to pursue?"

"You know it's not," she shot back. "I thought that... that because of the kiss we shared, you would have the wrong idea about me. Because I am now a widow... that... that you would... would think I am a loose woman."

"Ma'am, I don't know what you might have heard about me or what ideas you took from the kiss, but please rest assured I would never take advantage of any woman."

Isabel looked back at him, her hands moving around in her lap as if unsure of what the next best course of action would be.

"Then what did you mean... about what I could do for you?"

"Trust me with certain things that you know," Nicholas said, wondering how much real information Isabel had. He could tell she was intelligent, but whether the smugglers or the Halls had ever realised that was less certain. Whether she was involved or might have overheard the right bits of information, he wasn't sure.

The carriage paused at a junction, and Nicholas moved to sit next to her. "If there were crimes you were aware of in this neighbourhood, crimes you knew were being committed. If you had any information about those who were responsible..."

Their eyes met. Nicholas wondered if he should mention her being the culprit in the woods. Isabel's lashes fluttered, and Nicholas sensed she was wavering. Carefully, he edged closer, and in as much of a brotherly tone as he could manage, he said, "I would like to think you might one day be able to trust me with whatever you know. If it means betraying your dead husband—"

This got her attention, and she backed away from him, her initial calm gone. "How dare you?"

"I'm sorry. I simply meant—"

"He may not have been a perfect husband, but like so many other women, I had to make do."

"I meant no disrespect to Mr. Hall." Her choice of words had rather surprised Nicholas; he would have imagined the eldest daughter of a prominent and wealthy tradesman, with good connections and a beautiful face would never have struggled for matches. Of course, he couldn't tell her that.

"Yes, you did," she said. "My husband might not have been the perfect spouse, but he was never unfaithful. And there was not some perfect man available to swoop in and rescue me. Not... not like there was for Prudence."

Unable to help himself, Nicholas smirked. To his knowledge, Miss Pendleton and Heatherbroke's romance, which started with a kidnapping from the side of the road, included some highwaymen and an illegitimate child, could hardly be described as perfect. But it had at least ended happily for both Heatherbroke and Prudence. Nonetheless, it was not what Isabel wanted to hear because she gave him a hurt look.

It was frustrating; Nicholas had always been reasonably adept at knowing what to say and do with women, but not with her. She rendered him as incompetent as a schoolboy.

"I know Heatherbroke." Here he stopped himself; he didn't want to ruin her friend's reputation. "I mean... I meant no insult to you."

"But that is all you have done."

"Not at all."

"You could drive a saint mad."

"Are you a saint?"

"I try to be. I try as hard as I can to do everything right," Isabel said. "I am the eldest. I have to do the right thing."

"What about you?"

"What about me?"

"When was the last time you did something just for yourself that wasn't perfect? Something that just made you happy?"

Isabel gave him a strange look. Her ability to confound him annoyed Nicholas no end; her expressions and the movements of her face remained so mysterious to him.

"You implied Mr. Hall was not a good husband. It is not as if I had a choice," she finished as if this were a triumphant note to end on but then looked embarrassed before dissolving into angry tears. "You always make me say the wrong thing." She scrambled through her handbag, looking for a handkerchief.

Knowing that if anyone saw them, he'd be in trouble, but past caring about this, Nicholas moved closer and enfolded her in his arms. He assumed she would push him away, but she didn't. Instead, she snuggled into the warmth of his arms and cried against his chest.

Minutes ticked by like this, and Nicholas discovered that it was rather pleasant to hold her thus. Aside from her crying, which created a slight dampness just above his heart. But

Nicholas reasoned that it was rather endearing, especially since the lovely, refined Isabel looked refreshingly human when she leant back into her seat and sniffed loudly. The other problem was how to stop her from being this miserable.

She blew her nose and then told him, "You are to forget that this ever happened."

"I'll take it with me to the grave."

"You always seem to be joking with me."

"I am not. I promise." He still had one of his arms on her waist, and as much as he thought she was getting comfort from his embrace, he felt it would not be wise to push his luck. He had no desire for Isabel to know how tempting it was to try and make love to her in the carriage. When he held women, it was for a simple purpose, sex. This was more than that, more important than such a base motivation.

"I must look a fright," she muttered, almost to herself.

"I think you look very pretty," he told her.

Isabel glanced up at him. She still didn't pull back out of his arms. Instead, she even smiled. Her lips, delicate and fine like the rest of her, widened into a broad grin. "Do you know what I would have given five years ago to hear that? You would have made my year telling me that as a girl."

She made to pull back, and, unable to stop himself, Nicholas brushed a kiss against her forehead. Isabel made no comment but rearranged herself in her seat, her expression as dignified as a saint once more.

"That was very good of you," she said. "It seems the stresses of the day must have driven me to it."

"I take it there was not anything similar from your relations." It surprised him that no one in her own family had been comforting. But, Nicholas rationalised, it was more about the Halls. He had disliked Isabel's brother-in-law on sight. "From your husband's family."

"The Halls are not an affectionate group. It has been an adjustment."

The edges of Eastbourne floated by, and Nicholas knew that they were running out of time. "You know, I think your sister is wrong."

"How so?"

"There is everything to recommend staying in your home. It is yours. You have earned your liberty."

Isabel looked startled at his words, and Nicholas had been about to add more, but it was then that the carriage drew to a stop.

"My dear," he said as she moved to leave him.

"Mrs. Hall," she corrected him, "I would not want to get above my station."

"It may be unfamiliar to you, or it may be second nature, I do not know you enough to say." Nicholas paused. He wanted to give her good advice, even if she were a criminal. It was her presence that compelled him. Her vulnerability, and protectiveness of her family, when they did not seem to deserve her. At least, not from what he had seen. "Sometimes," he continued, "in order to stake a claim, to be able to embrace one's independence, one must sometimes be brave."

"Are you suggesting that I take up gaming? Is that why you mention risk?" Her shocked expression made Nicholas grin at her. How fun it would be to tease her, but he meant it in earnest. He caught her elbow and kept her in her seat.

"One must gamble what one has in order to get a better return."

"I do not follow. Explain it to me?"

"You could gamble with, say, what you know about any crimes in Sussex, tell me, risk trusting me...?"

"But you know I am ignorant of such matters."

"Of course." His response soothed and dismissed her lie.

"Give me another example."

"It might be riskier."

"But I don't know you."

"Then I would say: trust the people you do know, and gamble what you have against the people you don't trust. Confront whoever might try and stop you from... say, staying here, achieving your independence—"

"Me?" She grinned.

"You might do whatever you care to do, but only if you can take the risk."

"I took a risk before."

"You did?"

"By marrying, isn't that what all women do?"

"That was at your father's suggestion," Nicholas guessed as his arm moved down from her elbow, his fingers moving over the sleeve of her dress to hold her hand. "A gamble would be you making a choice."

"So, it does return to an indecent offer?"

"I wouldn't want to leave you disappointed." He stood and climbed out of the carriage first, proffering his hand to help her down.

The quiet street was lit up with street lamps as the evening set in. The surrounding townhouses had their doors decorated with festive holly and ivy sprigs. The lights from inside the nearby windows seemed to make the place sparkle.

Still holding her hand, Nicholas walked Isabel up to her front door. "No decorations this year?"

"We are in mourning," she replied.

"But still, the world turns."

"Not for us all."

"Only for those who are prepared to gamble. With the promise of greater rewards." With a last squeeze of her hand, Nicholas bounded back up to his carriage. He wasn't sure how much of what he had said would stay with Isabel, but he hoped to hell she never cried like that again. It had moved him in a way that he could not remember feeling for more years than he cared to count. There was an unnerving element to the sensation it generated in his entire body.

Climbing up into the carriage, Nicholas called out, "Home," and settled back amongst the pillows. Her jasmine scent lingered still and made him dwell on Isabel all the way back to Hurstbourne.

CHAPTER 7

Over the following few days and over Christmas itself, Isabel dwelt on what Lord Lynde had told her. Not so much about his implied offer of an affair, although in the darkness of her bedroom, she liked to play out what would have happened if she had said yes.

On the one page she had kept, there were coded words and initials she did not understand, but she was sure that *C.H.* stood for a man. This information had to be worth something. She was prepared to sell it to James to get her allowance from the Hall business and the promise from him that her father's involvement with the smuggling would end. She had a nagging suspicion on what *C.H.* stood for, but it kept slipping away from her. Isabel cornered her father on Boxing Day and asked him to arrange a meeting at his office on the 29th of December with James.

"Whatever for, child?" Her father loved her, Isabel knew, but he had never broken the habit of considering her little more than a dependent. He also had no faith that women knew much about numbers, even though Isabel had been better at them in her youth than Thomas.

"The Halls are withholding my widow's portion," Isabel said. "I need your help to smooth things over."

Mr. Blackman nodded his head low in agreement with the plan.

THE 29TH OF DECEMBER ARRIVED WITH A COLD, FRESH dawn, and Isabel found herself dressing with immaculate care. She had always favoured softer, paler colours, believing they implied a femininity that suited her pale skin. With that in mind, she selected her standard mourning clothes, a simple black day dress, but over the top of this, she placed a deep purple velvet pelisse that covered much of the black gown and implied maturity in her mind. It brought out the colour in her cheeks and made her fey silver-blonde hair seem brighter. As a final touch, and a rather grand one, Isabel placed a purple plumed hat on her head, which she tied around her chin with a black ribbon. Pleased with herself and confident that this would work, Isabel unlocked the safe that held remaining page as well as her household accounts, all the proof she had, tucking them into her handbag.

Then she walked through the quiet streets of Eastbourne to her father's offices, passing by red-faced sweepers and wrapped-up stewards. The only thing she kept hidden about herself, just in case, was the slip of paper that tied Hall to *C.H.* and then back to her father.

Her father's secretary, a small, Cornish man named Mr. Ramsay, was cordial when she entered. He nattered away to Isabel about Christmas, about problems he'd had with his turnips and the ordered goose until James arrived. Then Mr. Ramsay's wide grin slipped from his face, and he shuffled out.

"What's this all about?" James asked as he looked around

the room. His voice was hard and scornful. "I was expecting Mr. Blackman."

"My father will be joining us." Isabel had chosen her seat carefully. Close to the desk, she could view the room from a position of power. It was also angled with the back of it to the fireplace and near a vicious-looking poker. She would take great delight in beating James over the head with it if he came too close to her.

"Not that it isn't simply..." James paused as he looked her up and down in a way that Isabel knew was meant to be insulting. "...charming to see you. Especially with you looking so respectful to my brother's memory." His eyes lingered on her widow's bonnet its large colourful plume. "If you wanted to create the idea of being a bold woman, congratulations."

"I heard you were out at La Rue's." Isabel cited the famed gambling den and whore house located in Eastbourne. It was well known to be a site that James frequented. "I see family respect is something you care for greatly."

"Are you listening to gossip?"

Isabel gave him a slow smile. "It isn't gossip if you know it to be true."

James started to move around the study, filling up the space as he shifted from the bookcase near the door to staring out of the window, his expression restrained and polite. Isabel was reminded of a statue she had seen once of a tiger, all its aggression visible in the way its claws were held.

"Why not take a seat?" Isabel indicated the chair opposite her.

He ignored her, although his hands came to rest on the tips of the chair frame. "Keeping us waiting, is he?"

Isabel knew her father was fetching all the documents that related to her marriage. But she didn't think James wanted to hear that, nor did he wait for her reply.

"I know what this is about, by the way."

"Yes?" Isabel replied.

"Oh, yes." His voice was malicious. "It's all about the money with you. It always has been. I warned Pierre myself on that. Always said he could have done better than you. But then, where would that have left you?"

Isabel chose not to reply again. Her lack of response seemed to inflame James further. "I always said he should have married Sir Benjamin Wright's daughter. That plain little mouse of a girl. She wed that nobody Philips, didn't she? Already given him two sons." James stepped nearer to her, with the desk separating them. "You're in much the same position as you were before. Minus your maidenhead."

Colour rose unbidden in Isabel's cheeks, and she had a horrible feeling that Pierre might have discussed his marital rights with James. As she tried to think of a brisk and cutting reply, her father entered the room, and James stepped back, a more respectful look adorning his face.

Her father walked around the desk and then placed the papers down in front of him, rubbing his hands together. When he opened his mouth, it was Isabel who stood up. She had been preparing for this moment, and she needed to get it right.

"I have asked you both here today," Isabel looked around at the two of them, "because I know what has been going on with the Wareton Gang. I have all the details of the funding you have given them. What has been bought, how my father's investments were spent, and what Pierre was doing when he was killed."

Mr. Blackman was red-faced, mottled through with embarrassment at her words. James's expression, however, was blank. The only sign that he had heard her was his curled lip.

"I am prepared to offer a compromise," Isabel continued. "I will burn all of these papers, with the promise that my father will be cut off from any further connections with the gang and the mysterious C.H. But I have a rather good idea who he is." She looked between the two of them, wondering if they knew she was lying. It was a gamble but one she felt sure she could make; C.H. was a person. "In exchange, I will not ask for my widow's portion, just a lump sum from the estate upfront, thereby cutting all ties between the Blackmans and the Halls. Forever."

She knew this was a sacrifice on her part, one that might mean that she would have to become a companion or resume living with her parents, but Isabel reasoned it was worth the risk. Having looked through the papers, she was aware that there was enough material here to hang or deport James, and she suspected it would be enough for her father to follow the same fate.

James leant forward, his eyes on the table, surveying the household accounts. "This is all of the paperwork?"

Isabel nodded.

Letting out a grim laugh, James got to his feet. "I guess you think you have us there." He moved away to stare out of the window, watching the proceedings down in the street, and he made a strange gesture with his hands.

Isabel glanced at her father. He looked very weary, his guilty face so vulnerable. "What must you think of me?" he whispered.

"I know you were tricked," Isabel soothed him.

Mr. Blackman patted her cheek before walking toward James. "I would say that would even us out; wouldn't you agree, Mr. Hall?"

"I might." James hadn't turned around nor taken her father's proffered hand.

"Father," she said. There was an unpleasant stillness to the room, and then an almighty bang ripped through the study as Isabel opened her mouth to say, 'Get away from the window.'

A bullet smashed the glass, winging her father in his arm and spraying fragments and shards of glass everywhere. Mr. Blackman dropped to his knees before James, holding onto his injured arm. The younger man swung around and started to hit her father about the head, knocking him down to the floor.

Isabel moved without thinking, hurrying over to the poker. "Get the hell away from him." She rushed forward and hit James over the back. Her hit bounced off his shoulders ineffectually. He pivoted towards her, his expression furious. He pushed Isabel aside and strode away to the desk. Isabel bent over her father. Harold was still breathing; the bullet had grazed his arm, nothing more; he was more injured by the repeated hits to his face.

Pressing her handkerchief to his head, Isabel screamed out to Mr. Ramsey in the next room, "Get a doctor. Hurry, please. My father's been hurt."

"Too late for that," James said. He was stood by the fire, adding page after page of evidence to the roaring flames. "You shouldn't have read so many of these notes. Tut-tut," he added, dropping the last of the papers into the fire.

Beneath her hands, Mr. Blackman struggled to sit up. The movement seemed too much for him, and his eyes rolled back in his head as he fainted. Isabel tried to ignore the fact that her leverage was now reduced to ashes in the grate. And now, she was alone with James, the thing she most wanted to avoid in the world.

He walked back towards her and dropped to his knees beside her, his eyes drifting over the passed-out form of Mr. Blackman. He was so close she could smell the rancid scent of cigarette smoke and brandy on his clothes. When she tried to move away from him, James reached out and dragged her close.

"You know, I quite liked you." One of his oily hands had

clamped around her waist; the other was fingering its way over her face.

Panicking, Isabel tried to fight him off, but the poker was too far away. He rolled them over so that he was pinning her down to the floor, his hands roaming over her body in a manner she detested.

Isabel froze, her words stiff. "If I give up all of the money I am owed—"

"You're ruining the effect; I rather liked the spirited resistance from earlier. Are you just going to lie still and frigid as you did with my brother? How dull." His arms moved down to her waist. Suddenly, as if she had been pushed into a cold bath, she realised what James meant to do. Isabel felt her body tighten as if she were shutting down and closing herself off. That thought made bile rush up her throat, and then anger infused her limbs.

"Get the hell off me." She spat full into his face. The phlegm ran down James's cheek, and he looked surprised.

In response, he grabbed Isabel by the throat, his fingers tightening. His words were a whisper in her ear. "You never should have used his code name. Charles won't let you live now. That was it, that decided your fate. Still, we can have some fun beforehand."

Isabel twitched beneath him as he pressed himself more tightly against her.

His hands moved over her in a way that might have made her cry out, but Isabel wasn't going to let him distract her. She needed to focus. Her father's unconscious form lay so close by. Isabel's mind flitted around the options; how long would it take Mr. Ramsey to get to the doctor's? Would anyone hear her if she screamed? It was the festive season; most people weren't in the office.

She would need to save herself.

James was busy pulling up her skirts, lifting and shifting

them out of the way. As he did so, Isabel rolled onto her stomach. The poker was close by, and James seemed to have forgotten about it.

He gave a raw chuckle, and his hands moved up to grab Isabel's bottom. "Much nicer," she heard him say as she reached for the poker. The edges of it were within her fingertips. She stretched out, touching the very tip of it, before being able to drag it closer. The metal snatched nearer as James pulled her drawers apart. Reacting, she brought the poker around with as much force as she could, catching James full in the face. As she did so, the door of her father's office burst open, and with a muted curse, a man ran in. But all that Isabel was focused on was James, who had collapsed to the side of her, his hands on his face. Blood oozed out from between his fingers. She smiled at the sight with grim satisfaction.

Only then did she look up from her position on the floor to see Nicholas standing there. His handsome face was livid as he looked between James Hall and her. When his eyes travelled to Isabel, they softened.

"Get away from the window," Isabel said as she got to her feet. She used the poker almost as a walking stick to try and balance herself. She was desperate. Nicholas was standing near to where her father had been shot. "He's got a marksman outside."

"I saw that," Nicholas muttered. He crossed over to help steady her. He held onto her arms, and then once Isabel was upright, he pulled her against him. She could feel him shaking as he hugged her. His hands moved over her sides, checking her for injuries. "I thought he might have shot you. Otherwise, I would have chased after the blaggard."

"You were watching us?"

"Excuse me." Nicholas released her for a moment, crossing to where James was slumped. He bent closer, yanking the man up by his neck. James muttered something that Isabel couldn't hear, and Nicholas dropped him back to the floor. James slumped where he was, and Nicholas hit him several times in the face, only pulling back to stare at his own bloody knuckles.

Isabel watched in fascination as James took the beating he'd always deserved. It felt almost wrong to marvel at the strength on display from Lynde. Hastily she straightened her clothes before turning away and hobbling over to her father. Mr. Blackman's pulse was faint, but he did seem to be regaining his senses.

"Stop that," Isabel called out to Nicholas. "Help me with my father."

Lynde stepped back, the look on his face murderous. "I've got my driver outside waiting."

"The most important thing is my father." Isabel tried to wedge her arm beneath him and pull him into a sitting position.

"No, my child," her father said, "you are far more important. My Lord." Mr. Blackman lifted his own drained eyes to Lynde's. "Please, she knows too much. Wareton... they're going to come for her. I will tell you everything I know, just please, protect my daughter. She's done nothing wrong."

"That's not true, Father," Isabel whispered.

"Please, get her out of here. If they see her...." Her father's voice trailed off. He was very pale and shaky, but the bruises on his face and his injured arm would not be life-threatening. He would survive if they could all get out. "Get her away from here. I'll explain everything I know. I'll gather everything I have here. Just take my daughter away from here."

Before Isabel could protest, long, strong arms were around her waist, hoisting her up into a standing position. "You have my word, sir," Nicholas said.

Without looking at her, Lynde proceeded to half lift, half

drag Isabel from the room. She fought against him. Leaving her injured father with an unconscious James turned her stomach. The idea of there being a marksman nearby also did not reassure her, even if Lynde swore the man had disappeared. Once they were outside, Nicholas wrapped his large overcoat about her.

"Let me go," she said, trying to prise herself free.

"You know I can't," he said. "What is your plan? I only have the one pistol. Your father is injured. There's just my driver here. We don't know how many men Hall might have in the area. We need to beat a strategic retreat."

"My father? We can't leave him."

"He will find his own evidence, and I will take care of you. We're outmatched. I am certain your father has a secure room he can hide in whilst I make sure you are safe. The priority is getting you as far away from the Wareton Gang as possible." Lynde levered her into the carriage, then climbed in next to her.

"Walsh," he called out. "Get us out of here. Now."

The carriage set off so fast that Isabel fell back amongst the pillows. The anger that had been pumping through her when she'd been in the room with James, when she'd seen her father hit, when James had crawled over her, all those moments had energised her. But now, it was gone. She felt safe, even though Nicholas was telling her she shouldn't feel so.

"Sir," she said, leaning forward and snatching at Lynde's coat. "We need to go to my house."

"God, no, that's the first place they'd look."

"My family—the servants."

Lynde leant back and looked at her with a bemused expression. Isabel felt she must have done something wrong. Or humorous. "Today, you have been attacked, shot at, and your—your person was ravished..." He looked so kind that

Isabel wanted to cry. "And yet your first thoughts turn to others."

"I am safe now." Her eyes narrowed; he knew so much, more than she might have imagined. How much he must be judging her. "What were you doing here today?"

"I had a sneaking suspicion about your father. I wanted to put it to the test."

"He's not a bad man. He was tricked." Isabel thought of all the papers that James had thrown into the fire. That had been the proof of her father's innocence. Now there was just her word and the faint hope that Nicholas might believe her.

"It is safe to say we need a new plan."

"We?"

Nicholas did not reply; he was too busy watching the road out of the small window. The town was quiet, and there was not much traffic, so soon they were quickening through the wintry fields of the countryside. "We need to plan something for you and your family's safety."

"My sister, Mrs. Miles?"

"Your entire family," he said. They lapsed back into silence, but Isabel had a hundred questions she wanted to know the answers to.

"What is your plan?"

"Allow me a little time to plan." He looked back at her. "Do keep away from the windows." His hand shot out, and he pushed her back amongst the pillows.

"Where are we going?"

"You'll see," he muttered. His eyes were on the fields that they rushed through. Suddenly, a horrible thought occurred to her.

"God, have you been hit?"

"No, no, I'm not hurt," came his brusque reply. Still, he would not look back at her, and Isabel realised what it was.

He was disgusted with her. With having to help a traitor like her.

"I'm sorry." She wondered if perhaps he was angrier than she realised; being forced to protect someone like her had tipped him over the edge. To have to support and be made to risk his life for a family, like hers—infamous aiders of smugglers, tradesmen... people so beneath his family's notice, it must rankle against his nature. This was what she was reducing him to, she thought with embarrassment. "I swear to you, as soon as I am out of this carriage, I will tell you everything I know. You risked much to help me."

Nicholas glanced back at her, his expression steady. "You have nothing to apologise for. You think that is what I am upset about?"

"I assumed you were distressed by being forced into helping people you regard as scandalous."

Even though the carriage was moving at pace, Nicholas managed to get to his feet and place the pistol on the opposite seat, away from them, before sinking down next to her.

"I don't give a damn about any of that. I can't remember a time when—to see him maul at you, I could have ripped him limb from limb. But you didn't need my help." He reached out and cupped Isabel's cheek, holding her face as if it were precious. "You felled him with that blow. Like an Amazon."

There was such warmth and tenderness in his touch that Isabel could forget that they were hurtling along country roads in the Sussex countryside towards some unknown destination. That if someone in her society were to see them like this, she would be labelled a harlot. It didn't matter. His touch was gentle against her cheek, his hand warm and soothing, and she shuddered as the fear she had felt thirty minutes ago drained out of her. She reached out for him and lay against his chest. He held her so, and Isabel closed her eyes with relief. It was safety. He was safety.

CHAPTER 8

The carriage didn't slow until they were close to Winston Cottage. Isabel was still in Nicholas's arms, sighing and shifting but otherwise at peace. There were no tears this time, which might have been just as well because he had no idea what to say to her that would be of any comfort. He didn't want her to know how close he'd been to killing James Hall; that wouldn't help her. His mind whispered that it wouldn't have helped their investigation either, despite how much satisfaction he would have felt in wrapping his fingers around the man's throat and squeezing the life from him. The important thing was that he had extracted Isabel from that place, and she was held against him. She was safe.

There was some faint light from behind the clouds; the afternoon sun was setting, and based on the view from outside, Nicholas knew they needed to end their embrace. If nothing else, his thoughts were taking a more romantic turn, which wasn't fair. Isabel's frame was delicate, but it held surprising strength. She was completely feminine. Her elegant shape was rounded in all the right places, and from what he could tell, her stays were not the thing forcing Isabel into such a handsome shape. Having made love to a few women over the years, Nicholas preferred to think of himself as open-minded, but to his memory, he could not recall a more pleasing form than Isabel's. It would be a gift indeed to peel back the layers, both physical and emotional, that surrounded her.

"We're here," he whispered against her hair.

She leant back and looked up at him. "I need to tell you something." Her hand curled around the material at his waistcoat. "There was one piece of information I do know. Something that my brother-in-law was angry about, the initials C.H. He's in charge of the gang, I think, and Mr. Hall called him Charles. Does that name mean anything to you?"

Nicholas accepted her words in confusion. He wasn't just limited by the information she gave him but also by Silverton's refusal to offer more concrete details. It was time the two of them met, and then perhaps Silverton would see how desperate the situation was.

"He burnt most of the details, but I had copied up some of the codes they used." She offered him a slip of paper.

"What do the numbers mean?" he asked, glancing over the sheet.

"I don't know. They were written by my late husband. I thought it might be a bank account of some kind. Or perhaps a drop site. It might be nothing."

Nicholas got to his feet, and they descended from the carriage. "Come with me."

The little space in front of the cottage was neat and tidy. The cottage itself was made up of old-fashioned grey stone. It was two stories high, with a shallow fence that encircled it. Handsome without being grand, it needed a little care, but in the summer months, it would be delightful.

"Wait here," he muttered to her, before moving over to

Walsh up in the driver's seat. "I didn't see a marksman. Did you catch sight of his face?"

"He was masked," replied the Irishman.

"Rouse all of the able-bodied men on the estate, and go up to the big house. I should be able to join you by then," Nicholas said. He was loath to leave Isabel, but she would be safe with Silverton. The cottage was the best place for her. Besides, he needed to honour his promise to her by protecting her family. He hoped that Mr. Blackman had managed to have James arrested. That would make things simpler.

On turning away from Walsh and back towards the cottage, Nicholas saw that Isabel had vanished. Despite her feminine appearance, she had a blasted independent tendency to go her own way. The door to the cottage was a little ajar, and it was clear that she had pushed it open and gone inside.

"I'll see you at Hurstbourne Manor within the hour," Nicholas said as he strode away from Walsh and followed her in through the cottage door.

Isabel was hovering in the hallway, a nervous look on her face. "It's very cold outside."

"Come on," Nicholas said, feeling guilty. He took her arm and dragged her into the warmer sitting room. It had been greatly improved by his sister with added furniture that had once graced one of the lesser sitting rooms at the Manor but been transported here. Viola had added other comforts, like a handsome collection of alcohol tumblers and a fine pile of books. The curtains had been drawn and rugs added to the wooden floors, creating a soothing, snug atmosphere to the place as if it had been dipped in honey.

But the initial sight that greeted the pair of them was not one that pleased Nicholas. Silverton was sprawled out, at his leisure. He looked as if he had been rendered from some girlish fantasy—his shirt loose and untucked, his dark brown hair swept off his face, with his bare feet resting on a pillow. In his hands was a book of poetry. He raised curious eyes, looking between the pair of them with an ease that annoyed Nicholas to no end. He suddenly wondered at the wisdom of leaving Isabel in such company. His sister hadn't seen any appeal in Gregory Silverton but would Isabel?

"Oh, for God's sake," snapped Nicholas. "Can't you see we've got company?"

Silverton looked from Nicholas to Isabel. There was a flicker of appreciation on his face as he straightened, and for the first time, Nicholas was glad that his friend had an injured leg; he could hardly chase around after Isabel in such a condition.

"How do you do, ma'am?" He tipped his head forward, his expression engaging. Isabel bobbed a curtsy.

"This is Viscount Silverton. Mrs. Hall." Nicholas made the introductions, knowing what the reaction would be. Silverton's smiling sophistication slipped, and his expression darkened now that he knew her name.

"He is your friend?" Isabel asked, clearly aware of the hostility from Silverton.

Nicholas realised that this talk was going to take longer than he imagined, even though he had so much to do. The authorities. The Blackmans. The servants. Finding a safe location to store the latter two. Perhaps speed would be his best course.

"Silverton is the man you tackled in the woods. He wasn't killed, as you can see, but he fractured his leg in the fall. He and I are working to take down the Waretons." Turning away from Isabel, Nicholas continued, "Mrs. Hall is going to help us do so, as she is now wanted by the gang."

"You appear to be remarkably well despite your demise," Isabel quipped. When only Nicholas smiled, she added, "I'm sorry, my lord. I was ordered to shoot at you and retrieve the bag. I thought it better..." She turned resentful eyes on Nicholas, and he saw that there were tears in them. "I thought you were dead. I was informed as such. I can only apologise for my actions."

Silverton brushed away her amends with a wave of his hand. He was much angrier than Nicholas had seen him before. "You should never have brought her into this. Don't you realise the level of danger—"

"No," Nicholas snapped back, "because you won't tell me everything you know. I am left to clutch at straws."

"That isn't Lynde—his Lordship's fault." Isabel cut in. "He has tried his best to defend me. I gave him all the proof I had and the initials of the ringleader."

At this Silverton looked almost desperately keen. "Who?"

"C.H."

Silverton sank back into his seat. "God, it *is* Harlington. His first name is Charles. The arrogance of using his first name," he mused almost to himself.

"Yes, that was the name James used," Isabel clapped her hands in excitement, then realised this was an error. "Mr. Hall mentioned him."

"Have you ever met him?"

"No..." She looked flushed.

"I take it," Silverton said, "that we do not have any of the accounts?"

"I'm afraid Mr. Hall burnt them."

"They were shot at. She was." Nicholas controlled his breathing at the memory of watching the bullet fly through the window, and the feminine scream he'd heard from outside. How he'd torn up the stairs towards Isabel's cry, away from the masked culprit on the street, not caring that he was letting a potential murderer escape. "I am not sure who the man who fired at the building was. His face was masked. Walsh didn't see him either," Nicholas added, although this did nothing to soothe Silverton. "I think we both have earned the right to know a bit more about Harlington."

"I already told you; he's a dangerous man."

"Why do you have such an interest in him?

Silverton looked deeply uncomfortable, and then finally muttered, "He is my twin brother. With a ridiculous assumed name—Harlington is simply the last one I heard him use. But as I said, Charles is his real name."

"I never knew—"

"Don't you think I know to keep it quiet that I have a treasonous sibling?"

"Treason?" Isabel's question echoed in the room, and Nicholas could feel the betrayal squirm in his stomach. He had harboured a fear that Silverton had kept some details from him, but he hadn't imagined that his friend knew so much more than he was letting on.

"How deep are we talking?" Nicholas pressed, his mind darted to the shifting powers of the French, the Russians, and Silverton's employers, the Home Office to whom Verne and Silverton owed so much. "Well?" he pressed the friend who had kept such details from him, jeopardising Nicholas's life with the lack of solid information.

"My brother is as bad as you'd expect. They'll hang him if they catch him. I didn't expect to find him to be here, just his destructive influence from overseas. I've managed to keep it all hush-hush," Silverton replied. "But he must have come back to England, at least briefly. If you can have Hall arrested, we may be able to get my brother's location from him."

"The priority was removing Mrs. Hall." That was another charge to level against Silverton, endangering Isabel.

"Desperate to play the hero?" Silverton asked Nicholas, but he could not dignify such a sally with a reply.

"My father was left alone with Mr. Hall," Isabel said.

"I've got to collect all the Blackmans, it seems," Nicholas

said. "No one knows she's here apart from Walsh and yourself. We must keep it that way." Nicholas stepped forward and passed his pistol to Silverton. "She knows about Harlington and about the code words the gang have been using."

"Understood. She will need to stay to help us crack where their location is." Silverton accepted the pistol and levered himself into a sort of semi-standing position, his expression pained.

Isabel nodded, willing to help, whilst Lynde felt a mixture of relief at remaining close to her but guilt at her continued presence in such a dangerous conflict. He turned and strode from the room.

"Will you tell them...?" Isabel rushed after him, crossing out of the parlour and down the hall and catching him by the arm.

"Yes?" All his desire to get back to the town and lock up James Hall diminished as he looked down at her.

"Will you ensure that my family is safe?"

"I will make sure of it." Nicholas squeezed her hand. She held onto him in a way that was oddly moving. "You will be safe too."

"You didn't seem too fond of him. The viscount, I mean." There was an edge of nervousness to her tone.

"I am just disappointed he kept such a thing from me. That doesn't mean I don't trust him. He won't let anything happen to you."

She frowned but kept her small hand on his coat. Above his heart. Her nails tapped against the fine material before coming to rest against the weave. Nicholas realised in surprise that this was all it took for her to command him. He wasn't going to move until she let him go. He would wait and wait until she felt safe enough for him to leave.

"You lied to me," she said.

"About Silverton's injuries?"

"He's not dead."

"I had hoped that it would lead to you confiding in me. A regrettable choice on my part. My most sincere apologies."

It was then that Isabel surprised him. She leant up on her tiptoes, separating the gap between them, and kissed his cheek. Her lips were soft against his stubbled flesh. He would have preferred her to feel confident enough to kiss him on the lips, but he understood the gesture as a peace offering.

"I should have given you my trust sooner," she said, once she had leant back.

"I should have been worthy of it," Nicholas replied.

She took a further step back, raising her hand to say goodbye. "Be careful."

"Are you afraid for me?"

Isabel controlled her smile, but Nicholas saw a flash of her confrontational spirit. "More for my father than for you."

Nicholas left the cottage, borrowing Silverton's horse for the ride back to the Manor. He could not quite explain the rush of emotion it had released in him, to see her so, flitting between her gentleness and charm to a more teasing tone. Once in the saddle, Nicholas adjusted himself as he turned the horse towards Hurstbourne Manor. He hoped Walsh had all the servants ready.

Upon reaching the Manor, Nicholas was surprised but pleased to see that Viola had taken charge of the situation and was preparing the staff. Walsh had gone ahead with four of the grooms to fetch the local militia, who were stationed at Brighton.

"And I sent the butler to ask the Blackmans to come to stay with us," she said. "Walsh mentioned a woman?" she added in an undertone.

"She's safe," Nicholas told her. "Where is Father?"

"Taking his rest. I've told the servants not to bother him.

He will sleep through dinner; that should give us enough time to get everyone here safely."

Nicholas was already wheeling his horse around. He wanted to be back in Eastbourne already, to capture and question Mr. Hall. Walsh was right to head to the militia, with the Waretons involved with someone as dangerous as Harlington. As much as he tried to think through the practicalities, instead the red mist of rage kept trying to creep into his vision. His very fingers itched at the idea of returning to fight Mr. Hall.

"Lud, you look murderous," his sister muttered. She edged nearer his horse, catching hold of the reins and looking up into Nicholas's face. "Wouldn't it be better to have Mrs. Hall up at the main house? Safer for her?"

"I don't want anyone knowing where she is," Nicholas said. "You must keep it secret."

"Even from her family?" Viola asked. Her small face was gazing up at him, her expression fraught with worry.

"Even from them," Nicholas confirmed. His thoughts turned to what he knew about Harlington; he knew the man was a killer of women and that he broke the law on a whim. That was enough to keep Isabel locked safely away in the cottage for as long as possible.

He half expected Viola to protest, but she just nodded. "I trust you."

"All of the to-ing and fro-ing from the estate will keep any of the smuggler's spies busy."

"Busy and confused," Viola added.

Giving her a brief nod, Nicholas spurred his horse up and headed back towards Eastbourne. He had remained as logical as he could, seated beside Isabel. She had focused him, reminded him of her safety being paramount, but now he would be returning to the fray.

Over the last ten years, Nicholas had prided himself on

being a typical gentleman of polite society. His friends in the Set had centred him in a way that his scandalous family couldn't. He'd always been running to protect himself from what his mother had done. But here was danger, and intrigue, and caught in the centre of it was a young widow who stirred all of the sort of emotions Nicholas had preferred to keep hidden away.

The skies opened above Nicholas, and thick drops filled the air, making the horse beneath him shudder in the cold. The surrounding countryside was plunged under a thick blanket of rain. "I know, boy. I know," Nicholas said in a calming tone.

On reaching Eastbourne, Nicholas slowed his horse, steadying their pace. He dismounted when he reached the area close to Mr. Blackman's office. There was an ominous quiet surrounding the office buildings. The front door of Mr. Blackman's office had been left open, and Nicholas walked up the steps and through the doorway, keeping close to the walls. Once inside, he picked up a discarded cane from the floor. He had left his pistol with Silverton.

Above him, there was a shift and then the sound of footsteps moving through the space. Nicholas raised the cane over his head, waiting for the emergence of a person at the top of the stairs. The footsteps stopped, and then there was a cry. "Hello? Is that you, Lynde?" came Mr. Blackman's voice.

Nicholas lowered his weapon. "Are you alright, sir?"

Mr. Blackman started to descend the stairs. He looked pale and rather sheepish. "I saw you arrive through the window. They came back."

"Was there another attack?"

Mr. Blackman nodded. "They got Hall." He walked through the hallway and into the nearest front room. Nicholas followed him through, cursing himself for letting James Hall escape again. Mr. Blackman went to the cordial cabinet and poured out two glasses. "Mr. Ramsey does not seem to have been a trustworthy man. He let them in. I did my best, but in the end..."

"How did you survive?"

"I know my offices better than anyone."

Nicholas cocked an eyebrow at the older man.

"I hid," Mr. Blackman said, "and watched them escape."

Nicholas sipped his drink. It was a rather nice brandy. "French?"

"Of course," Mr. Blackman said, a touch shame-faced about it. "I am prepared, of course, to tell you everything I know. But I do not know how much use I will be. The paperwork is gone. And I don't know where the next drop site is. I primarily helped sell the goods."

"Very well," Nicholas replied.

"Is my daughter safe?"

"Yes," Nicholas said, not prepared to go into further detail. He was not even clear in his own mind. "I am prepared to protect the rest of your family."

"I—" Mr. Blackman looked embarrassed, his old, flushed face colouring.

"I have it from Mrs. Hall that you were forced into the smuggling. I would like to know how it happened."

"I have regretted asking my daughter to marry Mr. Hall since the day they wed. She deserved better. My wife thought she wanted her independence, so I assumed that Mr. Hall, that Pierre..."

"Stick to the smuggling side of things. Just the facts." Nicholas didn't like hearing too much about Isabel being forced to marry a man such as Mr. Hall.

"When they were wed, around two weeks after..." Mr. Blackman gazed down at the brandy, swilling it this way and that in the glass. "Pierre came to me with a proposition that needed investment. He said it was a guaranteed profit. But he would not provide me with any details." He downed his glass. "So I refused."

"I take it that this backfired?" Nicholas asked.

"That's right," Mr. Blackman replied. "It turned out that Pierre had placed all of Isabel's dowry as an upfront investment. It worked. It generated a large amount of return. But my name was involved. Across the documents. So, if I were to..." Mr. Blackman trailed off.

"He entrapped you?"

"It wasn't just him. My own greed played a part."

"How long did it take you to realise what you were backing?"

"Too long," Mr. Blackman said. "And then the gang came a-calling, and I realised my mistake. But I kept trying to defend the Halls, for fear it would hurt my daughter."

Nicholas nodded. It fit. He felt sorry for Mr. Blackman, despite the man's greed. Such things had affected better men and made them fall for schemes that slipped out of their control.

"What do you know about a man called Harlington?" Nicholas asked.

"Only enough to know to fear him. His reputation proceeds him. I never met the man."

"What else do you know about James Hall?"

Sighing, Mr. Blackman finished his drink. "He's more involved than my son-in-law was. He spends more than any man I know. Has creditors coming around night and day. At least I made sure that his suit, that offer of his, never reached my daughter's ears."

"We will need to get statements from you. A signed confession of what you know. But as I said, I will ensure you and your family are protected."

Mr. Blackman let out a little release of breath and looked close to tears. "I assumed I was to be hanged."

"No." Nicholas smiled. "I shall ensure that does not happen. But in exchange, I need you to follow my instructions."

He offered out his hand, and Mr. Blackman shook it, the deal struck. As he finished his drink, Nicholas felt the weight of responsibility sitting heavily on his shoulders. A strange, little thought ran through his head. *No matter how far you run, no matter what you do, the obligations you have will catch up to you.* He couldn't quite remember if it was a tutor or his father who had said that, but it seemed to be true. For a man who had prided himself on being laissez-fair, he was now willingly jumping at an opportunity to be far more.

CHAPTER 9

It had been a strange introduction to Viscount Silverton, Isabel reflected, once Nicholas had left them together. She should stop calling him Nicholas, but it hardly suited their dynamic to continually call him Lynde either.

"Perhaps you could tell me how everything is arranged? About the cottage?" Isabel asked. She did not step too much further into the room, watching Silverton cautiously as if he might strike. Despite the injured leg, Silverton resonated with a sort of power that unnerved her a little. There was a lurking threat even while he lounged, supposedly relaxed. He didn't have the sympathetic familiarity that Nicholas possessed. No, there was something calculating in the dark depths of the viscount's hazel eyes.

"Take a seat, girl. I don't bite."

Isabel edged closer. She didn't like being called 'girl' as if she were a servant and, having turned twenty-eight this year, she didn't think the vestiges of girlhood applicable anymore.

The viscount had eased himself into an upright position and was viewing her. It was not the cold disinterest with which Pierre had regarded her. Nor was it the same hungry stare James Hall frequently gave her. Nor was it the same as Nicholas's; no, this man was something else, as if bits of her were being summed up? But for what purpose, she had no idea.

"I apologise again for my actions in the woods. I thought it better to injure the horse than you by firing a gun," Isabel said.

"Have you ever fired a pistol before?"

"No," Isabel admitted.

The viscount smiled, but it brought no warmth to his eyes. "You would have missed, then, had you fired at me."

"Perhaps. Or injured you far worse."

"You rate yourself that highly?"

"No," she said. "I meant I might have enjoyed some beginner's luck. That is not a chance you would have wanted to face."

The viscount's inscrutable face flexed, and not for the first time, Isabel was grateful for the openness of Nicholas's feelings. He had no bones about showing her if he were angry, upset, or interested. With the viscount, one would need a crystal ball to decipher his feelings.

"You would have considered it lucky to have shot me?" Silverton asked.

"Goodness, no." At this, the viscount laughed. Isabel began to think him a very cold fish. "I am relieved to see that you are not dead. And my actions, whilst regrettable, were meant to minimalize your injuries."

"We'd still have the papers if you had shot wide."

"One cannot change the past," Isabel said. They would still have had the papers if a lot of things had played out differently. She sank down into the settee opposite the viscount. She would not have been so bold, but today had been exhausting, and she no longer knew what her future might hold. Convention would have to wait. She folded her hands on her lap and gazed at him. He could glower at her all he liked; she no longer cared. This wasn't some ballroom or society affair where she wanted to win a viscount's approval. Those sorts of flippancies would never happen to Isabel again. Any idea of what would occur next seemed beyond her. "One can only make the future better," she added.

He was the first one to look away. "It seems we are trapped here together."

If Isabel had had Clara's adoration of the romantic, she would have loved the idea of this. The handsome, hazel-eyed viscount with his injury nursed by some lovelorn heroine. She could have run around with a white handkerchief and looked dramatic. But Isabel felt too cynical to embrace such an idea. "Lynde will be back soon, I am sure."

"I am unable, at present, to manage the stairs, so I prefer to remain down here. Do feel free to have your pick of the upstairs rooms. Lynde's sister has placed some items up there."

Isabel felt his eyes move over her and wondered if anyone would have brought a change of clothes that she could borrow. Both her once-glamorous pelisse and her gown were torn. So much for projecting an ideal of elegance. Isabel reasoned that any spare items would be of the male variety, and the idea of donning those clothes did not fill her with relief, given the activities she had had to engage in the last time she was dressed as a man.

"There's also food in the baskets." The viscount pointed to the corner of the room. "If you're hungry, please help yourself."

"Would you care for some, your lordship?" Isabel asked as she walked to the hampers and opened them up. The delicious smell of food hit her nostrils, and Isabel heard her belly rumble. It had been hours since she had eaten, she realised. The dramatic action of the day had driven food from her mind. Faced with it afresh, she thought herself able to eat the entire hamper. Had she been alone, she would have sunk to her knees and devoured the contents.

Instead, she dragged the basket back into the centre of the room and started taking out each separate element to place them on the neat wooden table between the two settees as deftly as she could. There were spreads and pots of confits and jams. Crusty rolls, only a little hard at the edges and still edible. Cold chicken. Walnut cake. A small round of cheese. Two bottles of wine. The list ran on.

"Didn't you want to put it in the kitchen?" she asked once the basket was emptied out.

"What is the point? They'll keep just as well in here." The viscount leaned forward and grabbed one of the rolls. "Lady Lynde is prompt at bringing out a replacement hamper."

Lady Viola Lynde. Isabel felt her nerves fizz at the thought. She'd been introduced to the fine lady a handful of times. Read about her, of course, and heard the rumours. 'So very like her mother' was the constant refrain, and Lady Viola's recently abandoned wedding seemed to confirm that. That was the general agreement about Viola; the goodwill with which everyone tender-heartedly discussed Nicholas did not extend to his younger sister. She was seen as wild, and that her 'bad blood will out' they said. But no matter how much Isabel pressed, her own mother would only say that the countess had been a bad woman, a bad mother, and a bad wife.

"You have known the family a long time?" Isabel asked, helping herself to one of the buns. She hoped her question wasn't impertinent; it encompassed the entire family, not just Nicholas.

"I—"

"This should be interesting," came a chirpy voice from behind them, and Isabel turned to see Lady Viola Lynde watching the pair of them. Her angelic face smiled at Isabel with just a hint of mischief. "Hello, my dear Mrs. Hall," she said, her expression hardening when it shifted to the viscount. "I'm not sure if you remember me from a ball that we both attended a good many years ago in Brighton. It was before you were married, I believe. Given these circumstances, do you think we could let society rules be broken and call each other by our Christian names? If so, I am Viola."

"Isabel." She found herself unable to dislike Viola; there was something so refreshing in the way the younger woman squeezed Isabel's hand. She possessed the same sense of righteousness that Nicholas had about him. An easy, welcoming confidence that made the two of them immediately agreeable.

"I'm Gregory," Silverton tried to join in.

"Leave him with the food," Viola said, depositing a new hamper down next to him. "Lets you and I go upstairs." She took Isabel's hands. "I understand from Nicholas that you are to reside here for the next phase of the adventure."

"It isn't an adventure," Silverton scolded her.

"What else would you call it?" Viola shot back at him.

This seemed to stump the viscount, so he just gave Viola a withering look. It would have felled other women, but it just made Viola giggle.

"I know it is shocking of me to remain here, but I do have some vital information towards the, umm, the mission." Isabel supposed she could turn and run to the Manor with her family, but at least, in part, this was her mess, and she wanted to help.

"No, I think it's fabulous," Viola replied. "You have so much more freedom than I do as a widow. Come, let's go and talk."

Unable to think of a reason to refuse, Isabel nodded at the viscount and then followed Viola from the room and up the stairs. The cottage was on a grander scale than what would normally be called a cottage, at least to Isabel's eyes. It was the sort of place her parents would have rented when they were taking the waters at Harrogate or Bath. Big enough to house a family of least ten, she reasoned, larger if you were economising. Although, to someone of Viola's upbringing, it must seem rather pokey.

"I've always loved Winston Cottage," the younger woman said as they walked up the stairs. "It should feature in some romantic opera or similar."

"Perhaps a play?" Isabel asked, imagining the idea.

"Exactly." The two of them reached the top of the stairs. "Now rest assured, all of your family have been secured in Hurstbourne Manor. I've had to keep them a little out of the way as Father is..." She looked awkward as she considered her words. "He has not been in the best of health."

"You do us an honour in helping us at all."

"Lord, it's great fun," Viola said, her tone easier again. "Tremendous fun. So much better than being scolded for my most recent misadventure. I cannot believe what sticklers both Lynde and Silverton are being." She gestured in front of herself. "That's the master bedroom. I had it all restocked when I thought Silverton would sleep up here. But since he's fairly at home downstairs, perhaps you'd be better in here. Good to keep this as respectable as we can."

"It's kind—"

"Nonsense." Viola pushed open the door and strode inside. "Now, I didn't have any gowns that were long enough for you; I remember you being much taller than me. You are lucky; everything looks so much better on tall women. But I was sure that Lynde would forget such things; he is a typical male. So, I borrowed one of our housekeeper's gowns. I also thought that cap would cover up those locks of yours as they're quite distinctive." She gestured at Isabel's bright blond hair.

Gratefully, Isabel took the offered dress. It was a simple one, and she could see other items in Viola's possession that were equally unglamorous: an apron, a brown shawl, and thick, rounded boots. If this was a play, Isabel was not the sophisticated heroine she had hoped to be.

Stepping behind a large armchair in the corner of the room, Isabel stripped out of her ruined finery. She perhaps should have felt ashamed to do so in front of such a fine lady, but all that pumped through her veins was relief. She was happy to be out of the dress that James had pawed at.

When this was all over, if everything went to plan, maybe this was the sort of position she would need to fill, Isabel thought as she smoothed down the new dress. She could leave Sussex, even ask Prudence if she knew of any positions a housekeeper might apply for. With the recommendation of a marchioness, it would be possible to find a role with a family like her own. There was something encouraging about that. A future in a world she hadn't been able to imagine a week ago. Of course, it didn't fit with the dreams of her youth, but that was never going to occur now. With this new idea in mind, Isabel stepped back around the chair and raised her head to look at Viola.

The lady was perched on the edge of the bed. She clapped her hands. "Isn't this fun? Let me do you up." She hurried around and laced up the back of Isabel's dress, "There," she declared as she walked around Isabel, examining her. "If you leave the cottage, we'll stuff a lacy cap on you. That'll age you up a few good years. Not that Lynde would approve of that."

"I am not certain that Lynde approves of anything I do."

"Hah. My brother must hate all of it. He loathes anything scandalous."

"Yes?" Isabel tried to hide the disappointment from her

voice. Viola removed her white kid gloves and walked to the fireplace before dragging up her own turquoise dress to better bend her knees and build up the fire. "It's the effect of my behaviour, and our mama's, of course. He had a choice. Be like Father, which isn't very much fun. But it did mean that he at least got taken seriously. He made a much better choice than me. If he is seen as a proper gentleman, no one will question him too much."

"Do you think so?" Isabel asked. Here would be some real insight into Nicholas.

"Of course, he tries to be like Father, a true gentleman, but underneath it all, I know he's different."

"I'm sorry for the loss of your mother. That must have been very hard on the both of you." Isabel wondered how it had happened. She would have liked to have known. It would have had an impact on Nicholas. But she could not remember anyone ever discussing it when it had happened.

Lady Viola's eyebrow lifted in the same humorous manner as her brother's. Their faces were very similar looking, just for a second, before she laughed. "No, no, you misunderstand me. My mother isn't dead."

"Then..." Isabel tried to think of an explanation that would fit with what she had heard.

"We're not meant to talk about her." Lady Viola sat down on the bed. "But I don't see the harm in telling you. After all—"

"It's not like this is a very normal situation," Isabel finished.

Reaching out a hand, Lady Viola pulled Isabel down to sit next to her. "My mother, Alice, was a wealthy heiress. There was some part of her dowry that my father couldn't claim. It was set up by my rather savvy grandmother; it's called a settlement."

"It would always belong solely to your mother?" How Isabel wished she'd had that set up for her.

"Yes, that's right. Isn't it a brilliant idea? The only thing I can't understand is why my mother ever married. Imagine having that sort of power, of really being an independent woman."

Stifling a smile, Isabel nodded. She could understand why someone might wed if they wanted companionship. If they wanted love. If they wanted a family. If they wanted children. If they wanted not to be called a spinster.

"Being with someone like my father must have driven her mad," continued Viola. "I was very young when she left. When the divorce happened."

Unbidden, Isabel's face contracted. One never divorced. Ever. No wonder the local society, her mother included, thought the countess a scandalous woman.

Viola had been watching Isabel's reaction. She smiled and shook her head.

"I'm sorry," Isabel said. It had just shocked her.

"You're better than some people; you didn't back away as if I were infected," Viola replied. "But I can understand why my parents divorced." There was a real forcefulness behind her statement, a sort of defensiveness that spoke of loss.

"You must have missed her." Isabel stretched out her hand and squeezed Viola's.

"Of course, I did." Viola's youthful exuberance faded for a second. "But can you keep a secret?"

"Perhaps better than most," Isabel replied. It seemed her part to be forever hiding things. She hoped, however, that Viola would not ask her to deceive Lynde.

Dropping her voice, Viola leant closer. "We wrote to one another, my mother and I, over the years. And ever since I turned eighteen, we have been visiting each other in London."

"The countess and you—"

Viola's eyes glittered. "It has been the one solace I have found in the Season. Coming to know my mother."

Isabel struggled to think of how to reply; she could see that Viola was thrilled to have such a family connection, but Nicholas did not have such a luxury.

"She goes by a different name now. Lady Kingfisher." Viola saw Isabel's confused expression and smirked. "I know it doesn't make much sense. She runs a gambling hell near St James Square. A great many people in society don't even realise who she is. She wears a mask and a huge wig. Once," Viola leant forward and seemed fit to burst with her story, "she spent an entire hour with my father, and he had no idea who she was. Isn't that dashing?"

"She sounds quite extraordinary."

Viola radiated pride. "She is. She's a radical. When I reach my maturity... she has a settlement set up for me."

"Does Lynde—"

"No one knows," Viola cut her off. "I don't believe my brother would understand. He never talks about my mother. He doesn't understand how it is for us. To be trapped in a marriage and to yearn to be free."

Neither do you. Isabel bit her lip. There was something so keen and raw about Viola that it seemed too cruel to let her know of the harsh realities of married life.

"Besides, he was older when Mama left. So, he remembers her more than I do." Viola shrugged. "I have no great concern with being seen as shocking, but my brother does. He hates scandal."

"Yes, and the earl must have more expectations of him."

"Like whom he might marry," Viola replied. "When Nicholas does wed, I think he'll pick someone very dull. Unless he realises he has more in common with our mother than he would like to admit."

Isabel wondered how much of her desire had flashed over her face. She jumped to her feet and walked to the window. "Your mother is lucky not to have ended up at Doctor Hodgkin's hospital."

"It always sounded like a gothic horror when I was young, or a myth, we females were told to keep us well behaved. A tale told for thirty-odd years. What was the original doctor called?"

"I can't remember." Isabel whispered.

From downstairs, there was a click of the door, and both women froze, ears pricked for the sound of movements, each of them eager to know that it was servants or the returning Lord Lynde. Not something worse.

"Is that him?" Isabel whispered.

Viola nodded. "Shall we eavesdrop? I always hear more that way."

The pair of them crept down the stairs to listen at the door. From the snatches of garbled conversation, Isabel was sure both Nicholas and Walsh had returned.

"He got away." This was Nicholas, clear if rather tired sounding.

"Hall?"

"That's right."

"Not that surprising. We need more men."

"Do you think so?" The tone was mock serious.

"The militia won't know where to start. Their commander says smaller is better for undercover operations, but it's just a way of staying out of the situation. Wouldn't be surprised if he was taking a cut from the smugglers."

"You should have told me earlier about your brother." Lynde sounded angry.

"I never imagined it was this bad." Silverton's voice was quieter. "I made a mistake."

"I am increasingly tired of not being told things." Lynde's anger was mounting.

"I have asked Trawler to join us. He has been most useful—"

"Does Trawler know about your connection, about the gang, about the risks? Will he be straightforward with me?" The girls strained to hear more but it was Nicholas who answered his own question. "I see, it was I who was kept in ignorance, and I who risked my neck."

"Trawler has business ties that allowed—I didn't want to involve too many people in my mistake," Silverton replied, his tone heated.

"You could have trusted me. And as soon as you asked for my help, you should have done. As for Mrs. Hall, she's in danger too. Her brother-in-law would have—"

"We shouldn't be listening," Isabel whispered at the mention of her name. Viola might have been happy to hear any number of things about the smugglers, but Isabel wasn't sure she wanted to know any more than she already did. If she were to be able to escape this life after the prosecution of the crimes had been brought down, and if she did become a respectable housekeeper, then she would need lords like Silverton and ladies like Viola to be ignorant of her damaged reputation.

"Hush," Viola scolded back, and with enough volume to rouse the men, because the door opened, and Nicholas glanced out into the hallway.

His eyes travelled with amused ill humour from his sister up to Isabel. He straightened when he saw her. "Mrs. Hall. Would you care to step through?"

The two women greeted him in the half-lit hallway. Nicholas took Isabel's hand and tucked it into the crook of his sleeve as Viola brushed past him. "You'll be pleased to hear I collected your father from his office, and he is now residing at Hurstbourne Manor."

"Thank you," Isabel replied as they entered the little sitting room, which was just as cosy as when Isabel had left it. Walsh nodded at her. Silverton was now sat up on the sofa, with Viola close to the fire, her hands on the kettle, discussing the idea of tea.

Nicholas walked Isabel to the sofa, then fetched her some food from one of the hampers before removing the kettle from Viola's hands. "Sister, we must be returning to the Manor."

"My lord," Isabel piped up, "I wish to remain here. I can be of some use to helping you all. I would like to atone for my mistake."

Lord Lynde looked conflicted for a moment before nodding. "I trust Mrs. Hall will be cared for here. Her life is in danger, and I expect that both of you will protect her. And," he added, his eyes flicking between Silverton and Walsh, "that you will remain downstairs this evening." Lynde gave Isabel an encouraging smile before offering his sister his arm. "We must present the most unified front for the staff."

"Any number of your servants may be involved," Silverton said. His eyes turned to Isabel. "You never know who to trust."

"Quite," Lynde snapped. "I will take care of it. And I look forward to welcoming Mr. Trawler tomorrow." His eyes swept the room, not lighting on Isabel with anything more than a customary glance, and Lynde slipped away, with Viola giving her a cheerful wave in his wake.

Isabel ducked her head and started eating the food Nicholas had placed into her hands. She had once been talked into the idea of being a quiet woman, a silent one. It was a much smoother way of proceeding through life. But the truth was, she was hurt by the curt manner with which Nicholas had treated her. At one point, she would have been relieved not to be considered too passionate, but now she wasn't so sure. She had been docile throughout her marriage, and what good had that done her? It was time she took some decisive action, as she had done just now in insisting that she stay and help.

Once she'd finished her food, she asked Mr. Walsh to join her in the adjoining room. She was tired of feeling like a coward, and even if it meant that Lynde might never kiss her again, and it might make her too scandalous for him, she wanted to be as prepared as she could be.

"Sir," she said. He was a portly man but nevertheless, she'd seen him move with surprising speed and ferocity, and he smiled in such a way that made Isabel feel at ease. "I wonder if you could help me."

"Of course, my dear." He nodded.

When she told him what she wanted, genuine worry crossed his bearded face for the first time. "Well," he finally reasoned, after they had discussed the matter back and forth. "I would want my own girls to be safe, were they to be in such a situation as you find yourself in now."

The implication, Isabel thought drily, was that he felt his daughters would not be fool enough to wed someone like Pierre Hall. She hoped for their sakes that was true.

Although Walsh agreed, he had one stipulation; that she promise not to tell either Silverton or Lynde. Isabel agreed to this condition, and she went to bed much more easily than she would have imagined possible now that she would be learning how to shoot.

CHAPTER 10

For the next few hours, Nicholas berated himself for not speaking at greater length to Isabel when he had had the chance. There were a lot of things he should have told her, but finding the right words, in mixed company, seemed beyond him. It annoyed him no end to be rendered speechless. Nicholas always prided himself on knowing what to say and how to say it, especially with women.

His birth had blessed him with a title, good looks, and sufficient charm that he had never had to suffer from being tongue tied, whatever emotional damage his parents' divorce had wrought in him. But seeing Isabel in that servant's garb, looking so frail and vulnerable, had affected him more than he liked to admit.

It also made him angrier than ever, first with Silverton, but far more with the smugglers, the Halls, and with anyone else who was a danger to her. He had always assumed that he would react with distaste when faced with someone as scandalous as Isabel and her situation, but all he wanted to do was protect her. God, it made no sense.

He had been confused at catching her listening in on him

and Silverton. She was sat with his sister, the pair of them youthful and flushed as if they were playing a game. But this wasn't childish fun; this was life and death. If he had arrived at the Blackman office any later—or if Isabel hadn't reached that poker in time—Nicholas felt certain James Hall would have killed both Mr. Blackman and Isabel. The Wareton Gang were murderers; Walsh had told him so, and Mr. Blackman had confirmed that it was the gang's modus operandi. Mr. Blackman had given Nicholas an idea of the sums of money involved, and yes, people lived and died by those amounts.

Being in that hallway and meeting Isabel's gaze was all Nicholas could think to do. He had wanted to pull her close, to fold her against his chest. Instead, he had to settle for taking her hand into the crook of his elbow and finding a small slither of comfort in her trusting smile, her fine grey eyes, and her stance as she leant against him. It had all further unnerved Nicholas's shaky hold on the situation, as his mind whispered again and again, *What will you do if you can't protect her? And why does it suddenly matter to me so much that she us safe?* Shaking his head, Nicholas forced himself to ignore both questions.

The next day, when he marched downstairs to see the Blackmans and his sister around the breakfast table, his resolve didn't feel much firmer. He had slept badly, and his normally easy-going persona felt forced, like an act that Nicholas no longer saw the point of. The breakfast room was full, what with his sister, the entire Blackman clan, and the Miles family foursome.

"How are you feeling, sir?" He looked across the small room at Mr. Blackman. His face was bruised but he nonetheless appeared more chipper than the previous day. The other members of his family were nervous as they watched Nicholas.

"Where's Izzy?" Mrs. Blackman asked. She stepped forward and took Nicholas's hands in her own.

"She's being kept safe."

Mrs. Miles also moved closer, her expression mulish. "My sister is not to be taken advantage of, Lord Lynde. I don't know what her husband did, but my sister is innocent."

"Yes," chorused the Blackmans throughout the room.

There was a cough from behind him as Viola stepped forward. "I can assure you that Mrs. Hall is safe and will be protected. We aren't sure in these parts who can be trusted, beyond this room, of course."

"Due to recent unfortunate events," Nicholas said.

"With that in mind," Viola continued, "we thought it wisest to keep her hidden."

"For her own protection?" Mrs. Blackman asked.

Lynde nodded. Was it wise to do so, to keep Isabel separated from her family? She wanted to help, but was it sensible? And where was he to send the eight people now dependent on him? He had a vague idea of sending the Blackmans to his family's Mayfair residence but even then, he didn't know if that would be enough. His other idea was to ask one of the Set to house them, but most of them were secure in their own homes, far from London. When he'd floated these different thoughts to Viola, she had grinned and told him she would take them up to Verne's home, whose sister was a dear friend of Viola's.

"I have the perfect location for us to go to," Viola told the gathered throng. "Where you will all be safe and secure. We will be staying with Lady Caroline Briers; she is the widowed sister of Baronet Verne. The home will be very secure."

"I would prefer that my daughter—" Mr. Blackman started to say, but Viola held up her hand.

"You need have no fear; she is crucial in this endeavour. Is that not so, brother?"

Nicholas nodded wearily. Viola looked around the room and wetted her lips, about to continue.

"I would prefer if she was at least granted a maid, if you please." This was Mrs. Miles again. "You were kind enough to bring them all here. Why can't her maid go to her?"

"We will take that under consideration," Nicholas replied.

"Haste, I believe," Viola said, "must be our directive, and with that in mind, please be ready to leave Hurstbourne in the next hour." Her eyes moved to the small baby in Mrs. Miles's arms. "I will have the carriages prepared."

She slipped from the breakfast room with Nicholas in her wake, and they proceeded along the hallway, heading towards the stables.

"It is a lot to ask of you," Nicholas said.

"I am sure the Blackmans and I will have a grand old time of it."

Nicholas frowned, not understanding his sister.

"I think Mrs. Miles is correct; a maid would be a good idea for Isabel," she added.

"I hardly think—"

They paused by the entrance to the stables, and Nicholas shot out his hand to stop Viola in her tracks. "I don't know what Father might have said to you, or threatened, but I will always protect you as well as I can. If this is some scheme to get up to London and run off with a man, however—"

"Not everything involves a man. Rest assured someone as staid as Verne would never suit me."

Nicholas had hidden the scandal sheets from his sister after a duel was fought over her. They had featured explicit and implicit allusions to her antics with Mortimer. It might have been better shown if they put her off further interactions with men.

"Nothing scandalous," he said. "Nothing that will further hurt Father."

She gazed up into his face. "I love our father, and I will do my best to keep him happy, and I know you will care for him too."

"Vi—"

"When will you realise there are worse things than people gossiping?" She grabbed his face between her hands and reached up to kiss his forehead. "You will never be able to control everything just as you like it. Least of all me. But rest assured, I mean to keep the Blackmans safe. Just promise you will do the same for Mrs. Hall."

"You know I won't let anyone near her."

"I didn't mean anyone else," his sister told him. "I'm not a blind little fool, you know. I can see you like her."

Nicholas resisted the urge to grind his teeth. He had never discussed romance with his sister, and the idea of starting now... "It wouldn't be suitable," he finally said.

"When are you going to see that what Mother did means one simple thing: we can do whatever we like. Better to be happy and derided in the press than miserable but with the appearance of contentment."

There was a strange buzz in his head around the word Mother, and Nicholas tampered down all his recollections of their parents, and of the relentless teasing at school that had followed him after the infamous divorce. Viola had been too young to remember and hadn't lived through the whispers that had dogged his footsteps at Harrow. But it had lodged in his chest, and he couldn't let himself forget.

Nicholas turned away in annoyance as Viola headed off towards the grooms. He forced himself to stifle down his bitter response, and as he chewed it over, he saw Isabel crossing the lawn to the left of the stables with Silverton and Walsh, heading towards the Manor. His heart did a strange little flip in his chest, a rush of pleasure and fear at the sight of her. She had had the decency to hide her lustrous hair under a dreadful white mobcap, but otherwise, she seemed as bold as brass as she made her way towards the house.

Without really thinking about it, Nicholas made his way past the outposts of the stables and signalled to the moving group to follow him inside one of the outer buildings. With his annoyance mounting, he saw that Silverton was being supported between Walsh and Isabel, leaning on the latter with ease. Her left arm was wrapped around the viscount's waist to support him as he walked. An unpleasant surge of jealousy flared through him.

"In here," he muttered, ushering the lot of them inside. From the inner courtyard, they could hear Viola telling the head groom to prepare three carriages.

Nicholas looked back at the three of them. So much for keeping them safe and hidden. He had thought to scold the lot of them but satisfied himself with yanking Silverton away from Isabel and depositing the man onto a small stool.

They listened to the head groom move away, and then Nicholas opened the outpost and ushered Viola inside to join them.

Nicholas turned on Isabel, the calm good grace he was renowned for slipping further. She looked like she was playing at being a lowly housekeeper, except no lady would ever hire someone who resembled Isabel Hall, with all her good looks. Her blond hair was slipping beneath the cap and peeking out. Her bright eyes were alert and keen. Her gaze lifted and met his, holding him arrested for too long. God. No. No. He needed to be sensible.

"Couldn't you have stayed put?" he snapped at her.

"Silverton couldn't manage with just Walsh. He needs more care." She looked surprised. "We thought the plan was to leave as early as possible."

"Dearest Viola has volunteered for the role of escorting your family out of harm's way and up to Verne's home."

"It'll be exciting," Viola said. Her voice throbbed with anticipation. She had moved over and taken Isabel's hand in her own, "Now, you are not to worry. I will ensure that your family are well looked after."

"Thank you," Isabel replied.

Silverton jumped into the conversation. "I wanted to offer my own abode as a place for you to stay."

"Wouldn't that be rather obvious?" Viola replied.

"A new location might be wiser, my lord," Isabel interjected.

With a curt nod, Silverton said, "As you say, I am willing to play the sacrificial lamb and lead the smugglers away. In that way, the Blackman family could easily go to a different base."

"Agreed. Before I forget," Viola looked away back to organising everything, "your maid Lucy had a few things brought over from the townhouse. We thought it best she come join you in the cottage."

"That would be most kind," Isabel replied.

The two women turned towards the door as if to leave, and Nicholas grabbed the nearest, who happened to be Isabel.

"Now that you've sufficiently planned everything out, don't forget we're trying to stay as quiet as possible," Nick told his sister.

"Very well," Viola cut in. "I'll return to the house now, get everything set up. You two," she looked at Silverton and Walsh, "will want to leave an hour after us. Take a different, more prominent route." Then her eyes flicked to Nicholas and Isabel, and he quickly dropped his hand from her arm. "I suppose I will send Lucy along." Then she swished away. The door swung closed behind her.

"Walsh has chosen to stay with Mrs. Hall. We discussed it at length, and he knows the situation well. He has worked with my father before me and knows the whole sad story around my disgraced brother," Silverton said. "He will provide excellent protection, certainly more than I need. I'm of no use to you, as your sister pointed out."

Nicholas offered his hand to Walsh; the other man was something of a godsend in such circumstances. "I appreciate it."

"Besides, he will be able to predict Harlington's ways." Silverton shifted on the stool, his injured leg jutting out before him. He swore before fixing his gaze on Nicholas. "You will get him, won't you?"

"I promise," Nicholas said. The thrill of it, of being the centre of an effort to tackle a group of relentless smugglers, whirled through him. *I should ask questions of the man before me, I should trust him enough to give me an honest answer*. But as Nicholas looked at Silverton, he realised something. Gregory felt guilty, but he would never stop loving his brother. It had made him blind. It was just as well he was leaving. Clearer heads. Although that was supposed to be him, but he didn't know if he quite fit that bill, especially regarding Isabel Hall. Still, there was Walsh, and soon Trawler would be arriving.

From outside in the courtyard, they could hear the Blackmans descending. Silverton fidgeted on his stool.

"Time to be off, my lord," Walsh muttered.

Isabel had lifted her head to hear her family, and in the faint light, Nicholas could see the slight sheen of tears well in her eyes. He looked away, knowing the comfort he wished to offer her wouldn't be deemed appropriate. Instead, Nicholas moved closer to Silverton, easing the man upright to a standing position. "Trawler knows it all?"

"He has been involved since the beginning," Silverton said as they slipped from the outpost, leaving Walsh and Isabel hidden in the outer building.

The Blackman family were too caught up in getting into

the carriages and, with Viola directing them, Nicholas slipped Silverton and himself along the side of the building and back towards the Manor.

"He has used his business connections to track shipments and the like. There is so much I should have told you on that first day, but I hoped it wouldn't be necessary. I swear I had no idea that my brother would be involved," Silverton continued in an undertone. "There is nothing Trawler would not do to stop my—to stop Harlington." They paused as Silverton sucked in his breath, visibly in pain. "I can only apologise; I should have told you earlier."

"It is done now. Trawler and I will rectify this."

"If my leg—"

"I know." They had reached the shallow steps that led up to one of the small drawing rooms that looked onto the ornate gardens and slowly edged their way inside.

He deposited Silverton on the nearest settee and glanced back towards the stables, his mind filled with thoughts of Isabel.

"Go," Silverton said. "I'll listen for the sound of them leaving, and then take myself off to the carriage your sister has undoubtedly arranged for me."

Nicholas found himself moving forward. There was so much he wished to say to Silverton: that he understood shame over one's family, how what had seemed sensible at one point suddenly made less sense, but instead, he offered his friend his hand. "I will correct this."

"I have no doubt," Silverton said. "I wish I had asked for your involvement sooner. You are a good man in a crisis."

Nicholas slipped from the small room and headed towards the kitchen. He needed to find that maid, so that he could continue to protect Isabel's reputation. The problem was that he had so little idea of what they were up against, and reputations seemed rather petty in contrast to what he feared the Wareton Gang would be capable of.

By the time that Nicholas walked through the door of Winston Cottage, he felt he had lived through a great many hours of frustration. There had been Lucy to locate and keep secure. The grand exit of Silverton to loudly shout about. A visit from Doctor Forde, who checked on his father and prescribed yet more bedrest, leaving Nicholas in the uncomfortable position of being relieved his father was out of the way but also scared by how ill the earl now seemed.

Winston Cottage was an oasis of calm in contrast. He and Lucy had waited at the door and been admitted by Walsh, and then Lucy had disappeared to the kitchen, leaving Nicholas in the hallway.

"She's upstairs," Walsh said.

Making his way up the stairs, Nicholas knocked on the master bedroom door. It opened a little way, and in the gap was Isabel's upturned face. The half shadow over her seemed to further highlight the delicacy of her features, capturing the length of her tawny eyelashes and the way her mouth stretched up at the tips when she saw him.

"They're all gone," he said, as he stepped into the room.

"I watched them leave. I would have liked to say good-bye." Isabel moved to a seat by the window and pressed her hands against the frame of the chair, using it for support.

"You could write to them," Nicholas said.

"I'd like to go to Milbourn Street and get my belongings." Her voice held no sentiment towards her one-time residence.

"Lucy brought several items with her." The idea of her returning to such an obvious place seemed unnecessarily risky.

"She won't know want I need. Or my particular items. There may be another account book that I missed."

Nicholas shook his head. He didn't want her going back there; it was too dangerous.

"This could be an excellent chance to uncover more about the Waretons," she insisted.

"It would be quicker if I went alone. If you told me where to look," he replied. Isabel stepped closer to him and took his hands in hers. She was gazing up at him with such a look that his reply was sluggish, and Nicholas heard himself say, "We'll go at night, if we must."

Isabel looked to the little clock on the mantelpiece. It had just gone five. It would be at least two hours before it was dark enough. "You know," she said, as she released his hands and sank into a nearby armchair, "I believe that Silverton thinks me your mistress."

Nicholas's throat contracted at this, and he immediately felt self-conscious, although he had spotted the gleam in Silverton's eyes when he'd seen the pair of them together. "Nonsense," Nicholas lied.

"No, he does." She didn't sound sad, more as if she were weighing her options. "I suppose that could be my lot in life. Assuming we survive all of this."

"You shouldn't think like that."

"About my damaged reputation? Or about my chances of survival?"

"Either. Both." Now it was Nicholas's turn to pace around the room. It felt wrong to speak of anything involving scandal or death in such a place. The room was like the other bedrooms in the cottage, having a neat but large sleigh bed in the corner, a writing desk, and a chair, as well as the fireplace. He looked back at Isabel. He would need to reassure her.

"Then again, with a traitor for a husband and another for a father, what more can I expect?" she asked.

"Your father will be protected," Nicholas said. "I will ensure all records go before a jury, to acknowledge that both of you turned the Wareton Gang over to us."

"Only when it was too late for another option." She looked up at him from the chair, her fingers lacing into her hair. "That's not heroic, is it? Turning oneself in when you must. When you are threatened with death. No wonder Silverton thought so little of me."

"Better late than never," Nicholas tried to joke.

Isabel made a strange noise, halfway between a sob and a laugh, so it sounded more like a hiccup. Going to her, unable to resist, Nicholas knelt in front of her chair and took hold of one of her hands. Tenderly, he pressed a kiss to her palm. Her skin was like silk to touch, but he resisted continuing a trail of kisses. Now was not the moment. If he started, he felt sure he wouldn't be able to stop. Instead, he stayed still, close to her chair, near her long skirts, looking up at her.

"I promised to protect you, Isabel, and I meant that. Whether that be physically or financially."

She raised her kissed hand and placed it now amongst his own hair, each fingertip of hers touching and caressing his scalp, her movements encouraging Nicholas to lean forward. To his own amazement, Nicholas found himself resting his head in her lap. Once he was positioned there, his thoughts pulled him deeper.

"I never did this with Pierre," she whispered. "This sort of affection..." Her hand dropped away from his head as Nicholas moved to look up at her.

"Then he was a fool," Nicholas said. "If he never sought you out..."

"It was not that we were never intimate," Isabel replied. She had a faraway look in her eyes, and Nicholas felt certain she was remembering her past. "It was that it was always at night. It was always mechanical." She looked down at him. "Does that make sense?"

Nicholas was tempted to say no. No, not at all. The idea of anyone being able to be mechanical with Isabel confused him to no end. "Do you mean that was how your husband made love to you?"

Her cheeks bloomed with colour. "I suppose I shouldn't have raised it as a topic of conversation. But yes. I think that is why I could never be anyone's mistress. I would be a great disappointment."

Nicholas stood and moved away from her. It was becoming too tempting to pull her down onto the carpet and prove how wrong her dead husband had been. Keeping his back to her, Nicholas made sure his voice was steady when he spoke again. "In my experience, I have found that love making varies depending on whom one's lover might be. The experience of it, I mean."

"So, it can be better or worse with different people?"

"The same as when one..." His mind went blank, and he struggled to think of an apt comparison. Then it came to him. "The same as when one dances with somebody."

This made Isabel smile. She leant forward in the armchair.

"What is it?" He wondered if he shouldn't have encouraged her to view sex in that way; what if she wanted to 'dance' with any number of different people to test out his theory?

"No, I couldn't say."

"Please. After all, it is not as if you could repeat anything else we have said to each other."

"That's true." She got to her feet and went to him. Standing just a foot away, Nicholas could smell her perfume, or delicious soap, or whatever it was that was Isabel. An intoxicating, lulling mixture of jasmine, honey, and warmth. "I used to read about you all the time in the papers. The gossip sheets. It made you sound—your Set, I mean—it sounded ever so exciting."

"That wasn't so much me."

"No, that was the impression I got. But I thought you sounded like the best one." Here, she rolled her eyes at her own silliness. "Because I thought I knew you. You had your home here in Sussex, so you belonged to a world I was familiar with. I used to think about you coming back here. And that I would see you at one of the grand balls."

"What made you think of that?" When she was looking up at him that way, Nicholas couldn't think straight.

"It was you who said that it... it was like dancing."

"It isn't the same."

"But similar?" She arched an eyebrow, and Nicholas laughed. Then he put out his hands and encircled her small waist.

"Was this how you imagined it?" Tentatively, having never waltzed without music before, let alone in a bedroom, Nicholas started taking the steps. He kept them small, as if they were children learning to dance for the first time.

"Me in this old dress? Without any music?" She giggled as she adjusted her hands on his suit. Her movements were stilted and stiff, and every now and then she stepped on his foot. "No, this isn't how I imagined it."

Her eyes lifted and looked at Nicholas. It seemed to him as if she were able to absorb all of him into herself, able to see his flaws, his weaknesses, and all the worries he had ever had just by gazing at him. It terrified Nicholas, and yet it warmed his heart at the same time. He swung her round in a great wide circle, and Isabel laughed with delight.

CHAPTER 11

Isabel could not quite believe her own daring behaviour throughout that afternoon with Nicholas. She continued to act as if they were old friends. Or even as if something else might happen between them. It was nice to put off reality with such a fantasy. She could ignore that he was the son of an earl and all that that entailed. Whereas she was the daughter of a corrupt tradesman, who had attacked a dear friend of his. It was a miracle, all things considered, that they would ever even interact. These were brief, almost stolen moments, giggling as he danced her around a cottage bedroom.

She watched him now, as they sat opposite each other, heading to Milbourn Street in the carriage. He had offered her those precious minutes and Isabel didn't know why. They felt like golden moments. Or maybe they were a consolation prize. Perhaps he assumed she would be soon out of his life, or worse, he doubted her survival.

"What's the matter?" he asked.

He was getting better at reading her emotions. Or she was becoming less subtle. "Nothing at all."

"You won't have much time in the house. Be as quick as you can." They had waited until the cover of darkness had enfolded the town, and light rain hit the roof of the carriage.

This visit was a gesture of farewell as far as Isabel was concerned. The place had been Pierre's alone. It was a risk, but if there was a chance of discovering just a bit more about the Wareton Gang, it was worth it.

"Thank you," she whispered.

Nicholas gave her a rather hard look. She knew he wasn't happy about her decision, but he'd gone along with it. A bigger contrast between his ability to listen to others and Pierre's refusal to ever acknowledge her differing viewpoint could not be drawn. Then again, there was so little that Nicholas and Pierre shared, it was strange to think of them both as the same species. When Nicholas had held her in his arms, his hands moving over her dress as he spun her, it had been a thousand times more exhilarating than all the nights she had gone to Pierre's bedroom. It had made her blood sing, and she was grateful for the darkness of the carriage's interior that hid her face as she dwelt on their dance.

"We're here," Nicholas said.

Readying herself, Isabel pulled her housekeeper's garb about her. She had been lent one of Nicholas's old coats, and the thick brown tweed still smelt like him. Peppermint. Shoe polish. The seaside. It was odd how comforting such things could be as she walked along the pavement, past the other quiet buildings with their sleeping occupants. She was just planning where she would go first in the house when an out of place noise made her freeze. The sound was almost that of an animal, a sort of low whistle that could not have sounded more bizarre. Isabel looked back over her shoulder to check with Nicholas, and that was when it happened.

An explosion from her terraced house threw Isabel backwards several feet, as bricks, glass, and wood splintered and blasted out. The street shook all around her. There was so much noise and smoke that it blurred her vision. She could feel a liquid running down from her arm and into her eyes. Blinking, she rolled onto her hands and knees and started coughing. All around her were shrieks and the noise of the other houses along Milbourn Street awakening to the horror of the explosion.

"No one was inside," she kept telling herself, the words repeated like a mantra. No one, not Mrs. Gilbert or her butler or Lucy. But what about the neighbouring families, the Harts, and the Petersons? They....

Strong arms pulled her to her feet. She couldn't hear the person's voice, but somehow, she knew it was Nicholas. A loud ringing in her ears drowned out everything else. She was certain it was him, and that was when the wild panic subsided just a little. He was there. Something in the way he held her was all the safety she had dreamt of in her youthful daydreams, and she let herself relax against his chest.

He scooped her into his arms and rushed through the street, past the massing crowd and away from the burning building.

Their journey away from her burning house felt like fragments of snatched moments. Pieces that were held together by the sheer presence of Nicholas. He ordered the carriage off and away. She could hear his voice distantly, but none of the words quite made sense to her. She could feel his hands on her face and back, checking her for injuries, his expression one of deep concern. She thought she was fine, but it was nice—no, it was everything—that he cared enough to look that worried.

She remembered him insisting on carrying her inside the cottage. She could not find Walsh, but when she rolled over, she was inside her own room in Winston Cottage. The bedspread was familiar. Forcing herself to sit up, Isabel looked around the bedroom. For the first time, the darkness worried her.

"Nicholas?" she called.

"I'm here." He got up from a chair by the fireplace and made his way over to her. His hands took hers and squeezed. "I wanted to take you to the doctor, but we didn't know if that was too dangerous; the important thing was to make sure you weren't seen."

"I don't understand."

"Lucy checked you over, but none of us could see any major hurt." He sat down on the edge of her bed. "I should never have let you go near that building. It's all my fault. I'm sorry."

"I wanted to go there. I thought if I found anything more on the Wareton Gang or Harlington..." They would be gone now; that was for sure. She could picture the fragments of her one-time home and the smell of burning wood.

"God, you could have died. When I saw that blood on your face..." He trailed off as he looked at her again. "I'll never forgive myself..."

"You should put it about that I was killed in the blast." The idea grew in her mind. She felt clearer; the fogginess was receding. This, she reasoned, would be her opportunity to start afresh. "They'll stop coming for me then. The Wareton Gang."

"Walsh suggested much the same thing." Nicholas looked concerned. "I'll speak to the coroner and have it arranged. If this doesn't get the militia involved, I don't know what will." He got to his feet, leaning one way and then another, before heading back towards the chair.

"You can't sleep in that," Isabel said, sitting up. She was a little lightheaded, but other than that, she did not feel too bad. Perhaps her hearing had been affected, but she felt sure that was all.

"You asked me not to leave you," Nicholas replied.

"Then stay with me." Isabel shifted in the bed, moving to give him room to slide in next to her. She could not quite believe her own forwardness, but at the same time, she knew nothing untoward would happen. Nicholas was too much of a gentleman. And the comfort of his arms around her once again was the thing she needed in the cool darkness of the cottage. "Please."

Taking a hesitant step back towards her, Nicholas moved into the slim gap that allowed some moonlight to hit his features. "Are you sure? What about your reputation?"

"What does it matter? You're talking to a dead woman."

Bending, Nicholas removed his shoes and jacket and climbed in next to her. His arm slid around her shoulders and pulled Isabel against his chest. She could feel his heartbeat through the cotton of his shirt. It was steady and let her focus on her own breath, in and out. Isabel could feel each one of her muscles relaxing as she stretched out her body and curled it close to his.

"This is perfect," she murmured as she nodded off, the weight of the day and the memories of her home and family leaving, draining away from her with each moment that passed. She had been right; Nicholas was the safety and security, the comfort and solace she had always dreamt that he would be.

When the light woke her, she found that the fogginess from earlier had lifted, leaving her clear headed. Nicholas was sleeping next to her, his body close. His beautiful face was relaxed, and his long eyelashes fanned out against his cheeks. In the dawn light, Isabel could see the faint smudges of freckles that decorated his face and the beginnings of stubble on his jawline.

Cautiously, as if he might fade away, she put out her hand and traced the pattern of freckles down his exposed cheek.

He didn't stir, and she leant closer. His breathing was steady. Hadn't she dreamt of this previously? She had, constantly. She drew nearer still. His cupid's bow of a mouth was begging to be kissed. Would that be taking a liberty? Swallowing down her fears, Isabel brushed her lips against his.

"God, woman, you took your time," Nicholas muttered, his hands coming around her and hauling her closer, right up against him. It was wondrous as his mouth sealed over hers in a kiss that she could feel throughout her body, all the way down to her toes. The sort of kiss that would have produced poetry had she ever felt like writing it or music if she were better on the pianoforte. It warmed, turning her innards to mush, and pulsed sensation through her body.

Nicholas moved with precision and skill, rendering Isabel as giddy as if she had drunk brandy. Alongside this was the tenderness she felt as his hands grazed over her, never holding for too long so she did not become too insensible. She was overwhelmed by the sheer of emotion of it all. His hands moved over her with a lightness of touch that rendered her witless; it made her feel both exceedingly alive and yet lazy, as if she were a cat who wanted nothing more than to stretch out in the sun, to wallow in all these new, wondrously tingling feelings. One of his hands came to rest on her narrow waist, pressing her more tightly against his chest, whilst his other rested on her bottom.

She pulled back to look down at him, her hands resting either side of the pillow.

"Was that wrong of me?"

"All of it is," she answered.

"Do you regret it?"

"No." Again, Isabel felt she couldn't lie when looking at Nicholas. And yet this would never mean to him what it meant to her. He was used to having mistresses. Used to these acts of lovemaking being meaningless. That was what the papers had said. His Set had opera singers, dancers, actresses at their beck and call. Those women would be used to the sensations that he evoked in them, that bubbled beneath their skin. But Isabel wasn't. "It is all just a little new to me."

Nicholas raised an eyebrow. "Being held like this is new?"

"During the daytime. Mr. Hall liked us to have congress only once a month. In the dark."

"Fully clothed?" Nicholas asked.

"How did you know?"

"My God." For the first time today, Nicholas looked disgruntled and confused. He sat up underneath her, bringing his face close to hers once more. "You're teasing me."

"Not at all. It is what Pierre preferred. He said it was..." Isabel stopped herself. It was something private, something Nicholas might hold against her later, if he knew that Pierre had told Isabel it was the only way for them to conceive, even though Isabel had her doubts. For a reason she wasn't certain of, she didn't want Nicholas knowing she wanted a child. "He said it was how husbands and wives make love."

She shifted on his lap, and in response, Nicholas adjusted them both, slowly wrapping his arms around her. He started kissing the strands of pale blond hair at her temples, feathering kisses as he went.

"I take it you never enjoyed those evenings with Mr. Hall?"

"Not very much," Isabel admitted. "Thankfully, they never lasted very long, maybe a

minute or two."

She could feel Nicholas's smile against her skin, but he didn't say anything smart or anything that made her feel silly. His hand returned to her waist, and he stroked at her back, those cat-like feelings returning to her skin. Isabel had an urge to be rid of the housekeeper's gown.

"And did you ever, late at night in the dark, try and..."

Nicholas's voice trailed off, and Isabel was grateful he could not see her face. She had her nose close to his neck. But she wondered how much he might know of her fantasies of him coming to her, and if he had any idea, she'd fear that he would crow over her something terrible.

"I don't know what you mean." She pushed back against him, and Nicholas loosened his hold, putting a foot between them. When that was done, she slid off him and over to the other side of the bed. She didn't quite want to leave the bed just yet; it was still only early January, and the bedroom was freezing. But if she stayed, then she didn't want him prying into what she might have imagined.

A minute passed, and Isabel watched Nicholas from under her eyelashes. He was frowning at the ceiling, before he rolled onto his side, curving his body close to hers once more. "Come here. Closer. You don't need to worry; I won't do anything you don't want me to."

That might be the problem. Isabel did want him to continue kissing her. She wanted him to help her with the budding feelings that built up in her when he was close. It would be difficult to put that into words. She moved closer to him, with their foreheads touching. It was too awkward to look at him full in the eyes, so instead, she gazed at his mouth. So prone to merriment, it was now formed into a serious line; even his dimple had vanished.

"I'll tell you whatever you want to know," he said. No immediate questions came to mind; at least, not ones she felt able to ask Nicholas. "What did your mother tell you about your wedding night?" he asked.

Isabel tried to piece together whatever her mother had told her, all of those many years ago. She had talked about how it would lead to babies, how Pierre would put something inside her. Which Pierre had. It had felt solid, like a wedge. He'd wriggled around. Then he had stopped. It had hurt but it had been brief. It had helped to stare up at the ceiling, Isabel had found, and to recite the alphabet slowly in her head. By the time she was done with her recital, so was Pierre.

"She said it would be embarrassing at first," Isabel said. "But that I would get used to it. That it could be nice."

Nicholas waited for Isabel to raise her head and look at him before he asked his next question. "I take it that was not the case for you?"

"No." She felt upset, as if her mother had lied to her. There was something else at play too which was harder to define, but it made her feel as if Pierre had lied to her too. Kept something from her. Why hadn't it been nice? Wasn't she owed that?

"Don't cry," Nicholas soothed. "He can't hurt you again."

"I'm not upset," Isabel told him. She wasn't, at all, but she did feel a mixture of anger and annoyance throb through her chest. "Do other people enjoy it?"

Keeping a straight face, Nicholas nodded.

"That's why you have had mistresses?"

"I... You are very direct."

Isabel sat up. She pulled her knees up to her chest and held onto her toes. This was a whole world that had been kept from her, and she was only just starting to piece it together. "You said you'd answer any of my questions," she pointed out.

"Lord, it's like dealing with a virgin," he said as he sat up too.

"Not really," Isabel shot back. She was finished with being shy and retiring; it had done her little good so far. Being in her natural state, the one she had been raised to embrace, hadn't helped. Besides which, she had a growing desire to watch Nicholas blush. Something in that warmed her. Made him seem more human, more revealed, than in the fantasies she had entertained. "So, I take it you enjoyed it with those women?"

"One doesn't really discuss—"

"Your other lovers, you mean?"

"One does not tend to discuss such matters with respectable women," Nicholas said.

Cocking an eyebrow at him, Isabel laughed. "I think we can safely assume I'm not that anymore. Any one of your friends could say something—"

"They wouldn't."

"It is not like any one of them would ever agree to—" She had been about to say, 'Stand up with me at a ball,' but Nicholas, who had been growing more and more irritated, jumped ahead.

"You would like to be courted by one of them?"

Unable to help herself, Isabel laughed. The idea was beyond absurd. She had spent some time with Viscount Silverton, but there was something rather hard and unforgiving in his manner that Isabel did not warm to. He did not have an ounce of that easy, natural kindness that Isabel so... so... admired about Nicholas.

But Isabel had no chance to say any of this, because Nicholas moved forward and kissed her, rendering her speechless. His hands weaved their way through her hair and held her in place. His tongue rubbed against the seam of Isabel's lips, until she parted them, and he deepened their kiss. His mouth moved to her chin and down her neck. His stubble scratched against her tender skin, and Isabel moaned. That fidgeting, desirous feeling was returning to her limbs as she raised her hands and stroked them along Nicholas's back.

"He never did this," Nicholas muttered as he unhooked the front of her dress, parting the material with an ease that should have alarmed Isabel. But she was too busy enjoying the feel of his fingers as they traced the edge of her chemise.

Isabel leant back against the pillows as Nicholas feathered kisses against her décolletage. Every time his hand moved over her exposed skin, either at her neck or against the tops of her breasts, her hips seem to shift, to lift up and press against his body. It provided a small amount of relief for her, although it wasn't enough. Those sensations he stirred in her continued unabashed.

Shifting back and away from her, Nicholas laughed when Isabel let out a frustrated sigh. When he moved back and whispered against her ear, she could have died from sheer embarrassment, but she was too far gone to care. "Do you want me to show you why people risk so much for this?"

She muttered something as his hand moved once more over her hips, stroking at her legs, although none of her noises were exactly quiet.

"Was that a yes?"

"Yes, please," she cried.

Nicholas kissed her swollen lips as his hands lifted her rumpled dress, settling the material higher whilst his other hand started to trace its way over the front of her sex. Whenever Pierre had touched her there, in readiness for his insertion, Isabel had forced herself to relax. This time, though, Nicholas unlaced the front of her drawers, his fingers parting the folds of her sex, moving across the curls. Isabel raised her hips, welcoming the feel of him. He continued to kiss her lips and face as his fingers delved deeper, stroking, and moving their way around the intimate folds of her sex. Isabel felt sure she should be bursting with embarrassment at such an intimate action. But it felt too wonderful to care. Dignity be damned.

"How does that feel?" he asked against her lips, his clever fingers moving in a steady rhythm against the most sensitive part of her. He moved his fingers in an insistent beat, close to a small part of her that seemed buried deep.

"Yes," she said, as her hands pulled at his hair, forcing him to kiss her once again. "That's nice."

"Only nice? Hmm... how about this?" Nicholas angled his hand lower and sank a finger deep inside Isabel's sex.

At first, the movement felt like an intrusion, but Nicholas gave her time to adjust to the feel of him, to the shape of his finger, as she moved herself up against it, wriggling as she did so. Her eyes opened and looked into his. Tremulously, given how alive her body felt for the first time in years, she gave him a smile.

"I think I understand a bit better now. Why people make love."

Chuckling, Nicholas started moving his finger deeper within her, and Isabel leant further back into the pillows. Nicholas pressed on, his fingers playing against her soft flesh, parting her and driving her wilder. Her hips reacted in the same uneven beat, finding it difficult at first before she learnt when to lift and grind.

A small, joyous cresting started inside her that only seemed to ease if she continued to writhe against his fingers. It came from her core, building before rolling out of her in a series of little cries. The sensation like a wave, rocking through her body, until it eased its way through her. She shivered at her release as Nicholas kissed her forehead, cheek, and then her lips. Then he pulled her close against him, and she slept once more.

ON WAKING A GOOD FEW HOURS LATER, ISABEL HAD A faint hope that they might try something similar again. There must be other things they could do; that couldn't be everything. And if there was more, she wanted to experience it with Nicholas. But when she opened her eyes and sat up in bed, he was gone.

Pulling a shawl to herself, Isabel left the bedroom and went down the stairs. They would have breakfast, and then discuss how she would function for the next few days or weeks as his mistress. She did not expect to live much beyond that. And if she did, she would try and become a housekeeper—she already had the dress. It wasn't much of a plan but arranging everything was potentially too difficult with so much unknown.

When she entered the little kitchen, she was greeted by a red-faced Nicholas, who stood in the centre of the stone-floored room. "There you are. What is the meaning of this?" He shoved a piece of paper at her that Isabel had never seen before.

In surprise, Isabel looked down at the writing. Only when she reached the bottom of the page and saw Silverton's signature did she realise who it was from. He had supplied her with his secretary's address in London, with the suggestion of her writing to the man should she ever have need. The generosity of the statement, after what she had done to him, made a smile lift to Isabel's lips. Perhaps she had judged Silverton too harshly. Perhaps he wanted to make amends for his brother's actions by helping Isabel.

"Don't you smile about that. The indecency of him, offering you money. Can you imagine the scandal of the thing?"

"I'm not sure that was his intention."

"I cannot believe that he would write to you."

"What are you afraid of?" Isabel asked. "I have done nothing wrong."

"It is the implication of scandal."

"You are jealous."

The word caused the blood to drain from Nicholas's face,

and embarrassment washed over his features. She did not think that moment in the bed that they had shared had been something she could share with another man, but he had no right to assume the worst of her.

"Have the goodness, ma'am, to excuse me." Nicholas dropped the letter back onto the table and strode out of the room. "And stay here. Do not think about leaving."

With that, he was gone. Isabel swore at Nicholas's stupidity. Then she re-read the note. As she suspected, it was merely a courtesy on Silverton's part, and Nicholas had assumed the worst of them both. Her sadness and annoyance redoubled when she finished it. Silverton was trying to make up for his mistakes. She folded the note up and made herself tea at the stove, resolving with great sadness to never think of those few hours she had spent in Nicholas's arms again. Not if he was so quick to think the worst of her.

CHAPTER 12

Nicholas's mood did not improve with the arrival of his dear friend, Mr. Michael Trawler, to the Hurstbourne Manor. Trawler was the only one of the Set without a grand title to his name, but he was far more charming than Silverton had put himself out to be. He was also a magnificent businessman with one of the most fashionable department stores in London. Of course, Trawler was not without his own problems. He was base-born, and his father, the Duke of Grisham, was a hideous reprobate. The Set had never judged Trawler for the faults of his parentage, but Nicholas knew it weighed heavily on Michael. Sometimes the burdens of parents came down too greatly on their children.

Trawler was around six-two, with mid-brown hair that lightened at the ends. Nicholas supposed he had a firm, open, and handsome face. Madame Rebecca Dares, a renowned courtesan, had once said that he possessed the most arresting, amber-coloured eyes in all of London. Of course, the Set had teased Trawler about this for days. But now, suddenly, Nicholas did not see the humorous side. Bugger him.

Nicholas wished him a little less good-looking. Lynde's renowned good humour did not improve as his friend gave him a cheerful nod of his head.

Trawler reached out a hand and shook Nicholas's, then removed his hat and sighed. "Sorry to see you in such circumstances."

Nicholas continued to frown; he was furious with so many things, but he couldn't bring an order to them in his mind. His sister treating it like a game. His friends, managing such wild, dangerous affairs with smugglers and lawbreakers. And as for Isabel... he shook his head. He'd been able to ignore the former two issues previously, but now, it was beyond him. He had to take control, he had to play a part and be more responsible when all he really wanted to do was rush back and apologise to Isabel for being rude. He knew it wasn't her fault and that it had been his jealousy.

His friend was watching him with a wary expression, and Nicholas wondered if Trawler, like Silverton before him, would try and hide information about the smugglers.

"Silverton told me you'd been tracking, supervising a great deal of it—" Nicholas said.

The mild look of worry cleared from his face, and Trawler bowed his head. He sank into the armchair and crossed his legs, gazing back with so much ease that it frustrated Nicholas to no end. Why was he not more outraged? Why was he not more afraid? Perhaps he hadn't witnessed a bloody explosion, perhaps he had spent too much time pressed over a ledger rather than witnessing...

Trawler was speaking, and Nicholas had become too wrapped up in his fears again. "My connection at the Home Office gave me something of a tip-off, but clearly Robinson underestimated the scale of the problem with the Wareton Gang."

"You didn't know they were capable of setting explosives?" Nicholas's voice was harsh.

Trawler's eyes widened, and his hand moved to his waistcoat before lifting it and adjusting his cravat. "Was anyone killed?"

"No, thankfully. But I do not like being a step behind every move the Waretons make, and as for Harlington—I barely understand a thing about him, which does not help."

"You must understand what kept Silverton quiet on that front? Familiar embarrassments..." Trawler paused. "After all, a family scandal is something I am sure we all wish we could ignore."

"It wouldn't make you risk—"

"Your mother—"

"I am not prepared to discuss my mother." Nicholas was on his feet, his face flushed. He felt savage and resentful, his blood pumping through his veins. That night with Isabel had brought to his attention just how much risk she was in, and it drove him wild that neither Trawler nor Silverton had any protective measures in place. How could they remain calm when she was in danger? "I have to know more about the Waretons and Harlington. What are their patterns of behaviour?"

"Well..." Trawler hesitated as Nicholas stalked the room. Every refined piece of furniture, every miniature, even the thick blue curtains annoyed him. The refinement that built up his life now was just a thing that seemed designed to prevent him from acting as he should.

"Out with it," he barked at Trawler.

"I am choosing the best place to begin so that you have as many of the facts as I know, with none of my assumptions imposing themselves on you." Trawler moved forward as he spoke and rested his elbows on his buff-coloured trousers.

"There has been smuggling up and down the south coast, lasting for decades."

"You don't have to go that far back."

"Verne, Silverton, and I were approached... No, that isn't quite a fair summary. Verne's family has always been involved with controversy and the Channel. That is how his mother's friends were rescued from the guillotine."

Nicholas nodded. He'd heard as much before; he recalled the chat being similar at university, although he'd studiously avoided any discussion that might be too blackening to his own name, and now he was regretting that decision.

"When I left Oxford, I wanted to work—I needed to. My store gives me a great deal of insight into what is shipped in, what everyone pays at customs, and what is on the black market. Which is why I started working more closely with Silverton and Verne."

"And how does this tie into Harlington?"

"We did not suspect—one of my men, Robinson got a tip-off that Harlington was out of the picture. It seems as if Silverton does not believe his twin capable of staying away. He has visited England in the last few months, if he is not still here making trouble."

"Silverton said his brother trafficked in women?"

A pained look passed over Trawler's handsome face, and he grimaced. "He has a knack of taking well-placed women, normally servants or prostitutes, and manipulating them to his will. Sometimes through force, other times..."

"But none of them have been found?"

Trawler shook his head. "It may well be that he has changed his approach."

"How long has this gang been operating?" The fury Nick felt towards the smuggling ring was there but bubbling away was the knowledge that his supposed friends had kept him in the dark. That hurt too.

"It's been a good five years since Silverton discovered the truth about his brother's actions. And had him chased from the country."

"I'm glad I got Viola out of the way," Nicholas said, almost to himself. Although Isabel was still here; was that too risky? Should she have been sent to London too? Nicholas felt selfish for keeping her close, and his rationale for keeping her from her family was feeling flimsier with every passing minute. If he cared for her, he should have sent her to London; that would have been in her best interests. This interaction, this affair as she had labelled it, was rendering Nicholas incomprehensible even to himself.

At the mention of Nicholas's sister, Trawler got to his feet and moved across to the fireplace, his back to Nicholas.

"How's she keeping herself?"

"Viola?"

"Last time I saw her was at her almost wedding."

Nicholas smirked. That had only been a few weeks ago, but it seemed longer. The wedding that wasn't; it had felt like the end of the world. Now he'd welcome his sister walking out on every duke in the *ton* if it meant keeping Isabel safe. "Viola likes to get her own way," Nicholas finally said.

"I understand she's been sent away?"

"That's right," Nicholas said. "She's left."

"And the young widow who's caught up in this scandal, too?"

"How do you know about her?"

"Silverton wrote to me. The letter mentioned a Mrs. Hall and her dead husband. He also indicated that there was a dangerous brother-in-law. Is that correct?"

"She's taken care of," Nicholas snapped.

Trawler looked down at his hands, although Nicholas caught a slight smile at the corner of the other man's lips and guessed his friend was laughing at him. "Then I would suggest we locate the younger Hall, and ideally the other members of the Waretons, as quickly as possible. One suspects the former will be more likely to show himself around town. We're unlikely to get much help from the local militia."

Nicholas forced himself to concentrate. "Why do you say that?"

"I have my suspicions that one of the uppers is in on the scheme; that's why it's been able to operate for so long."

"What do we do then?"

Giving a matter-of-fact shrug, Trawler let his face relax. "We keep it simple. The fewer people who know, the better. It's about the ringleaders and finding their base. Is there any indication of where it could be?"

"I know for darn sure it isn't the Hall townhouse. I watched it blow up last night." The sight of Isabel's half-turned face as she looked back at him. The explosion that followed, with leaping blooms of smoke and flames. God, he wouldn't let himself forget how close she'd been to that hell.

"Do we have any idea of when they might get another shipment? And how they are moving it around?" asked Trawler.

"Silverton and I interrupted the last delivery."

"I was under the impression it was being moved through the Hall townhouse."

"You want to look through the rubble?" Nicholas asked. The wreckage would have at least cooled in the intervening hours, and the cold January showers would likewise help with that.

"Yes, to see if there's anything that would give us an indication of where they might try next. Who might they turn to?" Trawler got to his feet. He had more energy and enthusiasm than Nicholas, whose mind kept returning to Winston Cottage and everything he had said to Isabel. Or wished he hadn't said. All the things he should have told her. "Also, if she is still close by, I should like to speak with the widow."

"I would prefer if it went through me," Nicholas said. He was sick of endangering Isabel.

"I won't step on any toes," Trawler replied. "The sooner her in-laws are brought to justice, the sooner she'll be free of their dangerous association."

The truth of his words stuck in Nicholas's throat. "Let's go, then." He strode out of the room, with Trawler in his wake. "My father is not well. I'm trying to keep him ignorant of this," Nicholas said as they made their way down the front steps and towards the stables. "We'll go to town first, and then, if you're no clearer, we'll visit the widow."

"Mrs. Hall?" Trawler asked.

"If asked," Nicholas said with force, "she is in London with her family. We don't know where they have gone."

"Understood."

The rest of the journey into town was taken up with Trawler telling Nicholas about his New Year's, spent with his mother in Greenwich, and about the growing rumours of unrest on the Continent.

"From what they said," Trawler continued, as they neared the edge of Eastbourne, "there's more trouble from Russia and France."

"I thought everyone admired Tsar Alexander?" Nicholas asked. It was like whispering the devil's name to some people, the ruler who many had mixed feelings on. One of the few who had dared to defy Bonaparte and bring the despot to heel, but what did that say about the Tsar: was it bravery or madness on his part? Not that many people wanted to consider a choice between Russia's overweening influence or France's.

"Indeed," Trawler said, in a tone that did not imply respect.

They reached the cooled remains of the Halls' townhouse, where Walsh had gone that morning. Immediately Trawler and Walsh started chatting away in a familiar manner, while Nicholas made his way through the remains. The blast had only destroyed this one building. That took skill and precision.

Getting onto his hands and knees, Nicholas shifted pieces of the rubble out of the way until his hands alighted on a safe. The sturdy sort that would require a key. Unless one could cause a big enough explosion to render it apart. The dust bloomed around him as Nicholas prized the fragments of the case apart. It was broken, with bits of papers and old jewellery boxes in his hands. The papers were dusty, and as Nicholas looked through them, he saw the same code that had been written on the note that Isabel had kept. Perhaps it was more than he had suspected.

There was a noise close by, and Nicholas looked up, expecting to see Trawler. But it wasn't. James Hall was standing only ten feet away, a ridiculous expression on his face. Their eyes met. Nicholas scrambled upright in the dust and debris as Hall took off.

"Stop that man," Nicholas yelled. But there was no one close by to grab at James. Trawler was nowhere to be seen. Only Walsh seemed to hear Nicholas, but he was caught behind a gathering of clucking and umbrella-wielding women.

Cursing, Nicholas hurried after Hall himself. The other man knew the town better than he but based on his footfalls, the man was drunk. The terraced houses flickered past. Nicholas's breath caught in his throat, his shirt sticking to him as he ran to keep up with Hall. The man turned down a side street that opened onto the seafront.

The two of them made their way haphazardly onto the pebbles of the beach. Hall jerked wildly on the wet stones and slipped, unable to balance himself. Slowing, Nicholas approached him.

"That bitch is dead." Hall rolled onto his side and started to get to his feet. He didn't need to specify who he meant. "Weren't you there for her body?"

"Not before she told me everything." Nicholas tried to make his face form a lascivious smile, hoping to goad the other man. It seemed to work because Hall's expression darkened.

"She didn't know much," Hall spat. "Little tart was nothing more than an ignorant wallflower."

"I don't know about that," Nicholas replied. He was drawing closer to Hall. If he tackled the man, he assumed he could bring him down. It would be a fair fight unless the man had a weapon on him. Nicholas had him cornered; there was only the sea behind him, but Nicholas wasn't sure the man wouldn't dive into the icy waves. He relaxed slightly, as he couldn't see a weapon on Hall.

"I helped out the Blackmans," Nicholas said. "We could work out something similar for you?"

"Izzy would like that, wouldn't she?"

"She's dead, remember?" Nicholas lied.

"Still loyal to her memory?"

"Why don't you tell me about Harlington?" Nicholas pressed.

Laughing, Hall backed further away, the heels of his feet hitting the edge of the lapping sea. "I don't think so. That won't do me much good at all."

"I've heard about the loyalty that exists between men like you."

"How do you know that I'm not running the entire thing? For all you know, *I* could be Harlington."

Tilting his head to one side, Nicholas surveyed Hall. His assumed ignorance was what was keeping him alive. Did anyone else in Sussex know about Harlington's connection to the Set? To Silverton?

"Are you saying it's interchangeable? Almost like it could be a code name?" Nicholas guessed.

Hall's face was a picture of distress, and he muttered, "Don't know what you're talking about."

The sound of the waves was all about them, the cawing of the circling gulls echoed overhead, and the constant beat of rain drowned out the noise of anything else from the town. Large barriers funnelled the pebbles down to the sea. They somewhat limited the men's movements to either the right or left. Nicholas rolled up his sleeves. It was now or never. He would need to restrain Hall and drag him back for questioning. He didn't know whether Walsh or Trawler had ever interrogated a man before. He hadn't. The thought didn't appeal, no matter what type of man Hall might be.

Realising the situation he was in, Hall drew a knife from his coat pocket. So much for Nicholas's first assumption. It was on the short side but looked very sharp. He grinned when he saw Nicholas's expression. "You can't belong to the Wareton Gang and not come prepared."

It had been a while since Nicholas had had to fight someone, but it had been the routine of an elegant gentleman boxing, nothing beyond that. Not someone who had a knife and was prepared to kill him. The trick was to remain calm, he told himself.

"I don't think that'll be necessary," came a voice from behind Nicholas. Walsh was crossing the pebbles, and he carried a raised pistol. "Lower your weapon," he called out to Hall. The man's face tightened in fear.

"Come on," Nicholas tried again. If they could turn someone like James, they'd be able to bring down all the Wareton Gang. If that meant making a compromise and sparing the life of someone like James Hall, sacrifices would need to be made.

"That pistol won't work," Hall called back. "Not in these conditions."

"There's two of us." Nicholas reasoned. He was getting closer to Hall now, within striking distance.

A pistol went off. Nicholas looked back at Walsh as the man staggered where he stood. Nicholas realised then that it hadn't been Walsh who had fired. Hall was unhurt; in fact, the revolting man was laughing. Instead, it was Nicholas's colleague who had been shot. Walsh dropped to his knees on the pebbled beach before collapsing face down onto the ground. Keeping low to the stones, Nicholas scrambled away from Hall and towards the injured Walsh. He had to help him.

"Told you, you shouldn't underestimate us." Hall's tone was gleeful. Rather than making a break for it, he followed Nicholas over the rocks. Nicholas turned back to Hall. If he was going to be shot from god knows where, he would take Hall out of this world first.

He got to his feet, all semblance of being an earl's son gone in his movements, and grabbed the knife out of Hall's hand, surprising the man. Then with his free hand, Nicholas levelled a punch straight into the false handsomeness of Hall's face. Hall fell backwards. Another shot sounded, and Nicholas dropped to his haunches. It was darn near impossible to see where the bullets might be coming from. A thick sheet of grey rain tempered it all and rendered anything more than five feet ahead of them invisible. James scrambled away. Levelling himself up, Nicholas crawled over the rocks to Walsh's side; he knew better than to chase his foe in such circumstances.

"Where were you hit?"

"My arm," the man grumbled. "Don't think it'll be too bad. Clean through."

Through the rain, Nicholas felt the wound. There was enough moisture between his fingers to tell him that Walsh was a braver man than he. He was impressed that his comrade was still conscious. Keeping low and close to him, Nicholas pulled out a flask, which he pressed into Walsh's uninjured hand.

"Drink it," he said. Nicholas loosened his cravat and wrapped it around Walsh's arm. While he worked, he kept waiting for a third bullet to come, but none did. "Let's go," he said once he was finished.

Walsh was looking woozy, although Nicholas didn't want to speculate whether this was from the whiskey or from the wound. He wedged his leg against the injured man, bringing him upright. Then he proceeded to half carry, half drag Walsh over the rocky, uneven beach.

"If the wound doesn't get you," Nicholas said, trying to lighten the mood, "the cold might."

Walsh muttered something closer to a string of curses than a reply to the jest. They walked the rest of the way in silence until they reached the first tavern on the seafront, whose warm lights called out through the darkness. Shouting as he went, Nicholas gathered the attention of the staff. The landlord helped ease Walsh from his hands, and a stable boy was sent off for a doctor. Twenty minutes ticked by, and Nicholas stood close to Walsh's side, his back warmed by the fire as they waited until finally, the doctor arrived.

"You did a good job," the doctor commented as he looked over Walsh's arm. The man was unfamiliar to Nicholas. Walsh was unconscious, having been dosed with laudanum. "Is this to do with the smugglers who are about in these parts?"

"Can you keep him safe?" Nicholas turned earnest eyes on the doctor. This felt like a new threat. Every time Nicholas started to feel as if he knew what he was doing, someone reliable was taken from him. "Here," he said, handing a series of banknotes to the doctor. "That is for his safety. Keep him with you until he mends. Send any further bills to the Hurstbourne estate."

The doctor nodded, and Nicholas slipped out of the room. He hurried back towards Milbourn Street, anxious to collect Trawler, fearing for his friend's safety in the dangerous town. Then, he needed to return post-haste to Isabel. What had his friend gotten to? Thankfully, when he rounded the street, he saw Trawler. Rushing towards him, Nick gave only the briefest of overviews of the action on the beach as the two of them made their way back to their horses.

"Where were you?" Nicholas asked.

"Interviewing the neighbours, for anything revealing."

He didn't want to dwell on how much time they had already spent away from the cottage. He wanted to see her face. Isabel. She would make today better. She would smile and hold his hand. There would be an innate comfort in her. He had thought of little else whilst he had worked on Walsh's arm, making sure the man would be safe, conscious all the time that every breath he took might be his last if another bullet came.

"This way," Nicholas said. He'd had enough of Eastbourne to last him a lifetime; all he wanted to do was see Isabel. He could not believe that he had let this much time pass since their last, angry parting.

On reaching Winston Cottage, Nicholas tore inside, ordering Trawler to remain outside on his horse. Barging into the kitchen, where he'd last seen her, Nicholas was shocked to find Isabel poised with a knife in hand, her breathing erratic. Beside her stood a rather scared-looking maid holding a broom aloft as her weapon of choice.

"My God," she said. "You scared us."

"Leave us," he muttered at the servant girl, who scuttled hurriedly out of the kitchen looking relieved, broom in hand.

Nicholas marched forward and yanked the knife out of her hand, pulling her warm, alive body against his, so grateful to have her close. To feel her breath. To smell that faint scent of jasmine that was uniquely her and to kiss the clinging strands of her blond hair. She was alive. She was safe. She was his.

Isabel was struggling against him and fighting to loosen herself, to step away. He released her. "What is the meaning of this?" she gasped.

"I just had a frightful day." It was devastating to realise how much he needed the solace of her body, her mind, her voice. He raised his hand and touched her hair. It was as if the most beautiful of the moon's rays were caught on her head, tumbling this way and that, and all Nicholas wanted to do was carry her up the stairs and lay those strands on the pillows. Before...

Isabel's eyes were flinty, and she folded her arms across her chest. She looked like a disgruntled housekeeper, though a more beautiful one than Nicholas had ever seen. "You're all wet; your shirt is torn," she scolded him as she looked him up and down.

"It is raining," he muttered. Her sharp eyes didn't soften; they only changed when Nicholas muttered, "Walsh was shot today."

Isabel gasped, and tears well up in her eyes. "Is he alive?"

Nicholas nodded. "He's with the doctor now."

She let out her breath. "Couldn't you have opened with that? And couldn't you have taken a carriage? I don't want you to catch your death from the cold."

"My thoughts exactly," Trawler said as he pushed open the door and greeted Isabel. "You must be Mrs. Hall?"

"God, another one," she remarked, making a quick curtsey. "How do you do?"

"Another one?" Trawler asked as he entered the room.

"Another lummox of a man who apparently can't keep himself dry," Isabel replied. "You had better rebuild the fire," she told Nicholas. "I'll go and get some blankets." She marched out, and Nicholas went to the fire and started piling on coal. However, his eyes were soon raised to whatever was distracting Trawler. The man was hovering near the table, looking at pages of notes that had been spread out on the wooden surface.

Drawing nearer, Nicholas looked at the sheets. It was clear that Isabel had been hard at work. The numbers she had recorded from the slips of paper she'd kept and fresh speculations of hers were scrawled on the pages. When she entered, both men raised their eyes to her.

"What do you mean by this?"

"It is a code or the numbers that reoccurred numerous times in my husband's accounts. I think it's a point on a map."

Both men leant closer to her notes, pulling out the map she had drawn of the area.

"What's this place?" Nicholas touched a point she had marked.

"It's a site close to the town of Battle," Isabel said as she sank into a seat. "I don't know what's there, but I think it could be a meeting point. Or a site where they bury items. There aren't other buildings close by. I thought it would be a good sort of place for a drop site, no witnesses."

"She's right," Trawler whispered. His eyes moved from the map up to Isabel. "The location is the sort of place they've used for drops before. Clever woman. This is what we needed," Trawler said. "They have always used a drop site in the past. And this must be it. We've got them."

"The Wareton Gang have a set way of behaving?" Isabel asked.

"Most smugglers do. Using specific sites, normally close to the sea for obvious reasons. But the code you found would suggest they've been using this site more frequently. That's unusual."

"How so?" she pressed.

Trawler sent Nicholas a quick look. "Most smugglers vary their sites, but if they've used the same location again and again," he paused, frowning, "it implies something else."

"That they aren't only moving brandy. It would be something more valuable?" she asked.

Or something more dangerous, was the unspoken thought amongst them all. That had been Nicholas's fear. Silverton had warned them about Harlington's poisonous influence. That he had infiltrated the Wareton Gang from the Continent and was controlling things even now. Nicholas's eyes moved to the window to gaze outside as if he would be able to see through the cold January night and seek out Silverton's dangerous brother across the sea.

"That trade-off might be occurring soon," Trawler finished. "But I would need to see the site to be sure."

"We have to catch them in the act." Isabel stepped closer to Trawler, cutting Nicholas out from the conversation. As she spoke, her voice throbbed with a clear desire to stop the Wareton, and it terrified Nicholas to his very soul, the idea of her stepping into danger.

"You're not going anywhere," Nicholas said.

CHAPTER 13

It was clear to Isabel that Nicholas was furious in a low, quiet way, and she could not understand why. His anger seemed to be directed at her, even though he could not still be caught up on that silliness over Silverton. It seemed out of character for him, a poor fit with the kind, smiling man she was familiar with.

Carefully, she moved to the side of the kitchen where her cup was and sat down on a stool. She mulled it over as she sipped her tea and watched the two of them. Her thoughts were caught on so many things, and it did not help that she and her maid, Lucy, still had a lot of things to resolve.

Earlier in the day, Isabel had been downcast. She had believed that what she and Nicholas had shared meant something—it didn't have to be love, but it had been meaningful—only for his anger to break through at the oddest moment. It had lingered with her as Lucy and she had picked their way through lunch, neither uttering a word until Lucy broke the silence.

"Ma'am?"

Isabel had looked up from her plate and across the table,

realising if she didn't stop moping, she was little better than a lovesick fool. "What is it, Lucy?"

"It's about my cousin."

"I don't know if Jessica is still at the hospital. Mr. Hall didn't keep me informed on her wellbeing."

"Ma'am. I know she's there." Lucy leant forward. "His Lordship says we won't stay long here, and if we're for London, I want to get Jessica out of Hodgkin's madhouse first." She pulled a small purse from her skirt pocket. "I've got twenty guineas here. I'm hoping it'll be enough. I don't know if it'll cover the baby, though."

Isabel looked at the small purse and the indents of the coins against the material. It was likely Lucy's entire life's savings. The guilt twisted higher inside, and Isabel found herself nodding. She would do anything to help Jessica. She should have acted sooner to protect the younger woman. Something else prickled at her thoughts: Hodgkin.

"What's the doctor's first name?"

Lucy looked confused as she mulled on the question before she replied, "Charles. I believe, ma'am."

A buzz of excitement, of fitting the pieces together, had whizzed through Isabel. She needed to tell the men that she had another suspect who was involved.

Now they were here. *Focus on the tea.* The blend was familiar, strong, with a splash of wholesome milk. Isabel had never taken to having sugar in her drinks, but the comfort of something sweet was welcome on this occasion.

She knew she should have been more concerned about Walsh, and she was until Nicholas had reassured her that the man was recovering with a local doctor, and she felt there was little more she could do for him. Walsh was in good hands, she hoped. She would pray for him tonight. He might even be safer than the rest of them.

And as for Nicholas, it seemed that the two of them were

never to be alone. None of the things she wished to say to him could be uttered in front of another person. The newest arrival, Mr. Trawler, was another member of Lynde's Oxford Set. He was just as handsome as the rest of the men she had met so far. Perhaps the presence of Trawler was making Nicholas anxious.

"The bad weather won't help. Another thing to add to the list," Trawler said as he sliced cheese into smaller and smaller lumps and then proceeded to push them around his plate. None of them were hungry, although Trawler had eaten a few mouthfuls.

Neither Nicholas nor Isabel replied to him; in her case, because she had no idea of what he referred to. Did he mean Walsh and his survival, which was picking and worrying its way around Isabel's head in ever decreasing circles? Or something else? The drop site? She had some doubts and wanted to test them, but Lynde was adamant that she could not help.

The fact that there were only the three of them and the militia refused to involve themselves? It was all stacking up.

"But that's tomorrow's problem. I will see you in the morn." Trawler got to his feet and stretched, nodded at both in turn, and then made his way out of the kitchen, down the hall, and into the sitting room. The door clicked shut behind him.

"How did he know?" she asked, watching Nicholas. She wondered what had been said behind her back, what Trawler thought of her.

"What?" Nicholas shot her a studious look that she couldn't quite understand.

"How did he know where he was to sleep?"

"I said the upstairs was to be your and the maid's domain."

"That was only with Silverton because he couldn't manage the stairs."

"I thought you went by more informal names, ma'am."

"Nicholas," she whispered. She could not for the life of her understand why he was being so unpleasant. She had lain in his arms, let him stroke her and pleasure her, until she quite forgot where they were, who they were, which way was left or right. Until she no longer remembered the mounting danger they faced. The memory of the act throbbed through her, and she shifted awkwardly on her seat, embarrassed how much she still wanted him even when he was being an idiot.

"You know that note Silverton left, that it meant nothing." She pulled the first half of it out of her skirt pocket and handed it to him. "He just wanted me to know that if anything were to happen—"

"That he would swoop in. That you could always go to him? As if I couldn't help—"

"No, of course not. He's one of your oldest friends—"

"We're not that close."

There was a pause, they both laughed at the lie, and the tension in the kitchen eased a little. Nicholas crossed over to her and sat down in the nearest chair. He reached out to her and held her hands. His grip was calming, but something else worried Isabel.

"I'm sorry. I cannot think straight. I keep imagining the worst things. Thinking that you might go to him drives me mad."

"You are jealous?" She had suggested it before, and it had been dismissed. It seemed illogical, but she could not think of another explanation.

"Horribly so," Nicholas admitted. His hand stroked over her fingers, the touch bringing a warmth to her skin almost as much as his words. "Don't ask me what it means."

He pressed his forehead against hers and let out a sigh that seemed to echo through Isabel's body, his strength as well as his admission warming and touching every cell of her being.

Lynde leant back. He beckoned her to him, and gratefully Isabel got to her feet, walking to him, nestling onto his lap, welcoming the way his arms came around her and the feel of him as he rested his head against her back. The warmth of his breath stirred the thin cotton of her dress. It was solace. Comfort. But it was more too. Beneath the cotton, she was prickling, her mind darting here and there, imagining a great deal more. She shifted her legs. There was a heat inside, right at her core. After last night, she knew it meant that she wanted him. Desperately.

A wild wanton image of him making love to her fluttered through her mind, making Isabel's belly flip deliciously at the idea. She glanced over her shoulder, and their eyes met. He looked weary from a hundred worries that he insisted on keeping hidden from her.

"What is wrong, my love?" he asked her, his voice a little husky, and that tightening of his tone as well as the endearment further spurred her bravery.

She leant back, pressed herself against him, turning her face to place a long kiss against his lips, parting her mouth and darting her tongue out to run along the seam of his. She was invigorated by the feel of him as his mouth opened and he deepened the kiss.

Levering herself back against him required that she keep both of her feet on the floor, and to manage that, she parted her legs, finding that the movement meant his thigh was lifted directly against her sex. The unintended pressure made Isabel gasp. The noise echoed in the silent kitchen, and the two of them opened their eyes to stare at each other. A moment ticked by, and even though neither of them moved, Isabel could feel the tension in her body mount. It was centred, pooling almost like a liquid within her through her sex.

"God, you're so beautiful." The tip of his nose nudged against her ear.

Thoughts rumbled through her, and she pressed herself against Nicholas greedily. She needed him to know that as much as he had to find the smugglers and as much as she hoped he'd arrest Harlington and James, it was pressing that Jessica be saved before he sent her away. But when he touched her, God, those thoughts seemed to tumble from her head. Couldn't she just have one more night with him, one more night before she had to confront her own cowardice? Perhaps it was fear he would judge her for not acting beforehand.

She pressed her back against his chest and could feel the rumble of his breath on her skin. Warming her, sending thoughts of her mistakes, the Wareton Gang, even the public setting, straight from her mind. His lips touched the edge of her neck, the gap just above her lace collar, and she shuddered at the memory of how his fingers had felt inside her.

"God, I want you," he whispered almost to himself, and Isabel bit her bottom lip to stop her suggestion of them continuing in the kitchen.

Bending, Nicholas scooped her up in his arms and carried her out of the kitchen and up the stairs, with Isabel still half dazed. Her skin beneath her dress felt new and fresh, alive in a way that surprised her. Even the dark passages of Winston Cottage seemed almost snug now. On the top floor, outside her bedroom, he lowered her down to her feet. His lips brushed against hers in a chaste, delicate kiss as if their recent passionate fumbling had been imagined.

She took a step back from him. "Please listen to me. If I must stay here, then I need you to do something." She thought about sharing what she and Lucy had discussed and about her promise. "The place where the women are held—Doctor Hodgkin." She recounted the story Lucy had told her, about Jessica but more crucially about the doctor's name. "And his initials match the ones I found amongst my husband's notes. What if it's a code too?"

He watched her while she spoke, and his face remained passive in the dim moonlight. When she finished her request of going to save Jessica, he shook his head.

"I can't risk you being hurt. Once the smuggling ring is done with, I will close that madhouse down. I give you, my word."

Isabel thought of Jessica's baby. It would be born soon, if she had not delivered already. She could easily imagine something hideous happening to it. "You cannot command me," she told Nicholas. Pierre had tried to do the same.

The hallway was thin and poorly lit, with just a faint glow emanating from the doorway of her bedroom. Nicholas lifted his hands from her arms, moving them up to bury one in her hair with the other framing her neck before he dropped a kiss on her lips. It was as soft as if they were both innocent. As if they were courting, as she had imagined in her fantasies. But now it wasn't enough.

She moved closer to the door. Fury at being disregarded burned in her belly, and she pushed the doorway open but stopped in case he planned to follow her.

Nicholas let out a sigh. "I am only trying to keep you safe."

"You're going downstairs?"

"With you, I have to remain unselfish." He disappeared down the stairs.

Isabel made herself watch him go, the faint rays of moonlight alighting on his blond hair before she hurried into her room and closed the door. Slowly, she removed the housekeeper's clothes, stays, and cap, until she was down to her camisole. Finally, she let out an unsteady breath. As much as Nicholas tried, he could not understand the need she had to finally do something, to strike a blow against that madhouse, Doctor Hodgkin, and James Hall.

He meant to send her away; that much was clear. Crystal clear. She didn't care for it. She wanted to stay here. Sussex was her home. She had as much right to defend it as he did. Besides, she had stayed quiet and let whatever was going on with Doctor Hodgkin and those girls continue—she would be complicit. She hadn't been able to stop the smuggling, but she might be able to stop that wicked doctor. Climbing into her bed, Isabel tried to fall asleep, but it refused to reach her. Every time she felt restful, another horrible memory of James, or a mention of Hodgkin, would occur to her, until she cried out in exasperated frustration.

"Zounds." She flung her pillow across the room.

"It's not the pillow's fault." Nicholas's voice forced Isabel to sit up in her bed and pull the blankets closer to her.

"I didn't hear you come in."

"You cried out."

"Where were you?"

"Sleeping in the hallway."

"I thought..."

"I know we fought, but I needed to be near you. Was it a nightmare?" He had stepped closer to the bed and into a shaft of light. It illuminated his stark handsomeness, even in his nightclothes. Unable to help herself, Isabel found that she was moved by his confession, of wanting to stay close; she felt that allure of closeness too.

In the half-light, she could make out his eyelashes, his lips which were lifting in a slight smile, the slight curls of his hair. Her eyes dipped lower and saw his unbuttoned shirt, which seemed to have been hastily thrown on. It was adorable. Sweetly innocent. And yet the shape of his shoulders, of his muscles, made Isabel's throat contract with less than pure thoughts. She had pictured this before, but this time, it was different. Nicholas was in her bedroom; all the air around them seemed thicker as if weighed down with each of her wicked desires. Every movement was noticeable now. Whenever Isabel had gone into Pierre's chamber, she had disliked the moments before, the anticipation being worse than the actual minute or so in the bed with him. But this sort of anticipation, seeing Nicholas's eyes moving over her, made Isabel smile.

"What's funny?"

"I don't understand the question." She frowned back at him.

Stepping closer, Nicholas placed a hand on the end of the bed, his knuckles prominent against the wooden frame. In a flash, Isabel could imagine his fingers tracing their way down her skin, maybe to reach out for her breast hold it. Beginning there, before moving lower to...

"You were smiling at me. As if something was amusing."

Sitting up further in the bed, Isabel reached out her hand and laid it over the top of Nicholas's. "Perhaps I was just happy to realise how close you were."

He moved then, closing the space between them as if the thickness in the air had become alive. He let go of the bed, sinking down onto the mattress in front of her, her arms pulling him against her body. Isabel eagerly wrapped herself around him, her nightdress and the bedding pressing up against his body.

His lips were moving over her hair, kissing their way in a desperate passion over her face, her mouth, and her neck. Every time an item, be it the bedspread, his shirt, or her wrap, seemed to obstruct their movements, Isabel found herself giggling. It was delightful to feel as if this exploration was one of fun or joy...his hand encircled her breast, and she moaned. That was nice too, she realised, when the humour could move to desire just as quickly.

In one sudden movement, Nicholas was standing again, and Isabel was flat on her back, gazing up at him. Her nightgown was gone, and she held the sheet against her chest, the cotton cool on her warm skin. The rest of the bedding had been pushed to the end of the bed. His hands were on the waist of his breeches, at the buttons, ready to remove the final barrier. His body was beautiful. Isabel watched with unabashed interest. He resembled one of those statues in the British Museum, carved from marble. But this was far more exciting than anything she had witnessed there. Far more so than any moment she had ever shared with Pierre.

Isabel told herself she wasn't to compare them again. It was not honest, like comparing a bee sting to eating a slice of chocolate cake. One was brief and annoying, and the other delicious, possibly a little reckless, but ever so delightful. Nicholas's shoulders were broad, his stomach flat, and his waist tapered down into long well-muscled legs. Now she could see the biceps her hands had rubbed against. There was just the lightest covering of blond hair scattered over his chest, which had rubbed against her skin whilst they were kissing. Having him close to her had been intoxicating; the distance now was likewise making her head spin.

"Are you certain you wish to continue?"

In answer, with as much daring as she could, with the sort of bravery she hadn't even displayed in her fantasies, Isabel flickered the sheet off. The night air was cool, but the look that Nicholas gave her inflamed her body once more. He was out of his trousers and next to her once again, his hands caressing the length of her body with a fervent worship that made Isabel laugh once more.

"What is so amusing? You must tell me," he whispered as he nuzzled her neck.

"They are happy laughs, I promise you."

Nicholas, who was lying draped over her, raised his head and looked down at her. "What on earth do you mean by that?"

"Being here, like this," she admitted with an ease that surprised her. "It is what I used to dream about."

At her admittance, Nicholas looked bashful. "Is that so?" His hands moved over her rib cage, and she giggled once more. He had found a ticklish point.

"Yes, yes, I know it's very silly of me, but it's true. Before I was even married."

"And what did you imagine?"

"Oh, it never went as far as this." She gasped when his hand moved between her legs, dipping into the folds of her sex, tracing her flesh, and bringing out a small moan from her lips.

"Then what?" His voice was silken. "Tell me what you imagined?"

"I was a coward," she whispered as she watched him dip his head and capture the tip of her breast in his mouth. His tongue wetted her nipple, and Isabel cried out. The tension within her body was building. She could feel it itch against her limbs, and she wanted more. She rolled herself on top of him. It was thrilling to feel that much of him, the shape of his chest and shoulders, the beat of his heart beneath her. That sort of power could go to her head. She kissed him; this time her tongue dipped into his mouth, bringing forth a moan from Nicholas. "I would never have done this," she said when she pulled back.

"Sit astride me?"

"Is that what this is called?"

Nicholas's hands moved to her waist, shifting her backwards until she was positioned over his sex. "If you sink onto me, then it would be."

"I have never done so before," she said, uncertain of what to do but tempted to find out, nonetheless.

"I can help you."

Her eyes lifted and met his. He was looking at her so kindly, so warmly, that it obliterated her fears. In his eyes, she felt alive and dangerous, as if the risks were worth taking.

Nodding, Isabel shifted her weight lower, pressing her sex down and around his cock. Nicholas let out a groan.

"Let me help you," he said as he readjusted her hips, lifting her and then slipping the tip of himself inside her. Isabel's eyes opened wider. She was sat upright on top of him, his hands resting on her bottom, cupping her, and urging her to sink more fully down on him. It felt richer, fuller than his fingers, stretching her in a way that helped build the tension that ruffled and ran through her body. Enjoying the feel of him, the intrusion, she pushed, lifted, and shifted her hips, pulling him more deeply inside her. When she dipped her hips, the movement drew a cry from her mouth. One of surprise. One of discovery of something new and wonderful. Their eyes met.

"I never..." she started to say.

Nicholas sat up, levering himself upwards, and kissed her. As their lips met, he started to move his own hips, lifting and grinding in a slow, steady momentum against hers, causing Isabel to stretch herself and contort her back and stomach against the sensation that now arced its way through her.

With his free hand, Nicholas stroked his fingers against her left leg. His other hand was on the small of her back, keeping them in that tight, locked dance. Their bodies melded together, each shift of her frame causing him to catch his breath. Each movement of his hand caused her to gasp.

It was intoxicating, as absorbing as when one drank wine or danced... Now she understood why he had used that analogy, although the idea of 'dancing' with anyone else turned her stomach. She could not believe herself capable of moving, of sensing, like this with anyone else. The desirous feeling, which had caused Isabel's hips to buckle against his, drove them wilder and higher. It was so different from anything else she had experienced before, the contrast so marked that she could not help smiling down at Nicholas as they moved together.

"That feels..." she gasped. But no words seemed good enough to capture the budding climb of her desire.

He nodded in agreement, and she hoped he felt the same way. His pale hair had been knocked forward in their movements, and positioned as he was below her, Isabel felt her heart flutter. Never had she seen such beauty. Some men, she'd heard, objected to being called beautiful, but that was the only word for him. Nicholas's expression was fixed on her, so concentrated and earnest as she writhed and gyrated against him. Soon, their movements became less refined, and with each grind of Isabel's hips, she tried to keep in a steady, constant level of vibration.

"God," she muttered. She couldn't explain the feeling that ran through her. It was more profound, deeper, richer than what his fingers had enticed from her body so recently. It beat through her core, her chest, her mind. With each movement she made, this sensation seemed to grow as if she were dragging along with an ancient rhythm that only she understood.

"My..." she said, words losing meaning as she tipped over the edge, the tension releasing out of her limbs. She was pleased for the release, for she had been about to say, my love... and she had no idea how that admission that would strike him.

Beneath her, Nicholas shifted her hips up and off him, pulling her away from him, and Isabel found herself sprawled on the bed with his back to her. He made a few strange movements before he gasped, his back twitching. Then he turned back to her and brought her in close to his side. Slowly, he wrapped his arms around her and kissed the back of Isabel's head.

Minutes ticked by before Isabel spoke. "What happened at the end? Did you...?"

"Stop myself?"

"Yes?" She had no idea what he had done, the fundamentals of a male release not really known to her. "Was something wrong?"

"Not at all." Nicholas rolled her over, kissing her cheek and then her lips, gazing down at her face. "You're so exquisite," he whispered as he watched her.

"Please explain it," she said. Her experience of the end of love-making tended to be abrupt. It involved none of this tender holding or kissing. Yet still, she was perplexed by why he had withdrawn from her.

"I wouldn't have made love to you normally without... without... a barrier," he said.

Isabel racked her brain. "For safety?"

"That's right. It prevents disease and pregnancy."

"But you were not wearing one tonight?"

"That is why I withdrew. It is not foolproof, but better than finishing within you."

Isabel's cheeks flushed. "You do not have a barrier—"

"They are known as a French letter."

"I see." She did see. He had withdrawn from her. He had pulled out. Because he wished to protect her... That is what she wanted to believe, but another part of her felt differently. Felt as if he had withdrawn from her because this connection of theirs was brief and fleeting, and he did not wish to leave her with a child. Yet another man who could not picture her as a mother. She did not know why and could not formulate the words to express how much that stung.

"You look sad, as if I had done something wrong?" His hand moved over her head, stroking her hair, and in the moonlight, Isabel could see all of Nicholas's handsome features. She wished the comfort she felt in his arms extended beyond the physical. She had fallen into the role of his mistress. It seemed her lot would be to only have the memory of this night and little else to cling to.

"There is nothing wrong," she lied. Another idea had struck her; she wondered if that was why Pierre had only made love one night a month. Her naivety may have helped her husband stop her from conceiving. "How effective is it at protecting one from pregnancy?"

"If anything comes of this, you must tell me." Nicholas relaxed next to her. "I will do everything to protect you."

"With your other lovers—" she started to say.

"So much curiosity," he joked.

"I don't need many details. Just..."

"I was always careful with them."

So, he was like Pierre then. No desire for children. Although one day, an heir to the earldom would need to be provided. That was not going to affect Isabel. He would have his heir from a woman who demanded a lace veil and a fine church wedding along with it. Not a tumble in a cottage with his friend downstairs and smugglers encircling them.

Nicholas's hand found her back, his warm palm moving up and down, soothing her. "It'll be dawn soon. You're safe here. You don't need to worry about anything else."

Isabel lay her head against his chest. There was a distinct comfort, small but present, in holding him thus. At least, that is what she told herself. She disliked how a hundred things needed resolving, and yet Nicholas seemed to be ready to sleep. She leant up and caught his eye. "But—"

"Have I failed you?" He laughed as he rolled Isabel onto her back, his weight pressing her to the bed. Unable to help herself, Isabel smiled. It seemed no matter how she worried, how much her mind ticked over and fretted, there was still a comfort to be found in being held, in such a way by Nicholas. He was all-consuming for her, overwhelming in his manner, his laugh, his sheer good-natured manliness. "I need to do a better job at distracting you." His hand drifted once more down Isabel's naked body, and as his fingers nuzzled and stroked her, she lay further back amongst the pillows, allowing her worries to slip away from her. At least for the time being.

CHAPTER 14

Morning came sooner than Nicholas would have wished, but he knew he could laze the entire day away in this bed. With Isabel. More, perhaps. Hours just watching and listening to her sleep. When she slept, she made these adorable little half-snoring noises; he could imagine teasing her about when dawn broke. Or just waking her to make love again. Each act seemed to strike her as something new and exciting, as if she had never been married. From the brief mentions of her husband, Nicholas did not feel concerned; Pierre had been deeply inadequate, it seemed.

As much as Nicholas would have preferred to spend the entire day ensconced with Isabel, that wasn't a real option. Perhaps it was a relief because the amount of power she exercised over him unnerved him no end. And the other reason? He had an obligation, not just to his title or the numerous estates and tenants he was bound to. But to her, it was something else—not an obligation at all but something far stronger. In the past, Nicholas would have done his best to avoid someone as scandalous as Isabel. She was too damaging to his reputation. At least that was what his younger self would have told him.

He dressed in the clothes that he had worn the night before, but he could not quite bring himself to leave the bedroom. It was a little winsome, but he kept thinking of Winston Cottage with a special sort of reverence.

The bedroom was peaceful in contrast to the hours that they had spent loving each other, each minute seeping into the next until both of them had fallen asleep. Beneath all her fine clothes, Isabel's scented jasmine skin was all the more delicious. The fine exotic fragrance seemed to have been etched into her pores. Nicholas did not think he would ever be able to clear his mind of her leg thrown out and over the coverlet and her tiny feet sticking out. Her toes were so quaint he almost laughed.

Isabel was not gifted with great elegance or practised perfection but more with a semblance of ease that rendered her precise, neat, sophisticated beauty into a place where he thought she looked almost normal. She was less the goddess, as she had been last night when she'd ridden him; now she seemed like an everyday woman. Except she wasn't every day. She was uniquely special to him. That meant he had an obligation to her, one that he was more than prepared to fulfil.

On leaving her bedroom, Nicholas made his way down the stairs. He would not disturb her rest. He felt smug about his efforts to tire her out. But now, he had to make sure her reputation remained pristine. Once this was all over, once the Wareton Gang were rounded up, and Hall was on trial... God, there was so much to do. And his initial selfishness in keeping her close was not fair. He should have been the better man and sent her away. Her family and Silverton, not to mention the secrecy around the location they had all headed to, would have been more than sufficient to keep her safe.

"Good morning," Trawler called out. He was an early riser

and was already in the kitchen stirring up the fire and cooking toast. His honest, smiling face greeted Nicholas, who did not feel he could quite match the good humour on display. Being in love rendered one—

No, no, that was too far.

"Mmmh," Nicholas muttered.

"Didn't you want to wake her? Or her maid? I can't find the girl."

Nicholas gave him a furious look. "Do you mean to imply something about Mrs. Hall?"

"No, of course not." Trawler gazed back at him, his expression serene, with just a glimmer of a tease hidden beneath his calm veneer. "I assumed you had gone upstairs to wake her since the maid vanished."

Nicholas was not sure how much he wanted to pursue the subject. "When must we go to the drop site? Today?"

"It would be a good idea to scope it out as soon as we can. From everything I've read and seen, it would fit with the Waretons pattern to use such a site. Anonymous and out of the way." Trawler handed him some toast.

If, as Trawler had theorised, they could disrupt the drop site, confront several of the gang, capture them and their banned goods, this would be a start. Besides this, at least one of the ringleaders, ideally Hall or Harlington but perhaps Ramsey, could be rounded up. That was the answer.

"Might be worth taking a good number of groomsmen or manservants with us. Really, as many as your father can spare to survey the site. Set up a guard through that area. The drop site needs to be our priority."

"Agreed." As he wolfed down the toast, Nicholas grabbed some of the papers off the table and scribbled a note to Isabel on a loose piece of paper. The pencil felt odd in his hands. This was not what he'd hoped for after their first night together. There should have been flowers involved. Trawler shouldn't have been in the kitchen. There shouldn't be the oddness with her maid.

Nicholas glanced up to find his friend watching him, so he scribbled down the rest of his message. It told her that she was to be sent up to London and not to fear anything. Something to that effect. Nicholas had no desire to pour his heart out over a page. Besides, he was not certain how he felt or if could be summed up a small sheet of paper. Yes, of course, he cared for her, more than he had any girl before. But he had to be unselfish; he had to solve the smuggling crisis.

There was a knock at the door, and the maidservant entered. In her hand, she held a letter. "I've come from the main house, my lord, with a letter for you. And some breakfast."

"Your mistress is still upstairs; please go wake her up." Nicholas was still feeling guilty for bringing Isabel into this, let alone a country girl. He left his note on the table for Isabel.

The girl passed the letter over the wooden table, bobbed a curtsey, and slipped from the room.

Glancing at the scrawl, Nicholas recognised his sister's messy handwriting on the envelope. Trawler was still watching him as he opened his sister's note.

Dear brother,

We are safely ensconced in London. But not where I promised to go. In a location you would frown upon, I am sure, with all your mighty and brotherly scorn. As is your way. But please be reassured, if you can, that no one will think to look for us here. Do let dear Mrs. Hall know that I care for her family as well as I would my own. Tell Father I am with Verne's sister, or some such people that he would approve of.

Your loving sister,

V

THERE WAS AN UNPLEASANT CLENCHING IN HIS STOMACH AS Nicholas folded the note over, feeling the quality of the paper between his fingers. A strange, lurking idea stirred in him at the emphasis his sister had made on *my own.* Of all the places his sister might have taken the Blackmans, surely, she cared more for her reputation than...

There was a knock at the kitchen door, and Isabel entered. A small wave of contentment washed through Nicholas at the sight of her, even dressed as she was, in plain housekeeper gab. She smiled shyly at him and then looked to Mr. Trawler, her expression immediately formal.

"I hear that Lady Lynde has written," she said.

"Can you decode her note?" Nicholas passed it over. He watched her delicate face frown and then slowly clear before she handed it back. She settled herself at the table and helped herself to tea.

Meanwhile, Trawler was eyeing it. "Do I get a chance to read it too?"

Passing him the note, Nicholas shifted his weight back and forth as he viewed Isabel. He felt incredibly conscious of his body, his surroundings—the dripping of the tap, the frosted cold windows, the sound of the fire—all seemed to be closing in on him. Above all, though, there was a need to know what further scandal, if it were a scandal, his sister might have thrown herself into.

Confirming his suspicions, Isabel looked between the two men and then said, "I imagine she has taken them all to your mother. Lady Kingfisher, in St James Square."

Colour flooded Nicholas's face. This was what he had feared—further scandal, conducted when his back was turned. He trusted Trawler, and he loved—no, he... He dropped his eyes and turned his back on the pair of them. Years of humiliation ran through him, recalling how his parents' divorce had affected him, how Viola thought their mother's actions inspiring and worthy of a heroine, whereas... He wheeled around to look at Isabel, and behind her, cutting bread without a care in the world, Trawler.

"Have you no concern for your family being housed with a known gamester and... such a scandalous woman?" Even to his own ears, he sounded petulant.

Isabel lifted her eyes from her cup. "I would imagine, given my father is little better than a traitor, staying with individuals who might be classed as scandalous would not matter so much." She turned her face to Trawler. "Please cut me a slice, sir."

"Nothing like the immediate threat of death to make one think the *ton* all rather petty?" Trawler grinned at her.

Another bolt of shame and confused rage gurgled through Nicholas. Why didn't they understand? Maybe neither of them could. One of them was a woman, and the other was a bastard.

He swallowed the unpleasant, critical thought down. It was beneath him. It did mean that neither of them would ever understand the pressure, the expectation that weighed on him. Or the responsibility of knowing one day he would be an earl.

"We should go." His voice came out as more of an order. He wanted the smuggling business resolved. This whole affair had upset every plan he'd ever made, turned his well-ordered life upside down, and left him clinging, holding onto a woman he hardly knew. And yet, he felt certain he understood her better than his own mind.

"My lord." Isabel was on her feet. "There is some urgency to the request I made about the madhouse—I do believe that Hodgkin is involved in the smuggling ring. Why else would his initials keep coming up? The Halls were close to him. He could be the C.H. in the accounts."

Trawler had exited the kitchen, presumably to fetch his winter coat. And the pistols. The sharp sound of a January storm growing in strength came from outside.

Carefully, Nicholas took her hands in his, pulling her towards him, only inches separating them. "I wish you had told me about Kingfisher and what you knew about my mother. The situation shames me."

Isabel held onto his fingers; her face was kind, although she shook her head. "Not everyone can live up to your standards. Some of us must play the hand we are dealt."

Casting his mind back to the previous night, Nicholas wondered how truly honourable he was. Surely a woman like her should expect something from him, an offer of some kind. It was on the tip of his tongue to say so, but she spoke first.

"My maid's cousin is locked in that hospital; she is with child and due any day. I did nothing for her before, and I cannot leave her in such a place. My husband's notes indicated that the doctor is involved."

Brushing his lips over her knuckles, Nicholas let out a sigh. "I will resolve this. I will help her. The danger first and foremost is with the smugglers and finding their shipment. They must take priority. It may well have some connection to Harlington. And I'm afraid that is more pressing than some unfortunate maid." Taking a step back, Isabel dropped her eyes from his face, her shoulders slumped, and for the first time, she looked the part of a downcast housekeeper. Guilt throbbed through him. "I am not like your husband or James Hall. I will not allow any scandal to continue being wrought against these women."

She gave him a quick nod, but the kindness from earlier

was gone. Nicholas turned on his heel, leaving her behind with a hundred things unsaid.

"Let's go," he muttered as he entered the hallway and saw Trawler waiting for him. The two of them left Winston Cottage for Hurstbourne Manor and its stables.

The crisp January day chilled them both as they crossed the dewed lawns of the manor. Distantly there was the sound of the wind catching and throwing itself against the bare branches; soon, the storm itself would draw in from the hills and be upon them. There was such a contrast between the heat and passion he had experienced last night in Isabel's arms and the wet grass beneath his feet.

Trawler was talking, Nicholas realised. He forced himself to concentrate on his friend's words. "I like Mrs. Hall. I think you've chosen well there."

"What do you mean?" Nicholas's tone was icy, but Trawler seemed not to notice, his strongly built frame striding ahead, unconcerned with all of the boundless emotions he was responsible for stirring in Nicholas.

"Merely that she seems like a bright woman. It is a shame she never got a season in London."

"I would say it was a blessing." Nicholas was pleased that someone else saw the unique value of a woman as rare as Isabel. Then again, the idea of Isabel being in London society further unnerved him. He could not say why. It did not fit with what he had imagined for her. But he had little doubt she would be a success. She was too poised, too polite...

Then it hit him: her unconscious humour, her bravery, her delightful sexuality, and all the special attractions that had so captured him would be unappreciated in London society. In such a milieu, she would only be praised for actions that rendered her like the other *ton* ladies. The things he loved about her would go unnoticed.

There was that word again, Nicholas realised with annoyance. He kept slipping it into his thoughts, and that was a problem.

"When this situation is resolved—"

"If it can be," Nicholas said. He wished it could, but the obstacles before them seemed insurmountable.

"I've faced worse odds than these," Trawler said. This allusion to whatever Silverton, Verne, and he had gotten up to rattled Nicholas. He should have asked what skills, what unusual actions these men had taken. But he had considered himself rather more like Heatherbroke and Woolwich, who might fund such a protective measure but would not engage with them directly. That had been something that Nicholas had managed to avoid until now. "Mrs. Hall should be able to have a season once her mourning is passed. A handsome widow like that—"

"Hm." Nicholas almost coughed his reply. He didn't care for this sort of commentary or Trawler's train of thought. He had been angered at the idea of any of the Set admiring Isabel. But Trawler seemed to think that if Isabel were to enter polite society, she would be snapped up by someone else. The idea of another man going near her...

Aggressively, Nicholas swung his foot out at a stack of stones as he passed by, scattering them everywhere. He hated the lack of power he was experiencing, as if all things were beyond his control.

"Are you alright?" Trawler asked, glancing sideways at Nicholas. Unable to think of an answer, Nicholas strode on, his hands coming to dig into his pockets. Trawler was a teasing fellow, and it would be best for Nicholas if he ignored him. "She cares for you." Trawler added, then smirked, "Though that might make some people think her less than bright."

Nicholas swatted at him. The pathway they were on rounded a bend, and the trees thickened. Their dark and empty branches gave an almost gothic feel. But once through the brief woodland, they would be at the edge of the Manor, where the stables were.

They asked the stable master to saddle up the horses, and whilst they were waiting, Nicholas gathered four more men from the estate, fellows who could ride and shoot. They had armed and left the estate within the hour, by which time, the promised storm was beating its way down upon them.

"Should be a rather good cover," Trawler called out.

Nicholas nodded. It was a relief to be so focused on ordering the men. On plotting the route. On attempting to ignore every thought of his mother. His dratted sister. Or worst of all, leaving Isabel. That idea spurred back immediately to annoyance.

"I wished she'd told me that she knew about my mother," he snapped. His eyes were focused on the road, the way it wound to the left, and how the tree cover offered little protection.

There was a long pause in which Trawler made no reply, to the extent that Nicholas began to wonder if his friend had even heard him.

"There are a great many things I will never understand about women," he finally said, a slight grin playing around his mouth. "But I have no reason to doubt your sister's integrity, nor Mrs. Hall's desire for justice."

"I did not speak of them. My mother—" Nicholas could recall his childish cries for her and the way his father had explained she would never return. He closed his eyes against the day and against the memories. And how easily Viola had simply gone and found her. He did not know if he could have done the same.

"My mother is unconventional too." The rumours had always circulated around Trawler because of his birth. He was a foreigner, people said, his money was shipped in from faraway lands, his uncle was a notorious East End bruiser, his father one of Prinny's dearest wastrel friends... These tales ran around Harrow and Oxford, almost putting the divorced countess, Nicholas's mother, to shame. It had been a point of pride that Nicholas had never pressed his friend for the truth, but for the first time, Nicholas wished he'd asked Trawler.

The road narrowed and the moment for him to question Trawler passed as his friend overtook him and kicked on his mount to the edge of a bracketed field. Nicholas slowed the bedraggled men to a stop, allowing Trawler to cast a good look over the location. They had studied the map enough times to be sure this was where the numbers had indicated. Minutes trickled by, as Nicholas felt his body chill and then pinpricked against the cold. Finally, Trawler looked back over his shoulder, his eyes taking in the level of the grass, the surroundings.

"There's a building. I think there's someone—or rather some people—inside."

"The guns won't work." Nicholas kept his voice low. In this weather, any powder would be worse than useless.

"Wait for dusk then, hope it clears," Trawler answered. "We'll need to take up positions to surround it and agree on a signal."

It was the cold that made him feel anxious, Nicholas told himself as he moved between the men, telling them the plan, nothing more.

The wisdom of Isabel's earlier words came to him as he climbed off his horse, trying to stir up his normal good cheer. Her words lingered in his mind. What was society next to this overriding fear of smugglers who threatened his world's security? What were society's expectations compared to life and death? It seemed petty and small as each of them took up their position around the field, waiting with bated breath for the storm to pass and a new battle to begin.

CHAPTER 15

Isabel watched him leave, a mixture of frustration, annoyance, and fear pooling in her. How could they share so many hours together and not see eye to eye? He had been as tender and passionate as she could have wished, wiping away in a blink any memory she had of Pierre's touch, and yet in the cold light of day, he had changed. He was back to being a haughty lord, with the weight of expectation on him. One who couldn't see the plight of a maid as important and clearly thought Isabel far too scandalous for the likes of him.

He had told her to wait. She had engaged in such behaviour whilst being Mrs. Hall. But now, she was a widow. An infamous one at that, one who had affairs with eligible men, it seemed. She had risked her reputation for a night with him. It had been worth it, the throb in her bones and skin and muscles could attest to that, but was it worth it if he still didn't listen to her?

Nicholas would send her away; out of sight, out of mind, that was what she feared. She could envisage him being partnered with some attractive, little simpleton... No, she would not torture herself further.

Placing her hands on the wooden table, Isabel gazed up at the ceiling. Thinking such things was not helping her case at all. Fragments of weak sunlight began to appear through the frost on the window; soon, yet another cold winter day would arrive. It was clear there would be a storm.

Yes, that makes sense. Go outside on a day like this. Annoyance flashed through her.

The pair of them were going to go find the Wareton Gang. She wished them joy of it, she wished the case resolved, the men caught, and her father's name cleared. But in amongst this, what would happen to Jessica and her baby? Her thoughts kept creeping back to the hospital.

"There's only me." It slipped out of her mouth, and for a long moment, Isabel rather regretted her sentiment. She wasn't what those women needed. What possible good would she do them?

Getting to her feet, Isabel started to make her way through the cottage to the rear of the building and knocked quietly on the smallest room. It was cold when she swung the door open and looked inside. Kneeling by the empty grate was Lucy, her face stained with tears and her eyes red-rimmed.

"I'm sorry, ma'am. I just keep thinking, what if it's too late? You read all the time about girls, women, not surviving labour, and Jessica isn't very big-boned."

If that hadn't stiffened Isabel's resolve, nothing would have. But how? How would she defy what Nicholas had told her, and more importantly, how would she get away with it?

"I just don't know how either of us could get her out." Lucy had placed her bag of carefully saved coins in front of her and was gazing at it keenly, clearly wishing to switch places with her cousin.

Isabel's initial meeting with Nicholas flashed through her mind. Why not? She'd dressed as a man before for less worthy aims. What would be the harm in doing so again, and for a better cause?

"One day is too many to be spent there. We're going to save Jessica; you have my word." She reached forward into the cold room and pulled Lucy to her feet. "But first, I need your help."

❧

As she walked through the cottage, Isabel began to gather the items she would need. A straightforward collection of discarded clothes at first, and then her mind would turn to weapons. She would need something to defend herself with. No, she would need something to look after Jessica, too.

She looked down at her body. Her legs were encased in Walsh's breeches, the shortest of the men who'd been in the cottage. The material reached her ankles. On top, she'd layered the other men's shirts, tucking two in where she could and folding one on top of one another until there was at least a couple of layers between her chest and the rest of the world.

"If nothing else, it'll keep me warm," she quipped to Lucy.

Lucy needed to play her part and was donning some more feminine clothes that would give the appearance of a recently married lady. The plan was to pose as a couple, bent on 'doing a good turn' for the poor unfortunate Jessica.

"Hope so, ma'am," the maid replied as she tried to jam a borrowed hat of Lady Viola's onto her head.

When Isabel glanced up and into the mirror over the fireplace in the sitting room, she did at least look right. As if she were a handsome groomsman, or perhaps in a similar position to that of her brother Thomas, a trainee lawyer.

The last item she put on was Nicholas's. It was a faded, green-lined waistcoat that hung off her. Now that she had seen the chest and muscles that existed below, it made wearing such an item somehow like wearing a piece of him, as a form of protection that only he could offer her. Nicholas was almost hugging her through the material. It was a comfort to feel the waistcoat over the shirts, buttoning it up and enclosing her in a snug hold.

Once dressed, Isabel left Lucy to finish her face whilst she went to find whatever weapons had been left behind. Walsh had hidden three pistols in the cottage, and Isabel gathered them up, but he had only shown her how to load one of them. She did as he had demonstrated and loaded the easier pistol. Then she placed it in the large coat that Silverton had left behind. She would only get one shot; the time it took her to reload would be too long.

Gazing around the kitchen, Isabel's eyes hit on the cutlery drawer in the corner of the room. Once opened, it revealed a series of sharp knives. These were what she would have to use, far more than the pistol, especially in such inclement weather.

Then she slipped into Silverton's smelly black coat. It fell to her knees. Turning, Isabel made her way to the door and yanked it wide open. The cold of the afternoon greeted her, the air freezing her enthusiasm in its tracks.

"Lucy." She turned back and found her maid, grim-faced but nodding. Her sharp eyes no longer seemed so red-rimmed. The girl pulled a shawl close to herself and followed Isabel out of the warmth and away from the sanctuary of the cottage.

Cutting their way through the fields, Isabel and Lucy made their way down through the high grasses until they reached a small outcrop of land where boats on the river were housed. It seemed that they hadn't been used so far this year.

If they could get one of these going, they could make better time getting to the hospital over water than land. It would be quicker than walking, that was for sure. Besides, she wasn't too familiar with the route from here. From the town, she would find it easier to get to Hastings. The fare on the coach was only a couple of pennies. She didn't need to travel in any grand style. The pair of them focused on getting the little boat into the water and the oars into the current as they set off.

"How's your rowing?" Isabel asked as they pulled and yanked the frozen ropes free.

"I'll do it first," Lucy replied. That look of stubbornness overrode the cold as she scrambled in position. The task of rowing was a good distraction. It would keep the girl focused on the task at hand.

The boat moved off through the cold water, cutting an uneven line towards the coast. After thirty minutes, partly from sympathy at the way Lucy's hands were smarting and partly from the chill, Isabel took over. She vainly hoped it might stop her from thinking too much about Nicholas.

Her hands moved the oars roughly through the water with his image before her. It would happen. Either he would marry or take up with another woman, which seemed undeniable. She would not let herself dwell on it. The water flowed around their boat as she stuck the first oar into the water, arching her back with the movement. It was easier said than done. Her mind couldn't focus on the task in hand; it kept reeling back towards the inevitable presence of Nicholas Lynde.

Hadn't that always been the case with Isabel, though? Hadn't she had silly notions about him since she first heard of him all those years ago? *Wouldn't it be perfect*, she used to say, *he's two years older than me, isn't that ideal?* Not realising at the age of ten that gentlemen in society tended to marry women far younger than them.

When the press had copied down items about his mistresses, one attractive opera singer had been mentioned three years ago, and Isabel had gone off crying, heartbroken. None of her wildest or most fanciful daydreams would have permitted her to envision an illicit pairing between them that would happen in the real world. But it had happened. Now, if she survived this, perhaps rather than being a housekeeper, she could expect to be treated as any number of his mistresses had been. Of course, she had no idea what a mistress could expect.

Perhaps, she thought as she rowed, she might even prefer it? At least to being a housekeeper, although inevitably it would mean her family would cut her off...

Throughout the night, every time they had made love, whichever position he had turned or lifted or moved her body to, she had gone along with excitedly, with true passion for the play of his hands and the laugh in his voice. Willing him to see in her what had always been blatant. That she loved him.

But he had left her. He had withdrawn from her in much the same manner as Pierre had. Neither man was willing to consider her as a mother for their children. In Pierre's case, because it was not something he deemed necessary or financially prudent, she reasoned now. In Nicholas's... she supposed she could understand that a little better. A bastard child. No, he wouldn't want that. But it would be theirs. She was too far gone to much care for the consequences; after all, she had slept with him, hadn't she? Any consequence of their night together, any reminder, would be a sweet solace after Nicholas left her.

Tears formed in her eyes, and Isabel sniffed. *Stop being a coward*. The winter's day was fresh, the start of the year, a cold new start to her life. If it meant being a mistress, could she be selfish enough to demand a child from him? Would it be too cruel to the child she would bear?

Lucy shifted in her seat, and Isabel forced herself to give the girl an encouraging smile.

Hours later, when the river opened to the sea, it did so in spotting distance of the town that adjoined Eastbourne. She moored the boat at the edge of the town, and the two of them started walking through the suburbs. The pair of them made good progress.

The ease with which she moved around the town somewhat amazed Isabel. With her features covered and her hair hidden, very few people paid her any mind. Lucy was less lucky. Nevertheless, they made their way towards the coaching inn. Dressed as a man, Isabel could move through the place with a knack, and no one stopped with any of their usual glances or lifted hats. The day was dragging on when they finally reached the inn. She made her way inside and bought the pair of them seats to Hastings. Only fifteen minutes to wait and a forty-minute journey to the town. They would be there by mid to late afternoon, judging by the sky's light.

Hodgkin's hospital was located near the edge of the town, so Isabel had reasoned that the two would be better situated outside the carriage. Then they could disembark and make their way to the hospital on foot the rest of the way.

As their coach pulled in, Isabel saw her mother-in-law moving through the town square. Her distinct, fur-trimmed yellow pelisse was eye-catching and garish. Hardly the normal garb for someone in mourning. *So much for her lecturing me.* A small slither of pity went through her for Pierre, with his unconcerned mother. At least if Isabel were to appear in town, she would wear her black crepe dress. She looked down at her masculine clothes, borrowed and pieced together from what she had found in the cottage. Her morality seemed a little forgone, and she comforted herself with the idea that Pierre had betrayed her so much that her showing any loyalty to him was absurd.

Isabel bent her head closer to Mrs. Hall, desperate to catch something of her chatter, but the woman was in deep conversation with one of the drivers before she moved back to continue talking to one of her servants.

Her palish eyebrows were drawn close over her eyes, and whilst Isabel watched her, Mrs. Hall fidgeted and shivered, angry at finding herself in such a position. But she climbed up into the coach that was supposed to be conveying Isabel and Lucy to the madhouse.

Lucy's eyes had fairly bugged out of her head when she'd seen the older Mrs. Hall. "This won't work," Lucy whispered. "She's bound to recognise me." She passed the cloth bag, filled with money, over to Isabel. "Will you still go, missus?"

Isabel had been so focused on making herself move like a man, Lucy's hurried idea jolted her. The girl was probably right; it would be a dead give-away.

Isabel was loath to part from Lucy, but with reluctance, she slipped the money into the overcoat pocket and whispered, "Go tell Lynde where I'm headed. He needs know where the Halls are." She kissed Lucy's cheek and watched the maid hurriedly run from the coaching inn. It was just as well she'd told the maid about where the drop site could be found.

A cry echoed throughout the inn, signalling the departure of the Hastings' carriage, and with haste, Isabel made her way towards it. By the time she got to the coach, the outside seats had already been taken, and she was forced to climb inside.

"God, no," Isabel said to herself. It was a small, cramped space. How on earth would Mrs. Hall not recognise her in such close quarters? It beggared belief that they could journey all the way to Hastings and the blasted woman wouldn't know her. Isabel dragged her hat down low, a boyish cap, and closed her eyes tight. She was determined to get to Hastings, to the hospital. That was her task. Besides, if she tried to get out of the carriage now, all eyes would be on her. That would be more dangerous.

The elder Mrs. Hall was sat opposite her. Isabel was familiar enough with the sound of the woman's breathing, not to mention the acidic lemon and coy bluebell scent that she loved. Off the carriage went, the voices of their neighbours low and steady. Isabel adjusted herself, folding her arms against her chest and peeking out from beneath her cap. There were a total of five people in the carriage. Aside from the two Mrs. Halls, there were two youngish men, brothers, Isabel assumed based on their conversation, who were squished in beside her. There was also the man who was speaking to Mrs. Hall.

On the carriage went, battered here and there by the rain, until it drew to a stop. There were a set of quick-fire question and answers, and then both brotherly men disembarked, and the coach took off again. Isabel cursed herself for not climbing out, shifted more into her coat, and started to mimic a gentle snoring.

Mrs. Hall's voice was low, but the tone was clear. Her mother-in-law sounded nervous. The coach hit a bump, causing the sentence Mrs. Hall was uttering to come out louder. "Do be quiet, Jamie."

Midway through her fake snore, Isabel froze. How could she have been such a fool? She was accidentally journeying towards the hospital with one of the leaders of the Wareton Gang. All she had wanted to do was arrive at the hospital and free Jessica. And now, she seemed to be walking into a trap. Here she was, ensnared with her enemies... The pistol was in her reach buried in her coat pocket; dare she try to grab it, to fire it in such close quarters? If she missed him or just hit his mother... It was too much of a risk.

"He's been snoring for the length of the ride."

"I still maintain your guise isn't fooling anyone."

"It only has to be until this time tomorrow."

They lapsed into silence. Isabel's entire face itched, and she wished more than anything to be able to move, perhaps even to throw herself out of the coach. But that would just alert them, and she doubted James travelled without a weapon. The thought of facing off against him on the side of the road did not please her much.

"There's enough coinage on you to sink a ship," came the masculine voice and a strange sound as if James was patting something.

"Hush, will you."

"Sir, sir," James called out, directing his call towards her.

Isabel shifted as if in her sleep, the pistol growing a little warmer in her hand.

"Dead to the world," James snapped.

"Will you at least ensure there are passports?" Mrs. Hall said. Isabel had no idea what her mother-in-law was referring to.

A noise from outside the carriage made Isabel's head jerk forward. The falling rain had developed into sleet, and thunder sounded from the heavens above. The blizzard had finally arrived. She forced herself to settle back down whilst the Halls fussed over it. She thought she could hear Mrs. Hall talking about boats and the like. But it was the cry from the drivers that flagged where they were.

"Cooden Bay," they shouted out, and the coach started to slow down.

Dare she get out? Isabel had brought her scarf up to cover most of her face, allowing herself to straighten her body out. It was better to go wherever James Hall was not. The important thing for her own safety was to avoid him. With her coat dragged close, neither Hall paid her much mind as she climbed out of the carriage first, sloping to one side and hiding beneath the shelter where several people were waiting.

When James Hall hopped down after her, Isabel swore under her breath. The rain was falling in thick sheets of grey. James glanced around before setting off to the side as if making his way towards the beach. Her suspicions had been confirmed; he was going to the hospital, it seemed. What if he had decided to check on Jessica too? Was his fatherly instinct finally kicking in?

With stumbling footsteps, Isabel broke away from the stand she had been hiding next to, crossing from the coaching inn's shelter, trying to follow in James's footsteps. If he turned, she would shoot him. If she hanged for it, it would be worth it.

He crossed from the open pathway down to the beach, but Isabel kept to the higher ground, her pace looping, given what she hoped was the impression of being drunk. If seen, she would be ignored. If stopped, then she would claim to be heading towards the tavern.

The ocean cleared her head, the salted air refreshing to her face if stinging against her pores. Isabel drew her pistol. Finding a safe tree up ahead, Isabel took aim. Only when James started scrambling over the rocks towards her on the higher path did she pause. What was he doing?

She realised where James was heading. It wasn't just to the hospital. He was meeting someone outside, in the windswept grass before the building. Out of earshot, that much was clear. But when he was only twenty feet away from her crouching form, a man appeared on horseback. His countenance was striking enough and oddly similar to another man, although she could not place whom. Even at this distance, she could make out his hair, a buttery yellow.

She knew him by sight alone. His good-looking appearance did nothing to soften Isabel towards Doctor Hodgkin. He reached up in the saddle, and it was then that Isabel saw what the pair of them were about. The two of them exchanged papers. From this distance, it looked as if Doctor Hodgkin was in charge.

Hidden where she was, pressed flat against the tree, Isabel watched the two of them converse before they turned and headed towards the hospital. The exact location she had intended to rescue Jessica from.

Paused as she was, Isabel weighed her options, and then cutting through her thoughts came a low, soft cry of a woman in distress. It was coming from Hodgkin's hospital.

CHAPTER 16

With the onset of dusk, the weather had calmed and was now the soft, broken sort of rain that came on every thirty minutes or so. This was less than ideal, Trawler had assured Nicholas. It meant it was nigh impossible to see too far in front of them.

"But likely as not, those inside may not be armed," Trawler continued, huddled as they were sharing a tumbler of brandy from Nicholas's flask. "They may be lackeys and given nothing more than sticks."

"But you don't know that for sure?"

"Only one way to find out." Trawler's calm appearance did little to reassure Nicholas; it was an act, pure and simple. Nicholas was meant to convey the same to his family servants that he had brought with him. A stirring of guilt mounted in him as he wondered if any of them were likely to survive the encounter. The anxiety must have shown on Nicholas's face, for Trawler's bravado slipped, and his voice lowered. "If something were to happen, could I ask you a favour?"

Nicholas nodded. He wondered where he would begin on

his list of favours and requests if this hour were to be his last. He hadn't envisioned it ending without...

"Give my mother this." Trawler passed over a small golden chain with a ring attached. The ring had a simple moonstone at its base. "And..." Trawler raked his hand through his hair, his expression awkward, glancing at Nicholas hesitantly. "It was me, if you wondered."

"What was you?"

"The duel against Mortimer for your sister's honour." His sister's abandoned wedding seemed a century ago. "He was not polite about Lady Lynde," Trawler added. The statement dramatically underplayed the reality of whatever the duke had said about his sister, Nicholas was sure. He knew that he should care; society and his position demand that be the case, but compared to the ditch they knelt in, it did not seem remotely important.

"You wait until now to tell me about the duel? I'd never even heard a word about it."

"We thought it best—"

"We? The Set?"

"Some of us, those present in London, took it upon ourselves to..." Here, Trawler paused. "I do not think that Viola knows about the duel either."

The slight pause around the way he said her name instinctively made Nicholas look up. He locked eyes with Trawler, who blushed in the dying light of the day. Nicholas lowered his gaze and glanced back across the field.

"And you?" Trawler asked.

"If I don't survive?" A hundred worries would be laid suddenly at his father's door. On the estate. On the family name. But none of these were about Nicholas, the man beneath the title. He realised the thing that mattered more than any of the things he had always thought important was Isabel. If it came down to choosing between his societal obligations and her, it was no contest. It would be her every time. The thought made him smile despite the dire situation. "Look after Isabel—Mrs. Hall."

Their night together had meant more to him than he'd realised at the time. He had been caught up in the sheer enjoyment, in the utter delight at being with her. Inside her... All of it, the taste, the feel of her as she glided next to him. That handful of hours had stretched themselves out and put to shame whatever emotional connection he'd felt to any previous lover. With Isabel, it had been as if they were making love rather than just going through the motions of the sexual act.

He wanted more time with her. Infinite time with her. To discover her favourite flowers. To talk about poetry, books, and art with her. To find out if she got seasick. To make love until the pair of them were robbed of their breath, their thoughts, and she realised how much she had changed him. She's stolen away his fears of society and replaced them with the knowledge that it didn't matter. Other things mattered far more.

Images of her flashed through his mind. He liked to think her hair resembled moonbeams in a certain light, all luminous and glittering. The idea made him almost flush, despite the growing coldness of his current surroundings. They had rolled together over the bed, her skin peachy and firm, and every time he touched her, it seemed to elicit a new wonder in her.

His mind pulled him through those hours, each second relived. Part of Nicholas seemed convinced he would not get any more moments with her, and now that they were apart, it was consuming his mind, all the things he should have said. Or at least written. Too late now, if he never made it out alive.

Trawler was on his feet, ready to go. "I'll send one of the boys off to you. We'll move in closer after this spell stops."

Nicholas nodded, watching his friend slide away and be

replaced with a grim-faced boy of eighteen or so, Mattie Jordan. The lad crouched down next to him and silently started to recite a prayer.

What do I want my arrangement with Isabel to be? Nicholas huddled against the tree next to Mattie. Would it be better to have an ongoing relationship, keeping her in Winston Cottage until... until...? His thoughts would take him no further. He had little expectation that Isabel would sit around and wait. Nor did he want her to. Which meant...

Nicholas gave a violent shake of his head. He knew what was expected of him. One did not sleep with a woman of good virtue and birth without making her an offer. It just daunted him how much he wanted her to say yes. The predictable bride he'd half imagined proposing to in the summer, once he'd looked through the season's remaining Belles—the idea held little appeal. No, his mind would constantly be returning to Isabel. The sparkle in her sharp eyes. The purity of her vision and how strong she was beneath the gentle surface. The tilt of her head as she worked or argued her point of view. He would have found it tiresome with other women after a while, but not with her.

The rain ceased, and Nicholas prepared his pistol. Beneath his feet, the ground was spongey—a blend of water and mud, threatening to pull them all into the sludge. Hours had ticked by until a coat of darkness had shielded all of them, but each of them knew their positions. Knew not to break until the signal.

"I think Dexter's got something," Mattie said. The younger man had edged forward with Nicholas shadowing him. Nicholas was getting himself into a more comfortable angle, one of his hands cupped around his eyes as if trying to focus.

The base of operations appeared to be an abandoned shed. Its lonely grey roof offered little cover to the half dozen men positioned around it. Nicholas, Trawler, and the others had crept up, enveloping the Wareton Gang. He hadn't seen Harlington or Hall, but they might be inside the shed. What would they find within the little structure? Tea, brandy, cloth, or exotic wines; it would all be given over to Trawler either way and used to persecute the Waretons.

"What?"

"Look," Mattie said. His hand was raised and pointed to the field's opposite edge, where Trawler was stationed with Dexter.

Nicholas kept low to the ground, edging forwards, out of the trees. Behind him, Mattie moved up too. The boy wobbled where he stood, caught between a desire to prove himself and remain safe.

There was noise, a rippling bird cry that Trawler had informed them was the signal. It was followed by a rapid blast, and then a series of men, maybe five, broke out from the shed. They tentacled away, two of them making straight for the spot where Nicholas and Mattie had been stationed. Raising his pistol, Nicholas aimed and fired at the closest man, who dropped like a stone to the ground. He was glad that little Mattie had kept close and that the boy didn't have to shoot anyone. He didn't want Mattie to be responsible for something like that.

The other man tried to skate past him; Nicholas slammed the end of his pistol into the back of the runaway's head, sending the man crashing to the ground.

"Keep him there," Nicholas told Mattie, and he marched forwards towards Trawler, watching his friend wrestle another smuggler down. Crouching, he looked into the face of the restrained man. "Stop, why don't you stop? Look, we can help you. Where's Hall?"

The man stopped struggling, and Nicholas recognised him as Mr. Ramsey. Mr. Blackman's colleague, the one who had betrayed him to the Wareton Gang. Ramsey must have realised the trap he was in and how the gang had fallen into the encirclement. By the light of the stars, Nicholas could make out some of the man's face. Enough to notice the harsh lines, jarring as he opened his gaping lips and laughed.

"Yeah, right, I ain't a fool," Ramsey muttered.

Trawler rolled off him and went to check on everyone else, leaving Ramsey in Nicholas's care. A minute or two trickled by as Ramsey regained his breath, all the while watching Nicholas carefully, clearly hoping to make a break for it.

There was another blast close by. For all of Trawler's cheerfulness and peace-making appearance, he was ensuring that Nicholas's servants were safe even at the risk or danger of killing various gang members. One of them had used a cudgel against him, eliciting a loud anguished shout from Trawler, and now he walked away shielding his arm, having dealt with the culprit. His bravery made Nicholas straighten his own pistol at the man before him; he was pleased he had re-loaded it.

"Where is Hall?"

"Why should I tell you?" Ramsey's lip had been cut, and he swiped at it painfully.

"I would think that obvious."

"Nah, I don't think so. That blond whoreson knows how to punish you."

"More so than the noose?" Nicholas asked.

"Hall warned us about you. The fancy lordling." Ramsey eyed him with unmistakable loathing.

"That so?"

"Aye, you are a big wig, born with a silver spoon shoved up where the sun don't shine, but not too many brains."

Turning away, Nicholas surveyed the other captured or dead men. He had killed a man with his shot. The body was lying still in the grass, unmoving and scaring Nicholas more than he cared to admit. He looked back at Ramsey, but the older man had folded his arms against his chest and was staring at the ground with a look that said Nicholas wouldn't get much more out of him.

Trawler and Mattie had gone into the shed, checking there. If Hall were hiding inside, he would soon be captured. It should have been a relief, the knowledge that it might soon be over, but if anything, Nicholas felt the tension in his body double.

"Check for Mr. Hall. He's in his thirties. Reptile-like in appearance," Nicholas called out to Trawler.

Seconds ticked by. One of his servants from the manor had brought a lantern with them that could not be lit previously, but now they were over the worst, and the rain had stopped. The device created a warm glow amongst the captured men.

"No one here fits that description." Mattie returned from helping Trawler go through the building. "There's a teen boy; he was hiding inside. But everyone else. The others..."

Mattie had brought a youth with him who looked close to tears as he looked over his fallen colleagues.

"Tie him up," Nicholas said. "He can answer our questions. Since Mr. Ramsey won't oblige."

Trawler emerged from the small building, waving his uninjured arm. Even in the dancing shadows of the lantern, his friend's gestures were clear; he wanted Nicholas's help. Mixed worry about Hall and Harlington, combined with Trawler's reaction to the shed's contents, made Nicholas's mind whirl with frightening possibilities.

Nicholas reached Trawler, pulling his old friend close to him. There was real fear etched into Michael's face for the first time.

"What's the matter?" Nicholas asked.

Trawler pointed down at the floor of the shed, at the spilled pieces of paper scattered across it. Lowering himself, Nicholas shifted through the pages, which were illegible to him, They were not written in English, French, Italian, or German. He could only make out one or two words.

"These are written in Russian; that's what I'd place my money on," he said.

"It's not that," Trawler replied.

From his crouching position, Nicholas frowned up at his friend.

"What then?"

Looking sick, Trawler pointed at the insignia scrawled over some of the other pages. Nicholas stood up, taking the lantern off the table, before collecting up the pages indicated. Trawler had moved and was leaning against the wall of the shed. He looked quite wild-eyed.

"What is it?"

Trawler said, "But look, I recognise the paper. It's from the Home Office. I think someone inside is selling state secrets."

"Did you expect this?" Nicholas asked as he moved within earshot of his friend. The vagueness of Silverton's earlier actions made sense to him. They had been aware of the risk, it seemed. They had kept it from him. The real treasonous danger of Harlington. They had put Isabel in danger. Nicholas slammed his fist into the wood of the structure. "You should have told me of your fears."

"How would it have altered your actions?"

"I wouldn't—" A murderous fury that Nicholas had never experienced before was building inside him, directed not at the Wareton Gang but at Silverton and Trawler for keeping him out of the loop. Balling his fists, he again slammed one of them into the wood, too close to Trawler, who stepped away from Nicholas. "You didn't have the right to keep me ignorant. You should have told me."

"Isn't this about some girl?"

"I'm going to bloody marry that girl. You dared put my future wife at greater risk than you needed to." Nicholas was on a roll, the anger bubbling this way and that. If Silverton had been here, he would have happily fractured the man's other leg. Clearly, neither of them had ever been in love. *I love her.* It had scared him; in fact, he had admitted it because of anger. Now it kept running back through his mind with jarring persistence. *I love her.* With each repetition, it grew less daunting and more real.

Trawler appeared to consider laughing for a moment, but one look at Nicholas's face stopped him. "We suspected there was a traitor, but we didn't know for sure. Before. This means someone in England is selling secrets. Using Harlington to pass it on to the Russians. We have never had solid proof before. If we can determine who sent this information to Harlington, then we will have uncovered the spy in our midst."

"You could have told me."

"And then you would have told Mrs. Hall?" Trawler asked. "She's safe back at the cottage."

Giving Trawler a dirty look, Nicholas started to pace, all too conscious of the papers in his pocket, burning through his skin, taunting him with their dangerous presence. "What if the gang has other men? Who might have attacked the cottage?"

"Get back to the Manor for your romantic reunion." Trawler slapped Nicholas's arm in a joshing manner as they walked outside the building. "I can take the remaining gang members to—"

As Trawler spoke, Mr. Ramsey made a bolt for it, heading straight for Dexter, who had moved over to supervise the captives. Ramsey closed the distance, taking out the servant with a clobber to the face, sending the man flying. There was a scuffle as the other servants scrambled to help, but Ramsey bolted for the open road. Trawler snatched up his pistol.

"We need him," Nicholas said. As a witness. For proof of the treason the Wareton Gang had been committing.

"The papers will be enough." With as much precision as he could muster, Trawler shot through the darkness, catching Ramsey full in the back. The older man stumbled and then fell forward with a sickening crunch.

There was an unpleasant silence as everyone looked at the fallen man. Then the remaining young smuggler started to cry. Trawler lowered his gun.

Nicholas approached the lad, and in a gentle voice, said, "I will help you, boy."

The teen looked up, and Nicholas felt a pull of pity for him.

"Where is Mr. Hall?" Trawler pressed. "He's the ringleader, isn't he?" Despite his injured arm, Trawler lowered himself to the ground, wincing at the painful movement. "Do you know him, boy?"

"I don't know, sir; I only knows him as Jamie." The boy shifted where he was crouched. "And he's with the doctor. Hodge something. But he doesn't see people like me much. Please, this is the first time I've ever done a thing like this."

"A doctor—" Nicholas began when there was a cry from behind them, and Nicholas glanced across the field. It was uttered by a girl, a familiar-looking servant, whose clothes were different and who seemed to be wearing his sister's hat. Lucy. She rode a knackered old horse towards them as quickly as she could.

Her distressed face was etched with worry, but it lightened when she spotted Nicholas. "Ah, my lord. I was so scared I wouldn't find you."

"Where's Isabel?" he snapped, once she was off the horse and standing in front of him, Trawler, and the captured smuggler.

Lucy sucked in her breath and started to speak. "My mistress—she's gone," she sniffled. "It's my fault. She and I... We were to get my cousin from the hospital. But, my lord..." Lucy grabbed his hands between her small fingers. "We saw the Halls, mother and son, they're bad people—"

"The son too?" Trawler had stood closer to listen.

Nicholas's mind went blank with absolute terror as Lucy continued to speak.

"They got in the same coach as my lady. And I couldn't follow. She asked me to get you. I used my money to get a horse."

"You did the correct thing. Thank you," Trawler said to Lucy. "What will you do?" Trawler was watching Nicholas's face, a mixture of concern and fear visible through the darkness.

"I have to go to her." Nicholas looked around desperately for a sign of the horses they had ridden in on. Isabel had gone to the madhouse, to where the doctor was. The Halls were present, as was the doctor. The boy claimed he was involved in the smuggling ring, as Isabel had done. How had he been so blind? "Get fetch the militia. Tell them we have an act of war being committed if you have to. Follow me as soon as you can."

Scrambling up on the nearest available animal, Nicholas straightened in the saddle. Without a backward glance, Nicholas whipped the horse and headed for the infamous hospital.

CHAPTER 17

Isabel stayed quiet under the tree after Hodgkin and James Hall had left for the safety and shelter of the hospital walls. She was rooted even with them gone, holding herself against the wet bark, resting her head against the solid feel of wood while her mind raced. How long would it take for Lucy to find Nicholas and then for him to ride back here? How many hours had it been since she'd said goodbye to the maid? Would she risk it all to go in there? She could turn around and run. She could walk the rest of the way to Hastings, use a few of her own coins to buy herself a private room, some stew, a glass of wine, and order a fire... She could so easily pretend it wasn't happening.

With an abrupt shake of her head, Isabel cleared the image of the snug inn from her mind. "Pay attention," she whispered to herself.

The rain thickened around her as she huddled down in her low crouch. Soon her masculine clothes would be sodden and limp, of that she had no doubt.

If Hall was here, then who was at the drop site? Maybe her calculations had been incorrect? Or perhaps both Trawler and Nicholas were dead, James having dealt with them already? Isabel blinked away the image of either of them, especially Nicholas, being hurt, wounded... No, they would be fine. They had to be. He would survive, she had no doubt; she willed him to.

"Survive long enough to break my heart," she muttered as she pressed the coat more tightly around herself. It was she who was at risk of hypothermia.

Besides, hadn't she promised to save Jessica? It was hard to shake the obligation and the fear that had played over Lucy's face. But she hadn't expected Hall would be there. Whilst she might be able to convince some hospital porter that she was male, or even Doctor Hodgkin at a pinch, she had no illusions that her disguise would fool her brother-in-law for long.

"On your feet," she muttered. The answer certainly wasn't to freeze to death. Besides, if she were clever... She had been eyeing the hospital for at least an hour. There was the original plan of swanning up to it and offering to buy Jessica. But now she had another idea. She had seen the low, half wall that faced the roadside. A servant had left through it in the last thirty minutes, and several people had entered. If she could play her cards right, sneaking inside might be the wisest course of action.

Stumbling forward, her movements slow and jerky, Isabel edged her way towards the hospital. It was worse than she had let herself imagine over the years. Isabel had driven past the place, and she knew the shape and look of the building. It was an imposing size from the road. Now, approaching it from the lawns, cutting through the bushes and trees, it seemed even more ominous. An encircling dark wall encased the front of it; which was high and foreboding and had a locked gate. The building behind it was no more welcoming. It had been worn down by the sea breezes, and salt had pitted the black walls, with no fresh paint to brighten it. It was unusually tall, reaching up to the fifth floor, with bars on all the windows.

On reaching the low wall, Isabel straightened, adopting the pose she had seen arrogant young men around Brighton use. Head upright, shoulders back, gaze haughty. If she were stopped, she would claim to be a lost tourist if she had to. If only she'd cut her hair.

Marching inside, Isabel was almost surprised to find the small kitchen garden deserted. The carrying feminine cries from earlier had ceased, swallowed by the vast hospital and dingy walls. She proceeded to the door, which didn't budge no matter how much she pushed against it.

"You the new hire?" This was called out from behind her, and Isabel froze, her hands on the unmoving door. The accent was local to Sussex, thick and not unpleasant. She pivoted, pleased her hat hid a chunk of her face.

The speaker was a man of around forty, with a thickish beard and a reddened face. "Over with the Halls, right?"

Caught in the gaze of the man, Isabel found herself nodding. "That's right." She coughed hastily, realising that her voice was coming out far too feminine. "I'm here about Jessica."

The man frowned and for one wild moment, Isabel wished she had placed her knife in her coat pocket rather than her shoe. But then the man just shook his head. "Ain't it the way? The high and mighty don't want a perfectly sweet girl? I'm Peters."

"Lawson," Isabel lied, saying the name of her family's housekeeper, grateful she hadn't said Blackman or Hall automatically. They shook hands, and then Peters reached over Isabel's head and pulled down a key, which he slotted into the door and opened it. With only the thought of Jessica in her mind, Isabel willed herself to follow him inside. The room he led her through began pleasantly enough, a spacious kitchen filled with every day, if somewhat rudimentary, tables and chairs scattered about. It was not the horror setting she and her sisters had imagined. It only missed a well-placed vase of snowdrops or the like to make it homely. Isabel paused, taking in the scene, watching the man drop the key onto the wooden table.

"Where are the horses kept?" she asked.

"The doctor's horse?" Peters pointed to the left, and Isabel wondered if he just meant the one she'd seen Hodgkin riding earlier. It might be a struggle to fit Jessica and her on it.

She nodded, wondering if she did find Jessica, how the pair of them would get onto a horse, and then ride off at a great pace if they were being pursued. It did not seem wise, especially in such weather. But she was here now.

Isabel went across to the roaring fire and raised her hands to catch the warmth. "Good Lord, it's cold," she muttered. "Ain't like those fine toffs to care about us?"

In response, Peters chuckled and popped another log on the fire. "You can wait in here until they're done, I'd say. Or until you're warm. The girl's a resting." He gestured behind him to where Isabel assumed Jessica must be.

"And the babe?"

"Not born yet. Any day now." The man shook his head, dropping his gaze to look at the floor. "Such a sweet girl."

Hastily, Isabel looked back to the fire and waited for the feeling to return to her fingers and toes. It was good that Jessica hadn't delivered yet. It would be easier to move her.

A loud noise from the floor above made Isabel jump. The low-level anxiety that throbbed through her hadn't diminished in the intervening hour since she'd seen James; if anything, it had grown by having him so near after what had happened the last time she'd seen him. The memory of James pressing down onto her shuddered through her. To have him so close again—she could taste the bile in her throat.

Isabel forced a smile onto her face as Peters left the room. She waited for him to move further off, his footfalls echoing through the building until only the eerie silence remained.

"One step at a time," she said to herself as she walked away from the fire. She grabbed the keys off the table and followed the route Peters had taken.

The pleasingly large kitchen immediately gave way to bleak black walls that stretched out away from her like a labyrinth. This was more how the stories of this place always painted the hospital—windowless and cold, with damp on the walls. Some of the girls used to say it was tears.

Suppressing a shudder, Isabel continued along the corridor, stopping only to investigate the rooms, checking the doorways carefully before she stepped inside. Room after room proved to be empty. Nothing more than storage or a sparse and unoccupied servant's chamber, until she rounded the steps and stopped. The faint sound of feminine voices drifted through the wet bricks and caught Isabel's ears.

Eager and carried forward by adrenaline and fear, Isabel closed the distance and pulled roughly at the handle. The voices cried out, startled and scared, and she heard them scuttle from the entranceway.

Copying Peters' earlier movement, she tried the edges of the doorframe and located the key high above her head. She slotted the key into the lock. The door swung wide, and Isabel peered into the darkness inside. Squashed in the cell, a collection of bruised and dejected-looking young women were perching on the floor gazing back at her. Isabel's eyes darted between them, but she recognised none of their faces. They were aged anywhere from fifteen to Isabel's own twenty-eight years or thereabouts. In their rags, they looked like the sort of people who would go about unnoticed by most; small, slim women who would have been treated as forgettable. They had already been forgotten by most, Isabel thought with mounting anger. All six of them.

"What are you doing here?" There was a burst of defiance, and Isabel's eyes moved to the bed, to a body she hadn't noticed before. Jessica. Unmistakeable, despite the vast, nine months, elongated belly. She lay on the only bed, and despite it all, Isabel smiled. She had found her.

Yanking off her hat and causing her hair to fall around her shoulders, Isabel moved to the side of her one-time maid. "Lucy sent me to find you. I came as soon as I could. I'm just sorry it's taken me so long."

Jessica's eyes widened, and she let out a low moan, then burst into tears.

Isabel looked around at the others. The frowning and confused women were watching her with distrust on their faces. "I'm her old mistress," she said as a way of explaining her presence. "My name is Mrs. Hall, but don't hold that against me. Here." Isabel handed the kitchen key to the nearest female. "Go, now."

The woman who had taken the key frowned back at Isabel. "Where do you expect us to go? We ain't exactly like you."

"Head to Alfriston, to the Blackman household. I'll vouch for you." Isabel drew out Lucy's purse and passed a guinea to each of them in turn. "Get a private coach there."

The women didn't need telling twice; they took their proffered coins and fled. Only one lingered behind. "What about her?" She pointed to Jessica.

"What about her? We'll follow behind you." Isabel replaced the coin bag in her pocket and slipped the knife out from her shoe, preparing herself. Then she moved around to Jessica's side and helped the heavily pregnant woman into a sitting position.

Even in the darkness of the room, Isabel could make out the other woman's scepticism. Her eyes were on Jessica's vastly swelling belly. But nevertheless, she nodded, bit her lip, and exited, leaving them alone.

Easing Jessica out of the bed, Isabel wedged Jessica's arm over her shoulder. "Lean on me," she said as they tentatively started to walk forward. Each step seemed to take so long. "I'm sorry I never did anything before. It's all my fault—"

"Shut up," Jessica muttered as they made their slow way forward, "I'm trying to concentrate. I don't want it coming out yet."

Her steps took an age, each one pained and slow, until they reached the kitchen. All the while, Isabel was listening, trying to hear if anyone was aware of what she was doing. But the hospital was quiet. The escaping women had slipped silently out without drawing attention to themselves. They reached the kitchen. A wild burst of hope and light glimmered to life in Isabel's chest. *We're going to make it.*

"What's happening in here?" From behind her came a low cold voice that she didn't recognise, but she felt Jessica stiffen next to her.

Turning slowly, careful to put Jessica behind her, Isabel looked across the kitchen. She had seen the man stood there before, at parties, at a distance, his name keeping her away from him. Everyone knew the handsome doctor, but his good looks were frightening in their cold perfection. There was no warmth to his smooth cheekbones and chilled, slate-coloured eyes. Something struck her again, she had seen someone with remarkably similar features before, just put together slightly differently. She knew him, but she didn't.

"Hodgkin?" She played the fool.

"Mrs. Hall." Hodgkin bowed his head as if they were meeting in a ballroom, seeing immediately through her disguise. "I wondered if I'd ever meet you. Properly."

"Without your disguise in place?" Isabel dropped one hand behind her, pushing at Jessica to ease herself out of the room. "Perhaps I should call you by your preferred name, Harlington?" Now that she had met Silverton, there could be no doubt of their relationship. The man before her, who had gone through the county as a doctor, was, in fact, Harlington, Silverton's twin brother.

The blankness of his face contracted, and Isabel knew she was right. More dangerous than the devil, Walsh had said. Isabel drew herself back. She and Jessica were in touching distance of the door, of getting outside, but the distance might as well be a hundred miles. Harlington tutted and shook his head. Jessica stopped where she was. While his eyes were on the pregnant maid, Isabel slipped her hand into her pocket, her fingers grazing her knife. The room was almost contracting with the three of them inside it.

"How did you know?"

"I have the honour of knowing your brother—"

With a vindictive swipe, Harlington smashed the abandoned glasses off the table, causing both Isabel and Jessica to shrink back. Isabel removed her hand from her pocket, the knife clasped tightly between her fingers. Could she really use it if he came at them? Would she be brave enough? Before either of these questions could be answered, footfalls sounded down the stairs, and James Hall walked through the corridor and entered the kitchen, a look of shock and disgust painted on his mocking face.

"You little fools. The pair of you," James said.

"I am not the one running a smuggling ring," Isabel replied.

"Did you just decide to tell her everything?" Harlington's smooth voice cut off whatever James had been about to say.

"She's a nosy little bitch—" Whatever James was saying was stopped when Isabel moved forward; she had seen her chance when he had turned his back on her. Quickly, she lifted her blade to his neck, pressing against the skin by his windpipe. She locked eyes with Harlington. "Let us go, or I'll cut his throat."

Harlington's expression was neutral, as if this were an everyday occurrence.

"Go," Isabel said to Jessica.

As the maid moved, an ear-splitting gunshot echoed between the encircling walls of the room. Jessica screamed, and James reeled backwards, his body weight slamming into her. Isabel pushed at him in fear, and his body slumped away from her, dropping onto the kitchen floor. When Isabel opened her eyes, the shock of the sound having made her shrink back, she saw James sprawled at her feet. He was dead. His legs were at strange points, angled differently. His elegant coat of twilled navy was torn, and seeping through it was an ever-growing pool of blood.

Isabel looked up from the body and across the kitchen at Harlington and his pistol, which was now levelled at her and Jessica as they huddled in fear.

Ideas ran sluggishly through Isabel's mind, but they all seemed a hundred miles away, and none would come to her lips. The only thing she could do was stare in terror as she watched Harlington reloading his gun.

Think of something, anything...

From high above them came the sound of raised voices, shouting, crashing calls, and Isabel thought it might be a reaction to the sound of the gunshot for a couple of seconds.

With just a flicker of his eyes, Harlington glanced over his shoulder. Isabel pushed Jessica out through the open door with a shove, ensuring the maid was outside and free.

"Stay." Harlington levelled his reloaded pistol at Isabel's chest, forcing her to a standstill. The noises from above weren't ceasing, and he moved the gun to indicate that she should step closer to him. "I would have no hesitation in shooting you, my dear." His voice was smooth, strangely calm for someone who had just killed his associate and fellow criminal. Isabel had no doubt he would kill her too.

With tentative steps, Isabel stepped over the body of James Hall, grateful she could not see his dead face. "Why did you kill him?" she asked when she reached Harlington. He was more coldly beautiful up close; all of Silverton's polished looks were visible, but there was none of the guilt that humanised Silverton, nor any friendliness there. He was all chilling blankness as if he lacked any depth or kindness.

"He lied to me one too many times." He moved nearer to the corridor door. "Come, you may go first, my dear."

Reluctance bloomed within Isabel, and she could feel the cold tip of the pistol wedged into her back. If he pulled the trigger, she'd be dead. She shuddered at the thought.

"Focus on moving forward, one step after the other." His voice was soft, coaxing, as if he were teaching her something enjoyable rather than leading her through a deadly hospital before he killed her.

They reached the steps that would take them up to the higher floors within the hospital. Here the steps widened, and Isabel could make out some pretty, presentable wallpaper. This must be the part of the house used for social visits or his treasonous activities.

"Maybe not today, but one day." Isabel locked eyes with him as she reached the first step. "One day, you'll be caught, and you'll have to face up to what you've done."

"I have done nothing I wouldn't do again."

"This place is evil—I saw those women you kept here."

"A mere inheritance from one of my many connections. This place existed before I came here; I shouldn't wonder if it will continue after I've gone. There will always be a place for bad, scandalous, unwanted women." He grinned at her through the half-light of the hallway. "Rather like yourself if the gossip about you from your mother-in-law is to be believed. Now, up you go." Again, the weight of the gun pushed at her hip, and Isabel carried on up the stairs. She had hoped to sound more forceful than she really was.

Nearby, she could hear voices approaching them, their presence echoing ever closer as she walked up the stairs and into the lighter corridors of the hospital. She stepped out into the upper hallway and looked around, blinking in the candlelight.

To her left, all was smart gilt decoration, fine artwork, and polished chairs, and coming towards her, was Nicholas.

Her knees wobbled at the sight of him, but she remained standing. Her mouth opened, and she tried to think of the right words for the overwhelming sense of relief she felt upon seeing him. It was as if sunlight had entered into all the dark places, warming and consoling her. There was not a moment in all her life when Isabel could remember feeling more relieved to see another human being. He was safety, she felt that instinctively, the security he offered through his mere smiling presence—

Then Harlington appeared next to her.

"You came," she said. It was weak. But it didn't matter.

He gave her a tight-lipped smile. "All will be well," he said before turning his eyes to Harlington. "I'd lower that weapon if I were you."

"Is that so?"

Isabel shifted, turning in the hallway slightly so she could see the gun and the man behind her. Harlington had moved his pistol to point it at Nicholas's chest.

"No, I think Mrs. Hall will be accompanying me to the shore where, if I'm not mistaken, we shall be joined by my own form of transportation. Hurry up, my dear one."

He made to grab at Isabel, but Nicholas shot back, "I have something you want."

The man's nails dug into Isabel's forearm, and she swayed where she stood. He glanced back at Nicholas. "Very clever."

Nicholas had drawn his own duelling pistol, but it was his other hand that he waved in the air. "Recognise these? I'm afraid you won't want to be leaving England without these treasonous documents that are in my possession. That proof you have been on the receiving end of some rather important state secrets."

"I have no idea—"

"Been helping out the Russians, haven't you?" Nicholas's lip curled as he spoke, and, uncaring of the danger, he moved closer to Harlington.

"How sweet, how romantic," Harlington replied as he looked between the two of them. "What a lover's pair."

"Do you know what greets those who have committed such a crime? Treason is a hanging offence."

The nails gripped her but otherwise, Harlington's face was a blank mask, showing little to no emotion. "I will trade you. Tit for tat. You will tear up those papers now, in front of me."

"And give you time to shoot me while my pistol is lowered?" Nicholas asked.

"If you insist," Harlington pushed Isabel forwards, "Mrs. Hall will tear them up."

Step by step, she moved away from Harlington, conscious of the pistol he had pointed at her. Each movement made Isabel feel as if she were balancing on the edge of a giant lake; at any moment, she might fall off and into the water.

She lifted her eyes and looked ahead, absorbing Nicholas's dear face. Every angle. She'd remember his freckles, the delight she had taken in kissing him, watching him eat cheese and laugh with his friends, his kindness of describing love-making as dancing... There were a great many things she would have liked to have shared with him. But at least she had had this much.

"Easy," Nicholas whispered as she reached him. He passed her the papers. She leafed through them with shaking hands before looking back at Harlington.

"Tear them up," he ordered.

She glanced back at Nicholas, who nodded, his eyes focused on the traitor.

"As you do so, move behind me," Nicholas told her.

"Stay where you are." Harlington was walking backwards, close to the doorway. "Tear through the insignia of the Home Office, girl. Into little pieces."

Focusing on the action, Isabel started crying, the pieces of paper dropping onto the floor. Sections of it dotted around her feet like confetti.

Harlington was already close to the doorway, ready to run as soon as the last page was ripped up. Isabel glanced up and saw him move his weapon away from her and towards Nicholas. She dropped the remaining papers as Harlington's gun went off. Isabel flung herself at Nicholas, flattening him to the ground. A heavy layer of smoke shifted around them, the discharge of the firearm lingering. When Isabel looked up, Harlington was gone, vanished into the night. She returned her eyes downwards and drank in the sight of Nicholas below her, desperate to know that he was safe.

"My love?" she whispered.

Nicholas gazed up at her unblinkingly, and for one terrifying moment, she was sure that he, like James and Pierre before him, was dead.

CHAPTER 18

Isabel had hit Nicholas with a force that rather winded him. She had also called him 'my love' in such a way that also drew not only his breath from his body but most of his ability to function. He felt lightheaded but more from her words than his fall.

"Are you hurt? Can you hear me?" Isabel asked him. Her lovely face was pinched with worry as she leant over him, strands of her pale blond hair falling into his face. He was enclosed by her.

"I'm fine," Nicholas said. A new idea, a distant one, was prickling his conscience; he had allowed a traitor to escape. He had betrayed his country. His friends. He met her worried eyes, with their shades of blue-grey, and he knew he'd do the same thing again a hundred times to have her safely pressed against him. To feel her breath, her warmth, even the odd collection of the men's clothes she'd donned. It was so tempting to lift his hands up and hold onto her. "He's gone?" he forced himself to ask. "He's unmistakeably Silverton's twin."

"Yes. As soon as I saw him, I knew they were brothers."

She scrambled off him as she spoke, shivering in her thin boy's clothes as she collected up the fragments of the pages she had been forced to tear up. The proof of Harlington's crimes shredded into pieces. Hall's too. She gave him a sad little look.

Nicholas got to his feet after her and wrapped her in his own dry coat.

Her delicate face peeked out from the high collar, having slotted her hands through it. "It's my fault."

"What?" Nicholas asked as he took the pages off her and stuffed them into his trouser pockets.

From outside the hospital, through the walls, voices could be heard. Nicholas assumed they were the local militia, finally investigating this place. They would be here soon, and that meant Trawler would be too. He had passed a porter or similar, as well as the older Mrs. Hall, but otherwise, the place seemed empty. He had left Mrs. Hall in an armchair, claiming utter ignorance of everything. The rank conditions of the hospital had turned his stomach as he proceeded through the place, searching for a clue of Isabel's whereabouts. It would not have been a fit place to keep animals, let alone women. But this all fitted with Harlington's previous actions and that he'd used the cover of a well-meaning doctor.

This was the sort of place, the sort of thing, he had spent his whole life running from. The very air hung with the tale of scandal, of mistreated women, of treason too. Leaning forward, Nicholas pulled Isabel towards him. He needed her back in his arms. It mattered more than anything else. It was more important than the things he had clung to as protective armour, allowing himself to sail through life without being touched by anything too serious. And now, here was the woman who made him feel it all.

"All of this... it's my fault. I shouldn't have come here," Isabel said into his waistcoat. He could hear the tears in her voice, and it hurt him. "It is all my fault. All of that proof, gone in a minute."

"I don't care. It was worth it," Nicholas said. He was unsure how he would explain it to Silverton, Trawler, or whoever might ask him for an explanation. Would he be pulled in front of a court to defend himself and his actions?

"How can you say that?" Isabel asked hopelessly. She looked away as she shook her head. "Those awful men, and what they did to those poor women. He was evil. Hall too. We need to find Jessica; she's due so soon. What are you doing? Nicholas? Nicholas?"

Nicholas had dropped down to one knee before her. He supposed he had pictured a proposal in the most traditional of settings. It would have normally involved a drawing room at Hurstbourne Manor or at the Blackman residence, perhaps with some sedate piano music playing close by, played by either Viola or Isabel's littlest sister. The two of them would have been dressed in all of their finery. Her small, gloved hands would be held in his, and he would stroke the underside of her wrist, where a button might have come loose.

It would not have been in the faint dawn light of the day, with neither of them having slept for hours. It wouldn't be in this location. It wouldn't be with her back in men's clothing again. He would have received Mr. Blackman's permission first.

Perhaps he had thought more about the proposal than he realised. It had only been a short time since her husband had died, but society's rules be damned.

But he had to ask. He needed to know her answer more than he needed his next breath. Love was a rarity in this world; it should be savoured and protected. It could so easily be lost. If his parents' failed marriage had taught him anything of use, wasn't it that?

All these ideas of his didn't matter. He just needed her to say yes.

"Mrs. Hall," No. he didn't like that. Despite his desire for formality, the language was the only thing that could claim any degree of conventionalism. "Isabel, will you do me the honour of becoming my wife?"

For a second, her face broke into a wide smile, and she nodded, the question causing her eyes to gleam. Then suddenly, her face fell, and she replied, "No. No, you know I can't."

"Is it because I don't have a ring? That can be remedied," Nicholas said. A great many pieces belonged to the Lyndes and were kept in the family vault in their London home. A ruby would be a delightful contrast to all her delicate golden prettiness; or perhaps a more classical style would be her preference. Nicholas visualised leading her through the place and letting her choose something that pleased her. But she needed to say yes rather than no for that to become a reality.

"Oh." She sounded close to tears now. "For at least a hundred reasons." Isabel had moved over to him and grabbed his arms, forcing Nicholas to stand up. She swayed towards him and let him wrap his arms around her. She even allowed him to place a small kiss on her forehead.

Isabel leant her head against his chest, letting out a pained, rather damp-sounding sigh. Her skin was pimpled with cold. He needed to get her someplace warm, someplace away from this gruesome hospital. He wanted her back at Winston Cottage, a space where they belonged and had been happy.

"Give me one of those reasons?" he asked. She felt so right, held close to him. It made sense, and Nicholas told himself he would reason out all her denials. After all, she must feel as he did; she was cuddled close in his embrace.

"Your family. Your position." Her voice sounded rather

sleepy as if she was about to nod off. She shivered and closed her eyes as he ran his hands up against his coat, attempting to warm her.

"My father will be thrilled for me to finally have a wife. Any more?"

"An earl should marry a virgin," she murmured as she snuggled closer to him. "You owe it to your title. I am... not one."

"Neither am I. A virgin. So, I don't care a penny about that. Next? Don't we have another ninety-eight other points or so to go? You will have to speed up."

"My husband was a traitor. So is my father." Isabel shifted in his arms, and Nicholas suspected that this was her biggest fear, what society might say about their match. A day ago, a week ago, it would have been just the reason he resisted her, and now it seemed so insignificant he could almost laugh at it.

"You are not responsible for the actions of others. You have proven your bravery again and again. Your integrity. Your desire to help others."

Isabel leant back and looked up at him. Her face resumed its smile from when he had proposed to her. "That's very nice of you to say, Nicholas. But nevertheless—"

"Was that your biggest objection? Do you think I fear the scandal?" He looked her in the eyes.

Isabel blushed. "We have never once spoken of our feelings for each other, not without, well... I will not enter into another marriage without at least some sign of affection on both of our parts."

"Is that all?" he asked her.

"How can you be so—"

"I adore you, my darling."

"Then why didn't you say something earlier?" She looked

so annoyed, and despite the events of the day, despite it all, Nicholas laughed, pressing a kiss to her lips.

Pulling back, he looked down at her, pushing a strand of hair off her face. "Do you care for me at all?"

"Of course, I do. You know I do. You've known for weeks that I love you."

"That resolves that, then," Nicholas said. "Since I love you too."

Hitching her a little higher in his arms, Nicholas kissed her sooty, wet face. She had agreed, his heart sang, and now he could revel in the feel of her in his embrace.

The kiss was long and sweet, robbing them both of their breath until there was a noise from behind them, and they both looked back over Nicholas's shoulder and down the corridor. The toad-like Mrs. Hall stood with her arms crossed over her chest, watching the pair of them, taking in Isabel's loose flowing hair and strange male garb, as well as the fact that she was wrapped in Nicholas's arms.

"Get over here now, my girl. My son has barely been dead a month, and there you are—"

"I—" Isabel began to say, but Nicholas cut her off.

"Mrs. Hall, both your sons have the misfortune of a connection to the Wareton smuggling gang and were involved in treasonous activities. I would suggest holding your tongue."

"Well, I never," the older woman said. "If you expect your marriage portion now, my girl, James will put a stop to that."

"Mrs. Hall—Emma." Isabel walked closer to the older woman, her face surprisingly gentle. "I regret to inform you that James was shot. He was killed by his compatriot, Doctor Hodgkin." The older woman's face blanched, but nevertheless, Isabel continued. "I don't need my portion, but there is a woman who was badly treated by your son, young Jessica. She will be having your grandchild soon. I would suggest you give her that portion."

Mrs. Hall barely glanced at Isabel before she staggered towards a waiting chair, muttering to herself. There came more voices from down the corridor, and the space was soon filled with militia.

Pulling Isabel to his side, Nicholas forced the pair of them towards the door, whilst Isabel whispered to him that they needed to find Jessica. They reached the front door of the hospital, and Nicholas swung it wide before proceeding to march down the front steps, nodding at the soldier stationed close by. The man wore a uniform unfamiliar to Nicholas, and he had the distinct impression that the Brighton-based army had been too lazy or too uncaring to arrive; these men must belong to a different regiment. At least they were here now, and they could search the place for anything Harlington might have left behind. He could see Trawler talking to a heavily pregnant woman. Next to her was a weeping Lucy, clutching the other woman's hand.

"Sir?" The soldier stepped forward, blocking their path.

"I'm Lord Lynde." In the distance, Nicholas could see Trawler lift his head as he heard his friend's name.

"My lord, we were told to look for Doctor Hodgkin," the soldier said.

"He has escaped, down towards the sea. Your Doctor Hodgkin has scarpered. He also goes by the name of Harlington."

"We will begin by searching the grounds. Which direction did the doctor head to?"

Nicholas thought there wasn't much chance of these men finding Harlington but nevertheless directed him to the rear of the house. There, the walls gave way to the sea path, where the traitor would have had a boat waiting for him.

"My lord—"

But Nicholas was already moving away from the steps and towards his horse.

"Your Lordship—"

"I am returning to Hurstbourne Manor," Nicholas replied. He wanted to get out and have Isabel safely away from such a place, from the staring eyes and whatever grim realities might be unearthed. Lifting Isabel into the saddle, he led the horse towards the exit. "Report anything you find to Trawler there."

The soldier looked displeased, but it wasn't in his authority to stop Nicholas.

Turning, Nicholas looked at Trawler. "You have the right of it?"

"He escaped?" Trawler asked.

"It was life or death," Isabel answered. "He held us at gunpoint."

"And the papers?"

"Gone. He made us destroy them," Nicholas replied, ready to see fury on Trawler's face, but the man looked between Isabel and himself, and a glimmer of a smile brightened his expression.

"It is just as well that I held one piece of proof back then." Trawler tapped his breast pocket. "Which I think I shall keep hold of whilst we search for the doctor."

"Harlington," Isabel said. "They are one and the same. He was using a made-up name."

Nodding, Trawler cocked an eyebrow. "I will include this information in my report. I think it will be enough to prove what a traitor the man was, and to further blacken his name, we have the testimony of the escaped women. We met a gaggle of them in a private coach on our way here."

Behind him on the horse, Nicholas heard Isabel laugh, then she leant forward and touched Nicholas's arm. "We will take care of Jessica and the others?" She looked over to the two servants sat huddled in the cold.

"Consider it my engagement present to you both," Trawler answered smoothly, his eyes on the locked hands of the pair. "I took the liberty of sending the others to a fine establishment in Eastbourne, where they will be cared for."

"And Jessica and Lucy?"

"All will be well," Nicholas answered with a squeeze of her fingers. He could tell she was close to collapsing from exhaustion. He looked back at Trawler, reassured that his friend would resolve the issues with both Lucy and her cousin.

"Here." He passed his friend the small necklace back, closing the short distance between them, their earlier fears gone. "For your mother, yes?"

Trawler nodded, eyes downcast for a moment before he glanced up, his expression a blend of hope and concern. "About my mentioning of Viola—"

Nicholas was already moving off, back towards Isabel's swaying form. "I won't hold it against you," he called over his shoulder.

The ride back was peaceful. Isabel kept her eyes closed, her breath steady. Nicholas was certain she wasn't sleeping but continuing a conversation on horseback was far from ideal. After passing through the gates to his home, Nicholas manoeuvred the horse towards Winston Cottage. He wanted Isabel to have some privacy; he doubted the Manor would provide that. Once there, he proceeded to carry her inside carefully, up the stairs and to the bedroom. He went to tuck her back into bed.

"Let me change," she said sleepily as she struggled out of the coat, dropping it to the floor. Beneath the coat, Nicholas could see that she had donned his waistcoat.

"You were very brave." He moved away, allowing her to change on her own whilst he built up the fire in the grate. When he looked back, she was in a longish nightshirt, gazing back at him with a soft look on her face. It was so nakedly affectionate that Nicholas had to look away; part of him didn't feel like he could ever deserve her.

Isabel held out her arms towards him. Keenly, he stepped into her embrace, finally able to breathe. Happiness seeped through his limbs; just to hold her like this was something he had always thought beyond him.

"Your friend, Mr. Trawler—he will look after the girls?"

"Of course, and we can do anything you want to support them. Once we are wed."

"I will need to wait a respectable amount of time." She snuggled in closer, her hair brushing his chin.

"Two months."

"You know I will have to wait until December at the earliest."

Lowering his head, so he could gaze into her lovely features, Nicholas pulled a face, causing Isabel to laugh.

"Now who's being a stickler for the rules?"

"I thought you didn't care for scandal."

"I find myself singularly prepared to face every whisper."

Isabel rolled her eyes. "A year. At the earliest."

"Well—" He racked his brain for the right answer. "What if you were with child?"

"I thought you said that unlikely. Because..." Here Isabel blushed. She stepped out of his embrace and walked to the fireplace, warming her hands at the lapping flames.

Joining her and letting her lean back against him, Nicholas kissed her ear. "Yes, I did. But there is always a slight risk. If all else fails, I suppose we could try again..."

Giggling, Isabel snuggled in closer. "Perhaps by the autumn, once we have saved my parents from your wild mother. And sister." Isabel turned where she stood and gazed up into his face. "I should like to meet Lady Kingfisher, but only because she is your mother, not because she is so very scandalous." With her gentle hand, she cupped his cheek. "How many years has it been since you saw her?"

"Decades," he said, the words difficult to form. "I think I was waiting for someone as brave as you to help me."

"I always will. Help you, that is."

Looking down at her, he brushed his lips over her forehead. "Come, you must be exhausted; you can sleep as long you need to."

Reaching her arms up and around his neck, Isabel's lips formed into a delicious smile. "Strangely, I don't feel tired at all. Not now that you are with me."

Unable to resist those curving lips, Nicholas dipped his head and devoured the delicious taste and feel of her, every gift she offered him, swearing to God above that he would always try to prove himself worthy of her.

THE END

THANK YOU.

Dear Readers,

I really hope you enjoyed reading *The Lord's Scandalous Mistress* and that you are tempted to read the rest of The Oxford Set. If you want to read the prequel to hear more about the Oxford Set do sign up to my newsletter to receive a free novella, *The Debutante's Duke*.

Writing Isabel and Nicholas was a delight. Their love story was more of a slow burn, which I enjoyed hugely, building their dynamics until they flowed together, as well as blending a little bit the gothic with the smugglers and madhouse.

I love hearing from readers so get in touch using any of the below:

www.instagram.com/ava_bondauthor/
www.twitter.com/AvaBondAuthor
www.avabond.co.uk
www.facebook.com/AvaBondAuthor

And if you would like to write a review that would make me so happy!

Read on for a sneak peek of *The Spy's Elusive Wife*, the next in the Oxford Set series...

THE SPY'S ELUSIVE WIFE. SNEAK PEEK.

Paris, June 1815

Olympe De Lisle knew Paris, with its labyrinth streets, twisting pavements, and buttered smells, better than she knew the back of her hand. She was well-aware of the roads that surrounded her own publishing house, *Ma Grand Amie*, in Saint Marcel, and of every vendor, street walker, or artisan who lingered in this beautiful, if precarious, part of the city. It was not as sophisticated or spectacular as the area north of the riverbank, Place Vendôme, where aristocrats both new and old huddled away, drinking champagne, and reading in shocked tones whatever Olympe's publishing house had printed that month. As the eldest daughter of the Vicomte Sebastian De Lisle, Olympe could have found an existence there, but that was not her way.

Paris had been her home for ten years. So long that the other places she knew or had even lived in faded in her memory. She had no recollection of Milan, where she was born, although the Cornish countryside where she had grown up held a special affection. But she had gotten good at ignoring any lingering pull towards England and instead focusing on the work at hand, and that was being the scandalous literary editor, Madame O, at the infamous *Ma Grande Amie* publishing house.

However, everything was different now. And it was not just due to the recent fall of Napoleon. No, it was more personal than that. Etienne Toussaint, her fellow editor, had died in her arms, knife wounds scattered over his chest, his blood oozing across the kitchen floor and leaving Olympe with no time to run for the doctor, nurse, or even adequate bindings to help quench the rush of blood from him.

As blood oozed out of him, Etienne had begged her to publish his final pamphlet.

"Don't trust the spy," he gasped as he pressed his bloody fingers to the wound in his chest. This was Etienne's constant refrain on the man who had committed treason against the British crown, a spy whose name he wouldn't tell her.

"Hush. I know." In desperation, she had used her own overskirt against the wound.

"You must promise me to print the pamphlet. Else it will all have been in vain." His voice was already weaker, and while Olympe had not seen many people die, his breath did not seem easy; the colour in his cheeks and his movements spoke of a man without much time.

"I love you," she made herself say, a sentiment they hardly told each other so that it was unfamiliar on her tongue. In fact, it was more of an obligation than sincere honesty. They had been lovers once, years ago, but for far longer, they had been friends and colleagues.

"Promise me that you'll print it." He didn't seem to hear her declaration of love. And he didn't feel the need to express the same sentiment to her.

"I promise," she repeated until his eyes rolled back in his head, and she knew he was gone.

The Parisian authorities had come and looked through

the building, glanced briefly at Etienne's body, and concluded that it was a tavern brawl that had killed him, nothing more. Of course, it probably hadn't helped that Olympe admitted that Monsieur Toussaint wasn't her husband and never had been. But the officers had already made up their minds about her. They hadn't listened to Olympe as she talked through all the potential suspects who might target someone of Etienne's significance, in particular the spy he had spoken of.

When she'd finished with her rationale, the young officer had said, 'Well, if that's the case, what else can you expect, writing things that are so dangerous and so offensive?'

Thankfully, she'd been careful to hide the pamphlet. It had been lined up to be printed this spring, but Etienne had decided to edit it and include some new bits of information that had seeped through from his collection of musicians, returning soldiers, travelling authors, and even the occasional spy. This pamphlet would be especially shocking since it revealed that an English lord, Viscount Marcus Wilton, had been taking bribes from the Russians and describing English troop movements. It would be printed within the week, and with grim satisfaction, Olympe thought she would let the chips fall where they may.

Now that she was done with Etienne's funeral and the final pamphlet, what was her next decision? How could she write to her parents and tell them what had happened to her business? It galled her to think of asking for help, but did she have much choice?

Turning the corner of the street, Olympe saw *Ma Grande Amie*.

The overwhelming difference, though, came from the top floors, the unmistakable sign of flames. *Ma Grande Amie* was on fire. The handsome brick and stucco building with three floors featured attractive cream shutters that Olympe had painted herself eight years ago. But none of that mattered when the fire threatened to consume the building.

The blaze bloomed and swirled out of two windows on the top floor and had even started nibbling at the roof. Working its wicked way, its orange and red curving waves, consuming brick after brick, and even Olympe's grandmère's watered silk curtains.

Olympe took a step forward, a hysterical laugh bursting out of her lips at the idea of worrying overly about the curtains when her life's work would be gone within half an hour if she just stood there.

"Get back, madame," said one of the men nearest to her. "It'll be gone in minutes."

Olympe took another step forward. There were valuables inside that she cared about—family heirlooms, documents, and clothes. But more important than any of that was Etienne's pamphlet, and perhaps most crucially of all, her own manuscript. She had been working on a novel for the best part of four years, a collection of children's fairy stories that she had built on and added to. It had been gathered from every escaped immigrant or visitor to Paris and from every mouth that had a tale to tell, from their grandparents, sister, or cousin, from across Europe, Russia, and Africa who had whispered their stories to her. And now, it was compiled and ready to be printed. Yet it was lying inside *Ma Grande Amie*, which was burning down in front of her as she watched helplessly.

She could not let the book burn, could not lose it too.

Without even really being aware of it, Olympe was at the front door of the building and using her elbow to shoulder her way inside. She pulled her shawl off her head to cover her mouth and lips. Already there was smoke in the entranceway, blocking and seeping this way and that. Heat burned her eyes, and she knew it would be worse the further up she went. *Heat rises, doesn't it?*

From high up above her, she could hear the roar of the blaze, and added to the sound of it all was the occasional splintering of wood under the heated inferno.

"Focus," she whispered to herself, "just find it, find it."

She had always kept the manuscripts and Etienne's pamphlets in one specific location in the office, which meant she had to head upstairs. *Don't pay attention to anything else*, she told herself as she carried on up the staircase towards where the blaze roared.

Not for a moment did she think this was some unhappy accident. She knew that it had been started by the same person who had killed Etienne. They were back to finish the job. To end *Ma Grande Amie* once and for all.

On the second floor, the smoke was even thicker and much harder to break through even when she waved her shawl to try and see where she was going. There were three doors off the corridor, and she made her way to the office, groping along the wall to find her way to the right door.

As if to confirm her theory, the office was devastated, the chairs scattered and broken, documents ripped up and cast about. The desk seemed to have been smashed by someone deliberately. It was a cruel act to leave everything reduced to rubble.

Below, she could hear footsteps and the coughing of another human. Edging nearer to the wall, she looked outside to see a blond man of middling height exiting *Ma Grande Amie*. His walk was distinctive.

A spurt of anger moved Olympe forward, and she gripped the burning carpet up and pulled it aside. It smarted and hurt her hands as she did so. Then she dropped to her knees and plucked at the loose floorboard, where she had stored the pamphlet and her novel. They were there still. She let out a sigh of relief before coughing into the smoky room. With shaking and unsteady hands, she stuffed them down the front of her dress, which was baggy enough to accommodate them.

There was an acrid smell close to her face, and that was when Olympe realised her hair was on fire. Quietly singeing away, sending bright sparks out and burning away at her long lustrous brown locks. With her now free hands, she swatted at the clumps of her hair, tears falling rapidly as she put out the flames. Struggling to her feet, she swayed where she stood; the office seemed to have filled with more smoke, leaving no oxygen to breathe.

Tilting her head back, Olympe became slowly aware of a crashing noise coming from above her. Bits of the building's structure were already coming down. She paused where she stood. Was it a better idea to try and jump from the second-floor window? She might hurt her leg, but then again, she might survive. Or was it better to trust the rickety stairs that would take her down to the first floor and out of the front door?

Go for the stairs; you don't know if that man is waiting outside. If I jump, I might survive, but the assassin, the spy, the man who murdered Etienne, could be waiting there to slit my throat.

In a decisive move, she hiked her shawl once more over her mouth and hurried towards the staircase. Pieces of artwork, bits of furniture, and even her father's violin, a veritable museum to the original De Lisles, would all be ashes.

Forcing her feet to move, Olympe reached the staircase. The smoke was now so thick it was like cutting through gâteaux. She held her hands out before her, feeling her way. She held her breath as she proceeded step by step down the stairs. They wobbled under her weight. She took another step, but the wood gave way beneath her, and only because she was holding on to the fragments of the banister did she manage to steady herself.

She wriggled before realising that her foot was stuck, lodged between the wooden fragments of the step. Bending into the much thicker smoke that lingered around her knees, she struggled to loosen her trapped shoe. Each second seemed to last a lifetime as the wood stuck splinters into her hands. Finally, suppressing a cry as the final bit of wood gave way, she freed herself but could not stop the momentum of the release from causing her to crash down the remaining stairs to land as a heap on the floor in the thick, unforgiving smoke of the hallway.

Now it wasn't just that she couldn't see where she was going, as the downstairs was black and as foggy as the night, but her head was spinning from the fall, creating a sort of swirling spasm in her vision, where nothing seemed to focus for her.

Oh Lord, if this is where I die, will my parents know? Will they know how much I loved them? How much I've missed them?

There were so many good things she suddenly wanted to do. She needed to see her novel in print. She wanted to have a child of her own. She needed to see her mother again, and she would embrace her father until he laughed at her sentimentality. There were jokes to be cracked with her siblings. She was going to see a play. She would sing in the Cornish church near her home and dance at a grand society ball. She was going to fall in love. But those were things she had imagined, had promised herself, that she could look forward to in the coming years without Etienne by her side. But suddenly, they seemed an awfully long way away. Perhaps they had only ever been dreams. Then, there was another noise, the noise of footsteps that broke through those wild, frantic thoughts that pounded like a terrified horse through her head. Then she felt her body being lifted into the air.

"No," she said. She was certain it was the killer. He had returned to the building. His strong arms picked her out of the smoke until she collided with something solid, warm, and soft against the side of her face. It did not smell of smoke but of something else entirely. Something oddly familiar.

"I've got you." The masculine voice was inflected with an odd English twang that was unfamiliar to her. The man proceeded to carry her towards the street and the clean, clear air.

Trying desperately to focus, Olympe wondered if this was what an assassin would say before he killed her. "*I've got you.*" Yes, she supposed it would be something that a murderer would utter alongside an evil sort of chuckling before he did her in. Olympe forced herself to look into the face of the man who would be her end. But it was someone else entirely and not a stranger at all.

"You?" she croaked, the words heavy and tricky to form in her dry mouth. "Why are you always saving me?" And with that question asked, she slid into a dead faint in his arms.

ABOUT THE AUTHOR

Ava Bond has been a fan of regency romances since discovering Georgette Heyer on her grandma's bookshelf–especially *Faro's Daughter, Regency Buck* and *Devil's Cub*.

She studied Literature at university and has been writing since her early twenties. Ava lives in Scotland with her husband and small cat, Gwendolen.

www.avabond.co.uk

ALSO BY AVA BOND

THE OXFORD SET SERIES

The Debutante's Duke (prequel)

The Marquess's Adventurous Miss

The Lord's Scandalous Mistress

The Spy's Elusive Wife (forthcoming)

The Viscount's Reluctant Bride (forthcoming)

The Duke's Rebellious Love (forthcoming)

The Rogue's Brazen Lady (forthcoming)

Printed in Great Britain
by Amazon